THE ROAD TO CALIFORNIA

THE ROAD TO CALIFORNIA

LOUISE WALTERS

The Road to California
by Louise Walters

Produced and published in 2018
by Louise Walters Books

Email: info@louisewaltersbooks.co.uk
Louise Walters Books
PO Box 755
Banbury
OX16 6PJ

A catalogue card for this book is available from the British Library

ISBN: 9781999780906
eISBN:9781999780913

Typeset in Aldine 11 pt

Printed and bound by TJ International, Cornwall, UK

For Oliver, of course

1

THE ROAD TO CALIFORNIA

JUNE 2006

'Can anybody give me an example of a sympathetic adult in this novel?'

It was a simple question. It was asked with hope, Ryan thought, and a little bit of smugness. He could have answered. But he said nothing. It didn't pay to put up his hand in class. So he never did.

This was English, the subject he loved. This was the dreary supply teacher, who read from sheets of paper that she held in pale, disinterested hands. Her questions were so banal, so general, Ryan wondered if she had even read *A Kestrel for a Knave*. Ryan had read it nineteen times.

Mrs Marchant was away. She was Ryan's proper English teacher. She had been away a lot in recent weeks. Some said she was pregnant and being violently sick. Others claimed that she had a flesh-eating disease. Still others claimed that she had been suspended for kissing a sixth former. Ryan believed none of the rumours, especially the last one. Mrs Marchant was old, wasn't she? Too old to have a baby? She had grey hair. Her face was an old person's face. She didn't wear make-up. She dressed like an old person, in long skirts, polo-neck jumpers, billowing shirts. "Blouses," Mum called them.

And he hoped Mrs Marchant wasn't pregnant, because

she would have to take time away from school to take care of her baby. That's what the teachers did, he noticed, when they had babies. They disappeared and resurfaced months later, worn, snappy, a little bit sad. Some didn't even come back. Mrs Marchant was the only decent teacher he had ever met, and he would miss her kindness and her gentle voice. She always told Mum at parents' evening that Ryan was "gifted" in English. He had "something special". Mrs Marchant and Mum got along well, and Mrs Marchant had commissioned Mum to make a patchwork quilt. Mum had been working on it for weeks. And that was extra work on top of getting ready for the Melsham House Vintage and Craft Fair.

Ryan wasn't sure how Mum managed all her work, but he knew she stayed up late most nights. She had a greyish-purple rim around her eyes; but she was still pretty. Her eyes still shone. She was one of those people, Ryan knew, who never admitted to feeling tired, let alone complained of being tired.

Flick!

Ryan felt something land in his hair. He fiddled and pulled out a tiny piece of yellow rubber. He looked behind him but met a row of bored, inanimate faces. Ryan turned to the front again and the supply teacher frowned at him. He heard a stifled giggle behind. He felt something land in his hair again.

Ryan hated anything or anyone touching his hair. He hated that almost as much as he hated cats, and that was almost as much as bananas. So this was a big deal. His hair was like Mum's: thick and curly and blond, growing wild. He would occasionally let her cut it, but not often, and not recently.

He picked out another piece of yellow rubber, and looked behind him again. Beau Stirling smiled back at him, a wide, slow, daring smile.

'Could you please stop flicking rubber in my hair?' said Ryan.

Beau and his friends laughed. Ryan felt the eyes and ears of the entire class, and those of the supply teacher, zoom in on him. He faced the front once more. He didn't look at anybody.

'Settle down,' said the supply teacher to no one in particular.

Drone. Drone. Drone.

Flick!

Ryan turned and hissed at Beau Stirling to stop. The supply teacher passed around handouts. Beau leaned forward over his desk, staring Ryan down.

'What you going to do about it, freak?' he said.

Keep it pompous, Ryan told himself. It might work. 'I've asked you politely to stop,' he said. *Remember who you are.*

'Oo-ooh,' said Clarissa Cooper. She was always with Beau, always sitting next to him, always egging him on to do stupid things. Ryan and Beau looked hard at each other. Ryan thought he saw a shadow of something – regret? – move across Beau's face, like a pale wisp of cloud passing over the sun. Clarissa poked Beau in the ribs with her bedazzled fingernails and chewed loudly on her gum. Beau's face became hard once more. Ryan turned and looked to the front of the class. He concentrated on the whiteboard, wanting to avoid any trouble with Beau and his gang. They were bad news. They had no compassion. They were stupid, and they were nothing to Ryan. Why couldn't he become nothing to them? Why couldn't they leave him alone?

'I'll fight you,' said Beau, after a pause during which Ryan hoped the episode had passed. And once again all ears, if not eyes this time, were tuned in. A collective whisper sizzled around the room. Ryan sighed and shook his head.

'So. Class. All of you?! Any sympathetic adults in the novel at all?' intoned the supply teacher. Ryan thought that even if she had read the book, she certainly hadn't enjoyed it. Somebody asked what "sympathetic" meant.

'Chicken, eh?' said Beau, and Ryan could sense him smiling broadly at Clarissa and their hangers-on.

'No, not a chicken. More a kind of bored lizard,' replied Ryan, dropping the pompous, and hoping that his bizarre remark would be laughed at and all threats of a fight would be dropped. Saying stupid things could sometimes get him out of trouble; sometimes into trouble. Right now, anything was worth a try. Pomposity wasn't cutting it. Stupidity was his second line of defence.

'Listen to him!' said Beau. 'Bored lizard? What a freak. Let's do it.'

'All right, all right,' said Ryan, turning to face Beau again. 'Where and when?'

Ryan glanced at Clarissa, who smiled and chewed on her gum. She was ugly, he thought. What did Beau see in her? How could he even bear to have her sit next to him? She curled her hand around Beau's ear. He didn't appear to mind.

'After this lesson. Out the back, here.' Beau indicated the area between the canteen and the rear entrance to the school library, where the kitchen bins were kept. Ryan didn't like the mashed potato smells that lingered around that part of the school.

'OK,' said Ryan, and he turned away.

Ryan didn't fight. As far as he knew, Beau Stirling didn't fight either. Beau was popular and cheeky and lazy, and he liked to hang out with the popular girls, and in a way he was quite likeable. Beau didn't fight. And why did he want to fight him, of all people? There would be no glory in beating up year nine's number one weirdo. It made no sense.

'Mr Farthing?!' said the supply teacher. Nobody responded.

The bell rang and everyone hurriedly packed up their bags. There was going to be an audience.

Clarissa Cooper. Her hair was knife-straight and black and the silly large hoops in her ears glittered cheaply. She glanced at Ryan, and quickly looked away, her face turning red. So she did have a conscience, Ryan thought. Well, good for her. Perhaps she was a member of the human race after all.

Ryan lingered in the English classroom, taking his time in packing his bag. Nobody waited with him, and why would they? He had no friends in school, none at all. He left the classroom, ushered out by the supply teacher who wanted to lock up the classroom and get to her lunch. Ryan couldn't believe she hadn't noticed what was going on, and in that moment it seemed that the whole world had turned away from him. He thought of Mum at home, sewing, her machine whirring, the atmosphere frenetic and fevered. Ryan wanted to be there, more than ever, at home, safe.

He felt a rush of affection for his mum, despite the resentment towards her that so often nestled inside him these days. He had no idea why he resented her. He just did. She was nice, mostly, and she loved him, and apart from the occasional smack when he had been small and very naughty, she had never harmed him. But was she enough? Could she… save him? Ryan wanted a hand on his shoulder, an assured, deep voice in his ear – *walk away from trouble, son.* The voice he longed for. It was a voice that possibly didn't exist, or worse, a voice whose owner did not want Ryan to hear it. And that thought was unbearable. And now this ridiculous fight he seemed to have been drawn into. It was frightening to be alone. What was he going to do? Who could advise him, other than himself?

Word had spread, of course, and lots of kids were milling around by the dustbins, waiting for the action to begin. They made way for Ryan, and there was Beau, in the centre of the throng, looking at him; he was not sneering. He looked serious, but he hadn't rolled up his sleeves. He wasn't that stupid. Beau would never do that, Ryan conceded. He didn't make a fool of himself; not exactly.

Ryan put down his bag and removed his blazer. He moved slowly, purposefully, and he ignored everyone other than Beau. Was this how it felt to be "hard"? Whatever. This was it.

Ryan took three paces towards Beau, and they looked into each other, a brief moment of sanity in which Ryan knew neither of them wanted to be doing this. Then quickly, purposefully, Ryan punched Beau squarely on the nose. Hard.

'What the fuck…?'

'Shit!'

'Did you fucking see that?!'

Beau sat on the floor, blood pouring from his nose. He looked up at Ryan, stunned. Clarissa knelt down by Beau.

The teachers came, alerted by the crowd.

'Out of it!' The PE teacher, Mr Grant, thrust kids from his path and arrived in the middle of the throng, cross and red-faced. He helped Beau to his feet. Clarissa picked up Beau's bag. The no-longer-bored supply teacher put her arm around Beau's shoulder and steered him towards the first aid room. Clarissa went with them, casting a look of hate at Ryan. 'Wanker!'

The crowd dispersed, chivvied away by other teachers. Ryan put on his blazer and picked up his bag. He felt nothing; only Mr Grant's firm hand on his shoulder.

'To The Principal with you, Jones,' said Mr Grant.

'How much for this?'

She breathed in the familiar scents of history and age and storage. She crumpled the fabric and buried her nose in it, as she always did with fabric new to her. It was rarely brand new, of course. She only used new fabric as a last resort. This was one of the tenets of her business. She took great pride in using the used, a characteristic of almost all her work. *Road to California*: her business, her life, her living. Reusing, reclaiming, recycling, upcycling: whatever you wanted to call it – it was what she did. She looked carefully at this latest find, enjoying the funky clash of orange, purple, and green, in dreamy psychedelic swirls, pseudo-flowers, clouds, a strange repeated pattern with a fluid figure that might be a fairy, a girl, a woman. And was it silk? Nylon? She wasn't sure. The fabric smelled of tobacco, but that only added to its charm.

'It's a nice big bolt,' said the beer-gutted stall holder. Bob, she thought. He was a softie behind the gruff exterior. And the most unlikely person she could conceive of to be running a vintage fabric stall. 'A good five yards, I reckon. Genuine seventies, that is. Twenty quid?' Bob took a long, thoughtful drag on his cigarette. Joanna affected not to notice. But it smelled good.

She tried to get to the market most weeks, to pick up interesting finds. She had wanted to get out this morning, for an hour or two, just to get away from the sewing machines (she had two, plus an ancient Singer). She loved her work, but it was important to be healthy about it; and besides, new-to-her fabrics always inspired fresh ideas, exciting new projects. Her business thrived on it, and so did she. So these jaunts to the market were not a waste of time. They were essential.

'It certainly looks to be genuine seventies, doesn't it?' said Joanna, in her husky voice. She narrowed her eyes. 'I'll give you ten quid. How's that?'

Bob looked at her. She knew he remembered her, although they had never engaged in chit-chat. People did tend to remember her. She knew her bright green eyes and wild blond curls were striking.

'Fifteen?' he said. 'But I'm giving it to you.'

'You can't find your way to ten? I do come here practically every week.'

Bob raised his eyes to the sky and gave a little nod. He took another drag on his cigarette. The smoke drifted towards her.

She smiled and flourished a crisp note. Bob took it. He didn't offer her a bag, but she didn't need one. She had enough bags of her own.

'Thanks so much,' she said. 'I'll see you next week.' She checked her watch. There was enough time for a quick pit stop. She'd go to her favourite coffee shop, a small, independent outfit that sold no-nonsense coffee and tea in pretty vintage teacups with pot luck saucers, accompanied by a vast array of homemade cakes and biscuits.

As she turned from taciturn Bob and his wonderful stall, her mobile phone rang. She rummaged around for it in her handbag. She saw the caller ID and her heart didn't know whether to leap into her mouth or sink down into her toes. So it did both, in rapid succession, and she felt sick. There would be no coffee, no homemade cake today. Oh, no, no, no, not again. What now? *What now?*

'What on earth were you thinking?' said Mum, hands on hips. She swept her hair back from her face with an impatient swipe of her hand. She took one of her wide hairbands from her apron pocket and impatiently put it on, smoothing her hair back from her face, not taking her eyes from his. Ryan looked at the wall behind her. She shook out her hair and it fell in blond festoons over her shoulders.

'He asked me for a fight,' said Ryan. 'He flicked bits of rubber into my hair. They were *yellow* bits.'

'For goodness sake, Ryan, what difference does the colour of the rubber make?'

This was disappointing. He looked at the floor. He thought Mum would have understood. Ryan hated yellow almost as much as he hated people fiddling with his hair. Yellow was the colour of bananas. Mum knew this and he knew she knew. Why was she…?

They were at home. She had walked to school from the market to collect Ryan, and together, but very much apart and in silence, they had walked home.

'He asked me to fight,' said Ryan. 'I had to say yes. It's the rule.'

'You did not have to say yes! You could just as easily have said no. You should have said no. What on earth were you thinking? Ryan, you don't fight! I mean, you, Ryan, *you* don't fight. And on top of that you end up nearly knocking the poor kid's block off! God only knows what his mother thinks of me.'

Mum sent Ryan to his room to "mull things over". After all, she said, he had plenty of time to do that now. A three-day exclusion and a return-to-school meeting on Thursday probably meant the rest of the week off. Ryan secretly rejoiced. A week away from school without having to pretend to be ill! It was a dream come true. He stretched himself out on his bed, hands behind his head, and smiled at the ceiling. He could have walked away, he should have walked away. Of course. Mum was right. But not walking away had bought him time away from that dump, that centre of cruelty and tedium and shame, the place he hated above all other places. He would do it again. It was worth it, and by the look on Beau's face and the shocked reaction of the kids watching, Ryan was surprisingly good at it.

At times like these, stressful, Ryan-troubled times, she tried to focus on happier days, on good memories. So she remembered, four years ago, a man peering over the garden fence saying to her:

'Do you know you look like a chocolate lime? I could eat you all up!'

And she had been dumbfounded, just for a second, two seconds. She wasn't often dumbfounded, but this man, with his wide grin and frank eyes, threw her off balance, just for a moment.

'And you look like Chad,' she'd said, in the end, not as quick-wittedly as she would have liked, putting her hands squarely on her hips, taking up her default position. She trusted nobody.

Moving-in day. And a strange man, her new neighbour, peering over the fence and saying silly things to her. She liked it.

She habitually wore brown and she wore green. She wore a lot of brown and green. She wore pink too, in all its shades. These colours were, to her, colours of grace and harmony; they were natural and most importantly they "went with" her hair and her eyes. She knew the colours that suited her. Why wouldn't she know? Colour, pattern, harmony – these things made up her creative life. She wasn't a fan of rules, but she never, ever wore blue. On her it was too cold, and too unforgiving.

Chad, whose real name was Billy Plumb, and who was a plumber – "*Seriously?!*" – brought around cups of coffee and a packet of custard creams for her, and for himself, and they watched Ryan, nine years old, peer into the thick hedge at the far end of their new garden.

'He likes hedges,' Joanna said. 'Actually, he likes birds and nests and eggs. Which are to be found in hedges. You don't have a cat, Chad, do you?'

'Me?' said Billy. 'A cat? Good Lord, no. I hate the bloody things. All those revolting fur balls…'

'Dog?'

'No. I don't do pets at all, actually. Unless a woodlouse in my bedroom counts?'

He winked. But she was safe with this man, she realised. They were going to get along just fine.

Joanna looked out at Ryan peering into the hedge at the far end of the garden. The hedge was thicker than ever and badly needed to be pruned back, but there was no time. She was too busy preparing for the fair, too busy working on website orders, too busy working on Mrs Marchant's quilt. Maybe she could be cheeky and ask Billy to trim the hedge for her? Maybe she couldn't. He was such a great neighbour, and a good friend, and she would not take advantage of him. The hedge was not dissimilar to Ryan's hair, she thought, which was wild and curling and sun-bleached, like hers. Ryan, at thirteen, was just one inch shorter than her. He wore size eight shoes. It was disconcerting to her, mystifying. He had been born tiny, mewling and helpless. How could it be…? He still had his freckles, his limbs were still bony and awkward. His early-formed enthusiasm for birds, their nests and eggs, had not yet dwindled. Ryan was loyal.

The French windows were thrown open on this hot June day. Her "new" sewing machine (the other being the "old") had been whirring all morning. Now, she was jaded, and needed a rest. Yet the fair was less than three weeks away, and there was much to be done: the Melsham House Vintage and Craft Fair. She had attended for the past five years.

She thought Billy must be telepathic. Or could it be that he had noticed that her sewing machine had gone quiet? Either way, he flung open the gate that now separated their back gardens (constructed by him a year after she'd moved in), skipped into her kitchen, and with a flourish and a "Ta-da!" he set before her a jug of iced coffee and a plate of chocolate bourbons.

'You're amazing,' said Joanna, through a mouthful of pins.

'No, I've just got time on my hands.'

'Do you ever actually work, Billy?'

'When I feel like it.'

Billy now had four employees. So he was more of an administrator these days, he often claimed, a desk-hugging boss; he only really got involved with trickier jobs. Which was OK. And Joanna benefitted, obviously, so she ought not to complain too loudly.

'Oh, I'm not complaining!' she said sweetly, removing the pins and jabbing them into her ancient pincushion.

'Oi, David Attenborough!' shouted Billy, and Ryan turned from the hedge. He scowled. 'You want an ice-cool cola or what?' said Billy, pulling a can from his back jeans pocket and waving it at him. Ryan slowly walked back up the garden path, he entered the house, he took the can and thanked Billy. Cola was not generally encouraged. But Billy was kind. Joanna said nothing.

The mercury had reached thirty degrees, Billy told

them. Joanna murmured that she didn't doubt it. They drank their drinks. The iced coffee was delicious. She would just have the one bourbon, she said. "Things" were beginning to spread, just a little. You know? Billy did know, and he pointed to his own thickening waist, and with mock-wide eyes and a theatrical snarl, he bit two biscuits in half and chewed enthusiastically.

'No school this week, Ryan?' asked Billy, between mouthfuls.

'I look nothing like David Attenborough,' said Ryan.

'Oh,' said Billy. 'Right. I know that. It was a joke, you see?'

'In answer to your actual question, William, Ryan has had a fight,' said Joanna. 'At school. And he's been suspended for a few days.'

'Oh,' said Billy. 'I see. That's, er, that's not… ideal, is it?'
Ryan said nothing.

'Cola good, though?'

'Yes, thank you.'

'Want a bourbon?'

'Yes, please.' Ryan took one. He ate it quickly, cleanly. He finished his cola in three or four long gulps, and popped the can in the kitchen bin.

'Can I go back outside now please, Mum?'

'It's so hot, love. Oh, and cans in the recycling, remember? Fish it out later, would you? Wouldn't you rather stay in the house for a while? You've been out there for hours.'

'I'm searching for nests.'

'But you haven't found any. You've searched every inch of that hedge Ryan, every day, since March.'

'You have to keep looking. You can't find things if you don't look.'

She couldn't argue. She watched Ryan resume his careful searching. Billy watched her watching. He said nothing. She took up another biscuit.

Ryan always looked forward to the Melsham House Vintage and Craft Fair; it lasted all weekend, there was always a lot to do and see, and he got to have a look round Melsham House for free, in his capacity as stall holder (he and Mum got passes). He liked old houses, with their woody, leathery, dusty smells and their dark stillness, their gloomy corners. He liked the idea of all the untold stories that lurked in the creaks and sighs and whispers. Mum said he was a Romantic.

When Thursday dawned, Ryan covered his head with his patchwork quilt and wished that he didn't have to go to the meeting with "The Principal", as the head teacher called herself. Her name was Mrs Hunter, and she favoured a shade of lipstick Mum described (rather disdainfully) as "coral". The meeting would be awkward and embarrassing, because all meetings with Mrs Hunter were awkward and embarrassing. She would smile falsely and say things like, "Violence is not tolerated in The School". It was always "The School".

Mum knocked on his door at seven o'clock and told him to get up. She sounded weary and cross. It occurred to him that she probably didn't want to attend the stupid meeting either. She was busy and had "more than enough to do". For the first time he felt a pang of guilt over his fight with Beau Stirling. Why didn't he think of things? Why didn't he ever stop to consider? It was selfish of him. He thought he recognised in himself a glimmer of Mum's disappointment.

They ate breakfast, brushed their teeth, put on their shoes, all in silence. Mum fashioned her hair into a messy "updo", and they walked to school. Ryan walked as slowly as he could, Mum stopping every minute to nag him to hurry up. They sat in the corridor outside Mrs Hunter's office for ten long minutes on uncomfortable red plastic chairs. It was going to be another hot day.

Mrs Hunter finally opened her office door and beckoned them in. Her office was small and stuffy, with more uncomfortable plastic chairs. Bowing shelves were loaded with dusty books, folders, box files and manuals. The desk was huge and dark, with old teacup rings, all criss-crossing each other, forming a dense but uninspired pattern. A huge outdated computer took up one half of the desk, and an anaemic spider plant drooped from the high windowsill. Ryan glanced at Mum and he could see that she was, like him, slightly nervous. He didn't like this. He needed her to be strong and in control, at all times; especially now.

'Well, Simon,' said Mrs Hunter, which was a terrible start.

'Ryan,' said Mum, quickly; a little too quickly.

'Ryan. My apologies. Ry—an.'

Mrs Hunter appeared to scribble "Ryan" on her large notepad. She always carried around a large notepad, as though it was a shield, and her pen a sword.

'Ry—an Jones,' said Mum, fiddling with her hair. The updo was falling down.

'Thank you. Well, Ry—an Jones, as you know, Mr Grant has – umm – briefed me – thoroughly, about the unfortunate incident of Monday lunchtime. Ryan, as you know, violence is not tolerated in The School.'

Was Ryan supposed to say something? He looked at Mum. She looked at Mrs Hunter.

'So, I do hope your exclusion has given you ample time to reflect upon the serious nature of the… incident?' continued Mrs Hunter. Small beads of sweat formed on her forehead and her upper lip. She had coral lipstick on her teeth.

'Yes, miss.' Ryan felt he ought to say something.

'Ah-ah-ah?!' said Mrs Hunter, raising a finger and closing her eyes. Ryan dared not look at Mum. He would just say the things Mrs Hunter wanted him to say.

'Yes, Mrs Hunter.'

'That's better,' said Mrs Hunter, and she opened her eyes. 'Thank you, Ry—an. Well. I feel an apology should be made to the other pupil involved. If you are both in agreement, I'll send for him now.' Mrs Hunter's finger hovered over a suspiciously 1970s-looking buzzer.

'Will I get an apology too?' said Ryan, his sense of injustice wiping away his nerves. He was not going to "apologise" to Beau Stirling if Beau Stirling was not going to "apologise" to him. It didn't work like that. After all, it was Beau who'd flicked yellow rubber in his hair and it was Beau who had challenged him to a fight. Ryan was innocent, at least up until that point. He'd been quite happy minding his own business and not putting his hand up to say that the answer to the supply teacher's question was, of course, Mr Farthing.

Mrs Hunter appeared not to have heard Ryan. She pressed her buzzer and asked for Beau Stirling to be sent to her office.

'Excuse me,' said Mum, her nerves apparently vanquished too, 'but my son asked if this other boy is also going to be apologising. There were two boys fighting, not one. And Ryan was provoked. Absolutely, he was provoked. That doesn't excuse his actions, and God knows I feel as strongly as anybody else does about physical violence. I'm a p-p-pacifist, you see, so I don't... I can't support Ryan's actions... but this other child... it does... well, it does explain Ryan's actions and I think that should be acknowledged. Don't you?' She got there in the end, thought Ryan. What a relief. He loved it when Mum spoke her mind and stuck up for him, even if it was embarrassing at the same time. She meant it, and that was all that mattered.

Mrs Hunter looked at Joanna. 'Of course,' she said, coldly. *Pacifist?* – she seemed to be thinking. Ryan sank a little further down on his chair. Mum was great, and he knew he had every reason to be grateful to her and thankful for everything she did for him, which was a lot. But sometimes... sometimes she needed to keep her views and her politics to herself. She was just a little too sincere, and sometimes, Ryan knew, that made her come across as a bit naïve, and she wasn't at all naïve.

The awkward silence was interrupted a few moments later by a knock at the door.

'In!' called Mrs Hunter.

And Beau Stirling shuffled into the office, clearly embarrassed.

'Joe,' said Mrs Hunter.

'Beau,' Joanna said. She sighed and shook her head, but The Principal ignored her.

'Beau. Of course. Ry—an has something he would like to say to you,' said Mrs Hunter.

'I have not,' replied Ryan, earning himself a glare from Mum, and from the sweating head teacher.

'Yes, you have,' said Mrs Hunter. She smiled sweetly from Ryan to Beau to Joanna. She took out her handkerchief and dabbed at her forehead.

'Stop flicking yellow rubber in my hair,' said Ryan, shuffling his feet and concentrating on the floor. Mrs Hunter coughed.

'That's a fair request,' said Mum, 'and if Beau agrees to stop irritating Ryan, I'm sure Ryan will apologise, unreservedly.'

Beau stared at Ryan. Ryan finally looked at Beau. He used his well-rehearsed trick of looking at that part of a face at the top of the nose, between the eyes. People thought he was making eye contact, when he wasn't. Everyone seemed to regard eye contact as A Good Thing.

'I won't flick yellow rubber in your hair,' said Beau. 'I promise.'

'OK. I'm sorry I beat you up,' said Ryan.

'You didn't beat me up.'

'I'm sorry I floored you, then,' said Ryan.

'You didn't – all right,' said Beau. He was smirking, quite clearly, Ryan could see. The adults didn't appear to notice. Ryan didn't like it. Why didn't they notice? Mum? *Mum?* But she couldn't hear his thoughts. He'd learned that a long time ago. Probably he was worrying about nothing anyway: Beau smirked most of the time.

Mrs Hunter let out a sigh, and told Beau he could leave. He did so, not looking at Ryan or Joanna. Ryan was to return home and study "privately" for the remainder of the week, and return to school on Monday morning with a Renewed Attitude. Any more trouble from Beau Stirling, and Ryan was to come straight to Mrs Hunter's office. Immediately, straight to her office. There was to be no more violence, or the consequences would be serious indeed. Rules were rules, especially where safety was concerned. Ryan must respect those rules.

'I do!' protested Ryan. He liked rules. He made them up, all the time, and made himself stick to them.

'Many of the pupils were quite frightened,' said Mrs Hunter to Mum.

'I know,' said Mum. 'It's not like Ryan to fight.'

'Indeed. Let's put it down to an aberration, shall we?'

Ryan left the office feeling elated. He had received a promise from Beau that no more rubber would be flicked into his hair. And Ryan had said he was sorry for hitting Beau. Ryan wasn't convinced that Beau's assurance had been genuine, the smirk being a dead giveaway, but even so, the upshot of the meeting was: if he hit Beau or any other child in the school again, Ryan wouldn't break any promises, because he hadn't made any, and if he did hit Beau or another child in the school, Ryan would almost certainly be excluded again.

Perfect.

'Come on, Si—mon,' said Mum, 'let's go and get an ice cream. I reckon we could do with one.'

His favourite birds were robins. Not kestrels, or any other birds of prey, because they were cruel and hurt other birds. Kestrels were awesome, but Ryan preferred smaller, gentler creatures, and he liked the cheeky little robin best, with its fearless attitude.

Mum had killed one once, in her car, in the days when she had a car. The robin had just darted out from the roadside hedge, there was no time for Mum to react, and the poor little bird had been stuck behind a windscreen wiper, its wings fluttering in the wind, and Ryan had thought it was trying frantically to free itself. He'd insisted it was still alive, and made Mum stop the car. Ryan wanted to nurse it. He was going to be a vet, he said. He would take care of this injured robin and let it back into the wild once it had recovered. With a sigh, Mum had brought the car to a halt.

Ryan had climbed out and retrieved the robin. It was unbelievably light, weighing nothing in his shaking hands. It was hopelessly small. Perhaps it was a fledgling, fresh and trembling out of the nest, alone, inexperienced. He'd stood in front of the car for some time, examining the dead bird.

'Ryan?' Mum called, in the end. 'We need to get home, love.'

She apologised several times as they drove on. She kept looking at him. She was a nervous driver, and he asked her to look at the road. He was OK, he said.

'Just get us home,' said Ryan. He couldn't take his eyes from the robin, cradled in his hands. Its eyes were half closed, little black beads. Its legs were twigs. And its breast wasn't red; it was orange.

Ryan had buried the robin in a corner of the communal

garden that went with the flat; but the following morning it had gone; the grave was dug open, and just a small pile of earth remained.

Flick!

Ryan heard Clarissa's giggle, taunting and cruel. He kept his eyes locked onto the front of the class. He retrieved the rubber from his hair. He stared at it, his mind racing, computing, working it out. He had been one step behind Beau, obviously. And he thought he'd had it all worked out. Stupid, stupid... the rubber was red. RED. And that smirk in Mrs Hunter's office had said it all, of course. *I won't flick yellow rubber in your hair. I promise.*

Beau was full of clever little promises. Beau was the most hateful little prick Ryan had ever met. Didn't Beau know there were rules? Rules you should break, and rules you shouldn't. Did he have no sense of pride? Or rightness?

Flick!

Ryan struggled to ignore it. He once again could sense all eyes and ears in the class tuning in to the situation developing around him. It was happening all over again, only this time there was a bigger sense of expectation, and a lot more nudging. He kept his eyes fixed on the whiteboard, the words blurring. He tried to concentrate. Mrs Marchant, who had returned to school last week, glanced in Ryan's direction, but she didn't seem to understand. Had nobody told her? Mr Grant? Mrs Hunter, surely...? Didn't these people communicate? Ryan tried to focus; sweating, prickling. He felt sick.

And Ryan could read no more, because his eyes were full of tears. Why was this happening? Why did they have to treat him like this? What had he done? Why couldn't he just turn round and tell them all to *fuck off*?

Was it because he had no dad? His dad would tell them to fuck off, he knew. Anyone's dad would do that. It would be normal. His dad would defend him, or teach him to defend himself.

Flick!

Ryan's tears flowed, hot and toxic. He couldn't stop them. He sobbed, once, loud, trying but failing to strangle it. Somebody laughed. He trembled, he clenched his sweating palms into tight fists. He thought he said something like, 'Oh!', or perhaps it was 'Beau!', and Mrs Marchant looked over to him and said 'Ryan?' but her voice sounded far off, and was he dreaming all of this, was it nothing more than a nightmare? He thought of Mum, sitting at the kitchen table, busily preparing for the Melsham House Vintage and Craft Fair; and he thought of his father, who he couldn't remember, but had so often imagined, shaking his head wisely, telling him to ignore it all, because these kids were nothing but a bunch of *sorry-arsed dickheads*.

'Stop it!' a voice screeched, the voice of a person who'd had enough. And all that happened in a strange, convoluted order which later he would not be able to unpick; only logic was left to dictate what happened, and when. There would be no memory for him, as there would be for others. Ryan was aware of Mrs Marchant leaping up from her chair and pushing her way towards him... somebody crying out 'Ryan!' – probably it was Mrs Marchant – girls screaming... his chair falling with a loud crash – Beau's shocked but untouched face and a fist, Ryan's fist, tightly balled, smashing into Clarissa Cooper's face, her blood pouring down from her nose onto her white shirt, her mouth opening to join in the chorus of screams all around.

Mrs Hunter, in clipped sentences, told Joanna what had happened and that was that, Ryan was to leave and not return. Mrs Hunter would of course speak to the Governors and the Local Authority, but she envisaged total support. Ryan, for whatever reason, was a danger to fellow pupils, and to staff, and there was no place for him in The School. So Ryan left, feeling sorry for hitting a girl so hard, for hitting a girl at all. He'd not meant to. He'd lashed out. He'd been desperate. He said nothing to Mrs Hunter, who would not understand even if he tried to explain. Violence was not tolerated at The School, of course, and Ryan understood that only the mantra made sense to Mrs Hunter, while his futile explanations would not.

Mum was silent as they walked home; horribly silent. When they were home, she asked Ryan for his version of events. She bit her lip and listened carefully as Ryan told her the whole sorry story. He concluded by saying he was glad to have been excluded from school because he hated it more than anything in the whole world, it was hell on earth, but he had not meant to do it by hitting a girl, even though he hated that particular girl too. It was... unfortunate. That was all. He'd apologise if he ever got the chance, really he would.

Mum believed him. She believed him absolutely. There was not a flicker of doubt or even reproach in her eyes, about her mouth. It was what he'd hoped for; to be believed.

Joanna stared at her kitsch retro red telephone for many minutes before picking up the receiver one more time. She'd been making calls all evening, garnering clues, getting closer. She found herself stammering, a tic she had battled with all her life when nervous, and especially when speaking on the telephone. Really, it would have been simpler to email, or send messages on Facebook. But there was urgency, she needed to make contact today, she needed help today. She'd been needing help for an awful lot longer than that, but she didn't want to admit that just yet. One thing at a time. Recriminations could wait. She'd spoken to old friends, old acquaintances, people she had half-forgotten or half-remembered. They seemed to remember her. They all sounded delighted to hear from her. She heard gossip and rumours, baby news, she heard about marriages, divorces, affairs, scandals and tragedies. She reminisced. She fielded awkward questions. She even laughed; and she told nobody much about herself, or about her son. Many of the people she spoke to didn't even know she had a son.

Finally, she had the information she needed, and it was time. Every proud cell in her body resisted, and she swallowed hard as she finally dialled the number she had spent so many hours tracking down. She cleared her throat and tried to steady her stammer. *Speak clearly*, she admonished herself. *Get a grip*. Her hands shook as she held the receiver to her ear. The low buzz of the dialling tone growled at her, threatening, and she held the phone away from her, as though it would bite. Then she dialled the number, slowly, making sure she got it right. And the telephone rang, and rang. It rang. She cleared her throat again. She visualised the packet of cigarettes she kept in the secret little purple pouch in her handbag. Later, she would smoke one later, whatever the outcome of this call.

Pick up, damn you. Answer. About to hang up in disappointment and relief, she finally heard a click and an old, familiar voice say, 'Hi'.

'It's m-me,' Joanna said. She coughed. She tried again. 'It's me.'

There was a lengthy pause. She visualised herself taking a long, slow drag on one of her cigarettes.

'Shit.'

It was him, without question.

'Joanna? Is that you?'

'Yes.'

'Oh, wow. Shit. Again. God, how are you, honey? It's been so long. Give me a moment, would you? I got to sit down. Man…!'

She forced herself to speak, faltering at first, shy even. He listened, in respectful silence, asking only a few questions. She spoke with increasing fluency and confidence, as the years and the obstacles and her stammer slipped away from her. Some people were impossible to pin down, and he was one of those. But a promise was extracted, an agreement, of sorts, was reached, and as she put the phone down, she sighed, she rested her head in her hands, and she rocked herself to and fro. But – she had done it. And it hadn't been that bad, she had coped, and she'd said the things she'd needed to say. Now, it was up to him.

How could she not believe Ryan? He was her son, her only child, who rarely lied. There were no gaps in his account, nothing to jolt her into shame or panic. It was unfortunate, as he said, of course it was. Physical violence she hated, and her son, her sensitive, beautiful son, was becoming violent. It was unacceptable to her, but nevertheless it was a fact, and it was happening. She would have to accept that, and address it. Her telephone call… would he come through for them? Would he make a difference? It needed to be stopped. It was not to be tolerated. Mrs Hunter had been right. Ryan needed to learn that, and fast. This was one thing Joanna felt she could not teach him. Her boy was becoming a man and she was not a man, she could not fully understand that process.

But he would, or he should, the man she had phoned, and he'd said he would help. Give him a few days, he'd said. He had "shit" of his own to sort out. But he'd come. He'd help. He'd try to, honey, at least. OK?

JULY 2006

She had no idea what to do about finding another school. For a few days she did nothing. She had too much work to do. As it was nearly the end of the summer term, there seemed little point in rushing Ryan into a new school, dashing about the shops buying new uniform. She decided it could wait until September, and when she telephoned the Local Authority to talk about other schools, it was agreed that the summer holidays would provide a welcome "cooling-off period", time for Ryan to calm down and perhaps "reflect" on his actions; and he could start a new school after the holidays. The Local Authority would be in touch in early September. The woman spoke of educational psychologists; a Pupil Referral Unit, which might be appropriate, at least until a place in school could be found; psychologists, again. Her "troubled" son. Perhaps Joanna could take Ryan to their GP and request investigations or an assessment? Medications?

'No,' said Joanna. 'Stop right there. There's no need for any of that. Good God! What are you—? Ryan… he's OK. He's just a bit mixed up. And he gets bullied, doesn't that need sorting out more than anything? He retaliates. What does everybody expect? He's the victim of bullies. Get the bullies "assessed", why don't you?'

The woman from the Local Authority made conciliatory noises. Joanna ended the call. She was getting nowhere. Clearly the woman thought she was a hopeless mother. Maybe she was. Maybe that was the problem.

The summer holiday spread wide and flat in front of him like one of Mum's queen-sized quilts. He would be able to forget about school and about his exclusion. He could forget that Beau and Clarissa and all their revolting friends even existed. He wished he could forget Mum's disappointment. But he didn't feel disgraced. He was relieved that he wouldn't have to go back to that school. He was terrified of starting a new one, of course. But he could push that thought back into a far corner of his mind, the same corner where he would try to keep all thoughts of his father from now on.

For Ryan knew, his father was a no-show, he always had been and always would be. There was no "Dad". Ryan knew this. "Dad" was a dream, a person who existed only in his imagination. He had to put him out of his mind. He had to stop dreaming. He had to stop this yearning before it took over his life. There was just him, and his mum, the way it had always been. His dad had "run out" on them, he had not wanted "to know". A tale often told, and now believed. It was sinking in. Mum meant it.

It was Friday night, and tomorrow morning the Melsham House Vintage and Craft Fair would begin. Mum had been feverishly sewing all week, creating cushions, bunting, bags, pouches, table runners, finishing off throws. Her sewing machines had taken up permanent residence on the dining table, along with mountains of fabric, ribbons, buttons, pins, buckles and a vast tray of notions. He and Mum had taken to eating all their meals outside on the patio, but as the weather was so warm and dry, it didn't matter at all, and living outside was preferable to living in the kitchen. Ryan loved the feeling of being in the open, of his ceiling being the sky. It made all things seem possible, even if they weren't.

Billy Plumb's car was loaded with all the creations Mum would be hoping to sell over the weekend. Mum hadn't a car these days, but it didn't matter, because Billy was always willing to lend a hand, as well as his wheels. He usually stayed on at the fair to keep them company and look after the stall when Ryan or Mum needed the loo, or needed to get something to eat or drink. Gregarious and engaging, Billy enjoyed meeting new people. Ryan didn't understand him, but he liked him.

The fair was busy. People were stopping at Road to California and admiring the "signature quilt" Joanna had made, which was resplendent as the backdrop to the stall. It was green and brown and pink and white and made up of oodles of squares and triangles. The pattern was also called Road to California, and it was her favourite pattern to work on, and she had chosen it as the name of her business for that reason. It was the pattern Mrs Marchant had chosen for her quilt, and Joanna had brought along the half-completed project to work on at the fair. And people were watching her sew, and asking questions. She had brought along her old Singer sewing machine, which was much harder to use than either of her electric machines, and she only ever used it at shows; it was old-fashioned and romantic, and people were fascinated by it.

Mrs Marchant had chosen a colour scheme of blue and white for her quilt, so it looked different from Joanna's; crisp and stark. That was the beauty of patchwork: the same pattern, but in different colours, different fabrics. She loved these creative disguises and deceptions. She never tired of them. She never tired of talking about her work. She never tired of working.

Joanna glanced at Ryan as he sat beside her, quietly people-watching. He was grave. He looked tired. He slept badly in the heat. Her sleep was fitful and worrisome. It had been almost a fortnight since Ryan had been expelled from school; a fortnight since Joanna had made *that* phone call, to *that* man. And she had heard nothing. Presumably the "shit" of his own was holding him up. But she was not going to plead with him, or ring again. She'd told him what had happened, and it was up to him to come through, or not. He'd said he would, as she kept reminding herself; but of course, he said a lot of things. She'd all but given up.

This weekend, she would try to forget her troubles. There was work to be done, and fun to be had, and it would be good for Ryan to relax and enjoy the fair, as he usually did. It would be good for her too. She needed this. She needed to be positive. Late last night she'd sat out on the patio and smoked three cigarettes.

The craft stalls were in large white marquees, open all around the sides so there was at least a breeze. But it was still hot under the heavy canvas. They saw a girl walk past holding a large ice cream with a chocolate flake sticking out the top. Joanna felt Ryan looking at her.

'Great idea!' said Joanna. She fumbled around in her purse for some money.

Ryan watched Mum closely. Something was wrong, he could tell. He didn't know exactly what, but she seemed weird, jumpy; she was nervous. But it couldn't be the fair, because it was going well and she had attended this fair for years now. She was a regular. There was nothing to be nervous of here. Perhaps she was just frazzled by him and his antics at school, as she had described the events to Billy. And her face was pink, matching the dress she was wearing. The dress was one of her own creations, a "shift" she called it, and her hair was caught up off her face by a matching headband, and she was wearing the strappy brown sandals she'd found at a car boot sale for 50p. Ryan was deeply embarrassed by his mother's penchant for all things second-hand. He would never, ever consider wearing somebody else's shoes. It was disgusting, he often told her. Shirts and trousers, they were one thing... But shoes...! No.

'Nonsense!' was her usual response. 'They're as good as new with a few baby wipes and a squirt of antibacterial. What's not to like? Get over yourself.' *Beggars can't be choosers, Ryan. We've always lived this way, we have no choice. Don't be so surprised.*

Billy wanted an ice cream too, and after some arguing over who would pay for them, Ryan was dispatched with Joanna's money to buy three 99s-with-a-flake.

The ice cream van was popular and Ryan had to queue for a long time. He became anxious that the ice creams would melt before he got them back to the marquee. He splayed his delicate fingers around the three cones and walked, almost ran, as fast as he could, back to the stall.

Billy helped him distribute the ice creams, and he loudly smacked his lips while enjoying his. Billy was an enthusiastic eater, but he was messy, which Ryan didn't like.

'Keep your ice creams away from my stuff,' said Mum, 'or I'll—'

Mum stared across the marquee, open-mouthed. She speechlessly passed her ice cream to Billy, who took it from her, puzzled.

'What's up, sweet?' he said.

Ryan looked where Mum was looking, but all he could see was a throng of people. Then a man, dressed in black jeans and a white T-shirt and carrying a black motorcycle helmet, made his way over to Road to California. He walked slowly, but deliberately. Mum stared, her face growing ever pinker. Billy stared too. Ryan didn't know where to look, or what to do. So he remained in his seat and slowly licked his ice cream.

Ryan watched the man, and thought he looked a bit like David Beckham. Or a film star. He didn't watch films or television much, so he couldn't often tell one famous person from another. Was this man famous? Was that why they were staring at him?

The man stopped at their stall. Mum's face was red. Ryan noticed that she clung to the edge of the table. She tilted her head back in that defiant way of hers. Ryan felt apprehensive, recognising signs in his mother that so often spelled trouble.

'Hi, Joanna,' said the man. He smiled uncertainly, and nodded his head.

'Lex,' said Mum, quietly.

'Yup,' he said, half smiling, half looking scared to death.

'You're here,' said Mum. Her voice was squeaky. 'I didn't expect…'

'I'm here. Is that OK?'

'I—yes. Yes. It's OK.'

'I wanted to see the beautiful things you exhibit,' said the man. 'You told me about the fair when you called, remember? I looked it up… I figured I could… I'm here…' Ryan thought he had an American accent. He was a film star, then? How did Mum know him? 'I figured I could take a look at your work,' the man said, lamely. Pity. He looked so cool.

'I don't just exhibit. I sell,' said Mum, her voice stronger this time.

'Sure. I'm sorry.'

'I have to make money somehow.'

Mum's voice was normal again, unlike her first squeaky "Lex. You're here". And what a weird thing to say, Ryan thought. And what a weird name – Lex. And Mum's voice was now harder, louder, and she had more to say.

'I have my own b-b-business. Maybe you saw a feature I had in *Country Living* magazine? Back in May?'

'No, no, I didn't catch that.' The man looked embarrassed. So did Mum. Billy slowly licked his ice cream, studying the man, studying Mum, a quiet little grin decorating his face.

'It was a small piece, but it got me noticed,' said Mum. 'I sold a lot from my website after that.'

She looked away from this "Lex". She ignored Ryan's stare. Billy's ice cream was seemingly forgotten, dripping from his hands. Billy's eyes were large and staring.

'Oh, for Christ's sake!' said Mum. 'Can we all just... I'm forgetting my manners. Billy P-p-plumb, this is Lex Nicholson. Lex, this is my neighbour and friend, Billy Plumb. He's a plumber. Really. Billy, Lex is a... a... drifter.'

Ryan thought he heard this Lex man mutter, 'Jesus, Joanna.' But he wasn't sure.

Lex held out his hand to Billy, but of course, Billy's hands were full of melting ice creams, so after some shuffling about and awkward withdrawals of hands, Billy contented himself with a breezy, 'Hi, there!' Ryan thought his voice was almost as squeaky as Mum's. What the hell was the matter with him?

'And this is my son, Ryan.' Mum pulled Ryan to his feet and rested her hands on his shoulders.

'Hi, Ryan,' said the man called Lex. He had short black hair and stubble on his chin and under his nose. It looked like he hadn't shaved for a few days. His skin was golden and pink. Ryan supposed the man was handsome, like all film stars and famous football players. Ryan studied the black motorcycle helmet. There was a red scarf stuffed into it.

'Do you ride a motorbike?' Ryan said.

'Hell no, I ride a motorcycle,' replied this stranger who evidently was not a stranger, at least not to Mum. 'A Harley right now. But I've ridden a lot of bikes.'

Ryan liked motorbikes (motor*cycles*), and had always wanted to have a ride on one. He liked this man, even if Mum didn't. He had a motorbike. That was cool. Ryan ignored his mother's quiet tutting. So did this man Lex.

Mum, hands on hips, looked hard at Lex. Ryan knew she was accusing him of something. She sometimes spoke to

Ryan in the tone of voice she was using now, and she sometimes stood with her hands on her hips, just like this, her blond curls falling forwards from the hairband and partly obscuring her face, but failing to disguise her rising feelings. Lex looked from Ryan, to Mum, to Billy. It was as though he was hoping to find a friendly face. Ryan smiled at him.

'I like motorcycles,' he said.

'Do you have one?' said Lex.

'Of course he doesn't have one!' said Mum, swiping the hair from her face.

'I started riding little bikes when I was about six or seven,' said Lex. 'What are you – eleven, twelve?'

'I'm thirteen. I'll be fourteen soon.'

'God. Of course,' Lex said. 'The years…! Anyways, I used to ride in my old man's yard. It was a big yard. Good times.'

'Unfortunately, my "yard" is rather small, and Ryan doesn't even have a bicycle, let alone a motorcycle. We're not all made of money,' said Mum, and she took an elastic from her wrist and tied back her hair, shaking it off her face, knotting it at the nape of her neck. She adjusted the pink hairband. She was regaining her composure. Which wasn't necessarily a good thing.

Lex reached across the table and ruffled Ryan's hair. Ryan managed to suppress a wince.

'I'd better be going,' Lex said, smiling weakly at Mum. She didn't smile back. Billy, ice creams still in hand, nodded in an awkward fashion and Lex raised a hand to him as he backed away. Then he turned and started to walk off. Ryan didn't want him to go, but he wasn't sure why. He'd never met an American person before, especially not a famous one. He seemed nice, and Ryan was impressed that Mum knew him. Could he call him back? Run after him? Probably not.

Was he his d—?

But the thought was too much. He couldn't be. Yet he'd ruffled his hair. It had felt familiar, somehow. Dreams rarely come true, he knew. He had a feeling, and he couldn't shake it. He had felt something, something new and old and weird, when this man had ruffled his hair. And hadn't Mum once told him his dad lived in America…?

Mum sighed, muttered, 'Oh, fuck this, he is *not* getting away…!' and she snatched up one of her business cards and chased after the man. They stood together for a long time, just outside the marquee. Mum stood with her hands on her hips, listening intently to what the man had to say, which was, apparently, an awful lot. He took the red scarf from his helmet and wrapped it loosely around his neck. He took out a pair of black gloves. Evidently, he was preparing to leave, and in the end they parted. Mum walked slowly back to her stall.

'Who was that?' asked Billy.

'That was an old friend of mine,' said Mum. There was a long pause during which nobody spoke. She couldn't look at Ryan.

'Have you seen *Blade Runner*?' said Billy.

'Yes!' snapped Mum. 'Please don't say it, Billy. It's been noted before. The man's a big-headed arse as it is! No, really. He is.'

'Uh-huh,' said Billy, and raised his eyebrows at Ryan.

'He's coming to dinner tomorrow night. Would you like to join us, Billy?'

'Would I!' said Billy, at last dunking what remained of the ice creams onto the grass beneath his seat and noticing with disgust his sticky hands. 'What time do you want me there?'

Ryan knew. He knew who Lex was. Yet he couldn't remember him, of course. He'd been too young. But he wasn't supposed to know, so he said nothing. He didn't know what to say.

The dinner was going well. It had been difficult at first, with long awkward silences and surreptitious glances around the table. Ryan realised why Mum had invited Billy. He was chatty and funny and did his best to keep things from getting too quiet, for too long. He brought with him a bottle of wine too. Mum was nervous, but after a glass of wine she came alive, as she always did, and she talked more. She was celebrating. She had sold lots of things at the Melsham House Vintage and Craft Fair, and had been commissioned to make another quilt.

But mostly the three adults around the table talked about The Weather, The Government, Conglomerates, the extortionate price of petrol, the even more extortionate cost of flights; they even talked about Global Warming. Ryan could tell that none of it was what the adults really wanted to talk about, especially Mum and Lex. Why did people do that? Ryan wondered. Why couldn't people just get straight to the point?

After the creamy homemade mushroom stroganoff (Ryan's favourite), and crunchy salad, they had trifle with hundreds and thousands. The adults had more wine.

'This is good,' said Lex, studying the bottle. It was the bottle Mum had provided. Probably he was being polite, Ryan thought. Mum had no money for wine, let alone expensive stuff. This would not have cost her much. 'And such good food too. You always were a great cook, Joanna.'

She appeared not to have heard him, because she said, 'So where did you say you are staying?'

'I don't think I did say,' said Lex, unflustered.

'Would you say now, then, p-p-please?' Mum was going to get cross, Ryan could tell, because her voice was becoming high-pitched, and her eyes were slits of sharp, searing green. Warning signs, Ryan knew. He wondered if Lex recognised them too? He suspected he did. He knew who Lex was, all right. It was obvious. But nobody had told him yet, so he remained 99 per cent certain rather than the 100 per cent he wanted to be. Would he be expected to act surprised? Were they going to actually tell him, at some point? Did they think he was stupid? And yet – he couldn't believe this was happening. It felt like a dream, bizarre but real, concrete but fluid.

'I've rented a cute little cottage,' said Lex. 'Just out of town. I moved in on Friday. It has a fridge and a stove and not much else. I'll need to get my shit out of storage.'

'I see,' said Mum. She stared into her wine glass. But her eyes were no longer quite so angry.

'Is that OK?' said Lex.

'Of course it's OK. It's nothing to do with me, is it? Just try not to swear around Ryan, please.'

'Mum!' whispered Ryan. That was rich coming from her! And hadn't she ever been to school? There wasn't a single swear word he (or she) hadn't heard and hadn't used. Mum ignored him and continued her interrogation of Lex. 'Are you planning to stay around a while? Do you have a job or anything?'

41

'No job. But I am sticking around.' Lex paused. He looked around the table. 'OK, Joanna, I'm gonna level with you now,' he said, leaning back in his chair. 'I have money. My mom sadly passed a—she died last year.' A sympathetic murmur rose from Billy. 'And, uh, she left me her house, her belongings, her money, savings, pension, the whole damn kit and caboodle. I don't need to work again, if I don't want to. It's kind of cool but at the same time it's a little scary. Now that I really can live where I like and do what the fuck I like, well, I don't know where to live or what to do.'

'Please try not to swear, Lex,' said Mum.

Shut the fuck up, Mum! Didn't you hear what he said about the money and stuff? And his mum dying, who was my grandmother, probably. You should say you're sorry to hear it, or something.

'Actually,' continued Mum, 'I knew about your mum and your... situation. Someone told me when I was ringing... someone told me. I'm sorry.'

Well done, Mum.

'Well, it sounds bloody wonderful to me, you lucky thing!' said Billy. He winked at Ryan. 'I meant the not having to work bit. Not your mother dying... I'm sorry to hear about that.'

'Sure. I appreciate that,' said Lex. 'People die, right? No point in being coy about it.'

'Where are you from?' Ryan asked. Everyone looked at him. It was the first time he had spoken all evening.

'Well, I'm from the US, originally,' said Lex. 'The USA. My mom was American, a California girl by choice, a Texan by birth. She got bitten by the travel bug and came to England in, oh, I guess that would have been around 1970?

42

She was pure hippy. Do you know, and I'm pretty damn proud of this, my mom took me all the way to Woodstock. I was five years old.'

Ryan blinked.

'Ryan doesn't know what Woodstock is,' said Mum. Her sympathy for his loss was short-lived, it seemed.

'Yes, I do,' said Ryan. 'Blenheim Palace is at Woodstock. We've been there. It's not that far from here. It's where Winston Churchill was born. His mum was American too.'

'Is that so? Bless your heart, kid, but that ain't the same Woodstock. My mom and me went to the music festival at Woodstock in upstate New York, in 1969. Before we came to England.'

'Oh,' said Ryan. He didn't understand. Mum was right. 'Where were you born?'

'I was born in the States. My mom got… she got… she got knocked up when she wasn't married. In those days, back in the sixties, it was a little frowned upon, you know? But my mom, she was a real strong lady. Like your mom, actually.' Lex smiled at Mum, who stared frostily back. Lex continued his tale. 'She brought me to England with her. She'd thought of leaving me with relatives, or even my dad, she once told me… but in the end she just took off with me. She got work. She liked Britain, a lot. But it wasn't California. She felt kind of alone, I guess. And a little homesick. Europe was cold, she always said. Pure Joni Mitchell.'

Ryan was stumped. Mum tutted and rolled her eyes. Billy poured himself another glass of wine. They were now on Billy's bottle, Ryan noticed. Lex looked like he was waiting for the fierce pitch of a hardball.

'So,' he continued. 'My mom and I went back to the States, we hooked up with my dad for a year or two. It didn't work out. He bought me a little motorbike. But he wasn't really dad material.' Lex coloured, he stopped talking, and took a large mouthful of wine. He wiped his mouth with the back of his hand. Nobody said anything.

'Why are you called Lex?' said Ryan. 'The only Lex I know is Lex Luther.'

'Oh, well, my real name is Alexander. Lex is short for Alexander. You get it?' Lex seemed relieved to have something else to talk about.

'I always thought it rather pretentious,' said Mum, loudly. Was she getting drunk? She was becoming obnoxious, which wasn't like her, despite everything. Ryan willed her to shut up. She took a large gulp of wine.

'Yes, I get it,' Ryan said to Lex, ignoring his mum. 'I think it's a good name. It's better than Ryan.'

'What's wrong with Ryan?' said Mum, starting to ladle another portion of trifle into the dessert bowls, whether the guests wanted it or not. Lex put his hand over his. 'No more, thanks, Joanna. It was too good.'

'Oh, I'll have your portion, Lex!' said Billy. He shrugged. He muttered something about having a healthy appetite.

'Ryan is a boring name,' said Ryan. He turned to Lex. 'Why don't you still live in America?'

'Oh, that's a long story. I wanted to see the world, I guess. I'm my mom's son, all right. I went to college, in the States first, then over here. After college I travelled all over Europe. I followed in my mom's footsteps, you might say. I got jobs, bartending, that kind of work. I saved my money, and moved on.'

44

'On your motorcycle?'

'On *a* motorcycle, sure. It was such a cool time. I had a ball. Then I met your mom. That's kind of a nutshell version of events.'

'And then what?' said Ryan.

'I hung around for a while. I dated your mom. We got to be boyfriend and girlfriend. We had some… we had some great times.' Mum and Lex exchanged red-faced looks over the trifle. Billy coughed.

'Then what?' said Ryan.

'Well, then. Well. OK. Some shit happened… and then we broke up. It was my fault, of course. Your mom wanted something I couldn't give her. I messed up, kid.'

'Are you my dad?' said Ryan. He'd run out of patience. He might as well just say it, and he had. It was too bad if nobody liked it.

Billy glanced nervously from Joanna to Lex.

'Joanna?' said Lex.

'You are my dad, aren't you?' said Ryan. *Come on, out with it. Stupid grown-ups. Always thinking they knew better.*

'Ryan,' said Mum. 'Oh! Look, Lex is your dad, yes. I didn't know how or when to tell you. I'm sorry.'

Ryan got up from his chair slowly. He walked round the table to stand next to Lex. Ryan held out his hand. 'I'm pleased to meet you,' Ryan said. They shook hands.

'I'm pleased to meet you, too,' said Lex. He ruffled Ryan's hair. Ryan winced, but he liked it.

'What do you think of birds?' asked Ryan.

'They're OK, I guess.'

'I love birds.'

'Cool. Maybe you'll be an ornithologist someday, huh?'

45

'No, I'm going to be a vet. Or a writer. Mrs Marchant says I will be a writer.'

'Great.'

The conversation dwindled to nothing. Nobody ate or drank or spoke. Ryan returned to his seat opposite Lex.

'Lex,' said Billy, after a while, leaning across the table, his head leaning on one hand. 'Do you know you look exactly like a young Harrison Ford?'

'Shut up, Billy!' warned Mum, but she was smiling, despite herself. Billy apologised. Lex said yeah, he'd heard that, but he didn't get it. He was flattered, he guessed, and it was kind of droll, although he really couldn't see it himself, but hey… and the tension drifted away and the grown-ups laughed a lot and drank more wine. Ryan sat among them, watching Lex, listening to him, occasionally talking, but mostly trying to take in, through all his senses, the fact that it was truly his father who sat just across the table from him.

Ryan got to bed long after midnight. Lex stayed later than planned. Billy left them at about 11.30, claiming he had an early start in the morning, even though he didn't, and he complained that Mum's house was starting to remind him of The Waltons (whatever that meant), and he was going to be sick. He was only joking of course. But there was a strange atmosphere that evening, and Ryan felt it. His dad was there, in the kitchen, telling him about his life, how he'd met Ryan's "mom"; 'I met her at a party. She was the prettiest girl in the room.' Of course, Ryan had a lot of further questions, and some of them would probably not be easy for Lex to answer, but for tonight Ryan just wanted to feel the thrill, the sheer joy, of meeting his dad. He had a real dad with a deep voice and a soft American accent; a proper face framed by neatly cut hair; a handsome face, Ryan knew. At least, Billy obviously thought so. His dad looked a bit like Harrison Ford. Ryan knew him from the Star Wars films. And his dad was exactly how Ryan had imagined him and dreamed of him, which was the strangest thing. Maybe he did remember him, somehow, from when he was a baby.

The following day, Ryan felt listless, unsettled. He asked Mum a few questions about Lex, but she didn't give satisfactory replies. She was cagey, hiding something, Ryan felt sure. Ryan lolled on the sofa, watching TV. Mum sat at the kitchen table and worked on Mrs Marchant's quilt.

Ryan wasn't sure who heard the motorbike first, but by the time Lex hurled the bike to a growling, revving halt outside the gate, both Ryan and Mum were at the living room window; one of them agog, the other aghast.

'What do you think you are doing?' Mum asked, her head on one side, hands on hips, after she opened the front door. Lex strolled along the path. He carried with him a spare motorcycle helmet.

Ryan pleaded. So did Lex, in the end.

'Joanna, please, honey. I'm not that stupid. Just a gentle spin, is all.'

'Lex, you don't just turn up and expect to take my son out on your motorbike. It doesn't work like that. You should have asked me about it last night.'

'You're right. I'm sorry,' said Lex. He looked at the floor.

Ryan glared at Mum, and she glared back, but something softened about her face, her body relaxed. There was hope.

'I will be as sedate as you want me to be, Joanna, I promise,' said Lex, 'and I can show Ryan my cottage and maybe fix him something to eat. What do you say? We won't even be on the bike for long.'

'You promise to go slow and take care?' said Mum.

'Yes. Totally. You wouldn't recognise me,' said Lex.

'All right,' she said, finally, 'but if you have an accident, if you hurt my son, I'll never forgive you. And you'll never forgive yourself, will you?'

Lex looked suitably chastised; forewarned. He shook his head. He nodded.

'Oh, for heaven's sake!' said Mum. 'Just go, the pair of you. But I want Ryan home in time for his tea, six o'clock, sharp.'

'You got it.'

Ryan put on the helmet and it did fit, but he couldn't do up the strap, so Lex helped him. They climbed onto the bike and Lex told Ryan to wrap his arms around him, and not to let go, for any reason. When they went around bends, Ryan was to lean in the same direction as him. He just had to feel it. It was simple and easy and he'd get it in no time at all.

And with a roar of the bike's engine, they were off, the wind blowing all over and around them, the motorbike slipping and gliding through the streets and between parked cars like a dolphin swimming through the ocean. This was slow? This was sedate? Ryan held on tight, and he was exhilarated, gripping Lex's strong body, leaning around bends in unison with him, straightening up again, and feeling the backward wrench as the bike accelerated on straight stretches of road. He felt it, he knew what to do, and it was simple, Lex was right. Ryan felt he'd been doing it all his life; there was no need to learn. It was like a memory, buried, but there, and resurfacing, no effort required. Lex was impressed, giving him regular thumbs up, and Ryan glowed with pride.

On the edge of town, Lex slowed the bike to a low crawl, and they turned into a long, gravelled drive, flanked by trees and shrubs. Lex pulled up, turned off the engine and helped Ryan take off his helmet. Everything seemed so silent after the roar of the Harley's engine.

'Come take a look at my cottage,' said Lex, as he removed his helmet and ran his hands over his short dark hair. Ryan immediately wished he had hair like Lex's. But Ryan's hair was "pure Joanna", as Lex would say.

Ryan knew the house; he had walked or driven past it many times and glimpsed it through the trees and shrubs. It was large, not what Ryan would have described as a cottage at all. The windows were far too big to be cottage windows. Ryan knew cottages were small and thatched and white, and they had climbing roses all over them. This house was tall and red-bricked and it was posh. It had ivy on it, not roses; and it had a long, endless back garden with apple and cherry trees, and a wildlife pond.

Mum would probably describe the rooms as "cavernous". The kitchen was definitely the kind she dreamed of, with lots of cupboards and a big, red, weird-looking oven. The oven was called an Aga, Lex explained. Ryan had heard of them. Lex wasn't sure how you were supposed to use it, but he'd figure it out. There was a large fireplace in the living room, and not much else.

'Where's all your furniture?' said Ryan, looking around the near-empty living room. 'Where are your… things?'

'Good question, kid. Well, I don't have much. Some of my stuff is in a crate someplace. And the rest my old girlfriend kept when we broke up.'

'When did you break up?'

'A while ago. I pissed her off. Anyways, I went off for a ride out on my own, gone about two weeks, and when I got back there was just a note and an empty apartment. Finito.'

'In America?'

'No. Here. I haven't lived in the States for four or five years now. My girlfriend was British.'

'Oh. I see. I thought… so what did you do?' Ryan lowered himself to the floor and sat cross-legged. Lex lowered himself to rest on his haunches, one hand on the floor to steady himself.

'I quit the apartment and took off to Greece for a month. I had no plans at all. Nowhere to go. Can you imagine that? It was there I got the call from your mom.'

'My mum rang you?' Something nagged at Ryan. *You told me about the fair when you called, remember?* Of course. At the Vintage and Craft Fair. When his parents had faced each other, forcing out a conversation of sorts, his mum rude, his dad embarrassed. Mum had called Lex? Why? Why now?

'Sure she did. She asked me to come here and help sort stuff out. She told me a little about what happened in school. So I, well, I kind of wound things up in Greece and I came home and rented this place. Just for the rest of the summer, at least to begin with. We'll have to see how it goes. But maybe I shouldn't be telling you this?' Lex looked confused and ran his hand over his hair. He sat down, stretching out his legs. 'I mean, I'm glad she did call me,' he said. 'I was looking to maybe reconnect.'

'Reconnect?' said Ryan. He picked at the carpet, weeding out fluff.

'Yeah. With you and your mom. Maybe try to make things right. I feel pretty bad about being out of your life so long.'

'It may as well be all my life.'

'All your life? Oh. OK. I guess you're right,' said Lex, as though he had never thought of it before. He smiled awkwardly.

'My mum told me it was impossible for you and me to meet,' announced Ryan, as though quoting. He was quoting. *You cannot meet your father, Ryan. It's impossible. He doesn't want to know and I'm sorry, but that's the way it is.*

'She said that?' said Lex. 'Shit. I mean, wow. I don't see why. It wasn't *impossible*. I gave up trying to keep in touch after a long time trying. Your mom wouldn't return my calls or reply to my letters. Nothing.'

'You tried to… keep… in touch with me?' Ryan leaned forwards. Lex leaned back on his outstretched arms. He crossed his legs.

'Sure I did. But not recently. You must have been two, maybe three, when I gave up. I wrote your mom. I sent her money. She would never cash the cheques. But maybe you should be discussing this with her? I think I've said too much already. I'm not sure what you understand.'

'She said you didn't want to know…,' said Ryan, his voice trailing off in disappointment. This was horrible. It was as though he was seeing his mum clearly for the first time. His vision of her was suddenly sharp and clear; but it was altered and deformed.

'Well. That's almost the truth. For her it *was* impossible, I guess,' said Lex. He stood up and stretched. 'I was pretty crappy towards her, Ryan. I was nothing but a great big kid.'

'And that… pissed her off?' Ryan stood too.

'Yes, it did. I was such a jerk. Don't think badly of your mom. You see, we fell in love and we did what people who fall in love do, fooling around, I guess you know about that stuff, and then your mom was pregnant, bam! It was OK, I thought it would be OK, but it wasn't. Not for me. I was frightened, Ryan, I was so scared. And I took off.'

'Took off?' Lex wandered back through to the kitchen, and Ryan followed him.

'I went back to the States for a while. I left her all on her own to deal with it. I guess she learned to fend for herself. It was wrong of me. So when you were… oh, I don't know… one? Eighteen months…? I came back. Just showed up one day and we tried again. But it was hard. You were… you were quite a kid. Kinda sullen and watchful. When you weren't being sullen you were screaming and hollering, and kicking. You kicked out a lot. Your mom and me, we argued, like, all the time, and so I took off again. No excuses. It was shitty of me, there's no doubt. I see that now. I sent money, letters, offering my help. She never replied to one of them, she never cashed the cheques. I called. She must've changed her number. Letters and cheques are one thing, but… I should have tried harder, maybe…do you know what my old girlfriend put in her note to me?'

52

'What?'

'She said she was second in my life. She meant second to my bike and my travels, so in that respect she was wrong, I guess. But it got me thinking and I realised that actually she was right, she just didn't know it. She was second. But you were – you are – first. It just took me too long to understand. I went to Greece to try to figure things out in my head and my heart, and I was thinking about you and your mom a lot and then as if by magic – your mom called me out of the blue. Serendipity.'

Ryan had no idea what serendipity was. He would look it up in the dictionary. The world was full of words, and he felt they were all there to be mastered. There were so many he didn't know the meaning of, and many more he was sure he'd not yet heard. He had to learn if he wanted to be a writer, which he suspected he did. But he liked animals. He liked the idea of fixing them. They didn't let him down. The only animals he didn't like were cats, because they were cruel to birds, and they made strange noises. He had a lot more questions to ask Lex. Ryan felt something growing in him, a tiny little nut starting to crack open. It was anger. It was anger towards Mum, and it was new and raw and he didn't like it. He didn't want to show anger or feel angry. He wanted to be happy and smiling and glad. So he buried the nut inside, and shut his ears and mind to the questions uncoiling within him. Money. *He offered money*. Why didn't she take it?

'Let's go get something to eat,' said Lex, opening the fridge door. 'I haven't had time to get to the grocery store yet.'

Ryan peered into a bright empty fridge.

'Do you like pizza?' said Lex, slamming shut the door.

Joanna watched her son glide off down the street on the back of Lex's Harley. She would have to trust the man to take care of her boy. Lex was a speed monster, and always had been. But she knew him well enough to know that he'd take it easy with Ryan on the back. He was not stupid. Ryan would love it, she knew. This was all about Ryan, and not about her, or Lex. Yet how marvellous it was to see him again, she admitted to herself. Almost thirteen years! And nothing much about him had changed. She wondered how many lovers he'd had in their time apart. He probably had one now, some young woman, slim and beautiful, skulking in the shadows of his life. Lex had an issue with commitment, and Joanna had known that from the beginning of their acquaintance. But she had dropped everything, including her then boyfriend, to be with him.

Lex told her many times that he was in love with her. She'd believed him, and she'd loved him back, perhaps that little bit more, that little bit too much. And when the pregnancy she'd suspected, but said nothing about, to begin with, was eventually confirmed, she'd felt a thrill of delight, a conviction that it would be all right, she and Lex would be able to make it work, somehow. She didn't expect their parenthood to be conventional, of course not; she didn't expect marriage or even a permanent home. But she thought they would be together, she thought that Lex would be around, and only in her darker moments did she think at the very least Lex would be a father to their child.

And to begin with, he was. For a month or two he "stuck around", changing "diapers", rocking and hugging the squalling baby to sleep, fixing meals for her when she was too exhausted to fix them herself. Then he drifted away, making excuses to be places; going back to America for a "few weeks". Joanna became a single parent. After a few months, he drifted back, sad and sorry. Joanna, exhausted, lonely, started to believe in him once more.

When he finally left there was no warning. He went out to "the store" for milk and bread and he failed to return. He took nothing with him aside from his motorbike, his wallet and the clothing he wore. At first she thought there had been an accident. But later, when it became apparent there had been no accident (she had phoned the police to check, and had felt like a fool) Joanna had been bewildered, confused, and hurt. Overnight, Lex became her enemy. And weeks later, once he had "calmed down", found "someplace to live", he called her (late at night, long distance; she guessed he was back in the States) because he had "fig-yured it all out". He offered her money. He could get a job, wire the money every month. She would need money, right? Joanna?

She had unplugged the telephone. For almost thirteen years.

'Wait a minute. You don't have tomato sauce on your *pizza*?' said Lex, incredulous. 'Are you nuts?'

'It tastes like tins.'

The waitress waited, pen poised over her pad.

'What, like tin cans?'

'Yes.'

'Weird.'

The waitress took their order. Their food was brought. They ate.

'I hit a girl,' said Ryan after a minute or two of enthusiastic eating. 'Mum told you that, I expect?'

'Yeah, your mom told me a little about it. Not cool, kid,' said Lex, licking his fingers.

'I didn't mean to. I thought it was Beau.'

'Who's Beau?'

They were in Pizza Hut. In between mouthfuls of pizza and gulps of cola, Ryan heard himself telling Lex all about the rubber flicking, the fight, the sneaky promise from Beau not to flick yellow rubber, and then the dreadful day when he, Ryan, thumped a girl in the face and got permanently excluded from school.

'I hated that girl,' said Ryan, 'but I didn't mean to hit her.'

'Sure. I've felt that way myself about girls. Well, about people. Girls or boys. Not the hitting part, hell no, but maybe the hating part. I understand. If they switched seats and you didn't realise… well, easy mistake, especially when you're all fired up. Just don't let it happen again, OK? You could land yourself in real trouble one day, pulling a stunt like that. But I guess you know that already?'

Ryan nodded enthusiastically and gulped down the rest of his cola. It was sweet and cold, and he felt rebellious. And he was sitting in Pizza Hut with a cool American who was being stared and simpered at by huddling, giggling waitresses. They probably thought he was a film star. And this man was— he just *was*, and Ryan was already hanging on his every word, taking in all that he said. Ryan Jones, a nobody, was becoming somebody, somebody who didn't need to dream about his dad anymore because his dad was there, right there, eating pizza and drinking cola with him.

'Mum was upset because she's a pacifist,' said Ryan.

'Yeah, she says that. But you know she was probably just worried about your state of mind. She doesn't want you to end up in a whole lot of trouble. She loves you.'

After they had finished their pizzas and eaten too much ice cream and "candy", they went for another ride around town. When they reached Ryan's old school, he tapped Lex on the shoulder and pointed it out to him. Lex gave the thumbs-down signal and revved up his engine to zoom past. Ryan held on to Lex as if he would never let go.

When they got home, Mum was in the shower. Ryan invited Lex into the house and they sat together in the kitchen. Ryan wondered if he ought to offer to make coffee. Lex made a joke that Ryan didn't understand, but he laughed anyway.

When Mum entered the kitchen, wrapped in her large vintage rose bath towel, carrying a pile of dirty laundry, she let out a small yelp, dropped the dirty clothes, and scurried back upstairs.

When she returned, dressed, she rattled on about trying to catch up on housework, after all those weeks getting ready for the fair. She was tired. She would have an early night. Might be sensible to lay off the coffee and have a hot chocolate instead. But she'd run out, damn it. She hated tea, as no doubt Lex could recall. She must remember to get some in. Hot ch-ch-chocolate, she meant. Not tea. Lex and Ryan listened politely to the litany of uncomfortable small talk, until Mum ran out of steam.

It was past seven o'clock, but she said nothing about that. There didn't appear to be any supper waiting for him. Perhaps Lex had sent her a text to say they were eating at

Pizza Hut? She was stammering again. Ryan didn't like it when she stammered, and thank goodness it didn't happen often. But it was happening now. Why was she nervous?

'Did you have a g-g-good time?' she eventually asked, leaning against the kitchen counter, arms folded across her chest.

Lex told her about their afternoon, the motorbike riding, the pizza – 'This kid has no tomato sauce on his pizza!' – and Mum listened and smiled and nodded. Ryan kept quiet. He didn't want to look at her. But he couldn't stop looking at her. Almost, he didn't recognise her anymore. Had she lied to him? Could she have been in touch with Lex long before, possibly years before, she finally did get in touch? Why had she turned Lex away, and refused his help? Who exactly had "abandoned" who? His mother's stupid pride made Ryan sick. And what was Lex supposed to do now? Ryan wondered, and that little nut buried inside him started to grow. It felt like poison, it felt like rising vomit. He would have to ignore it. Pretend it wasn't there. Push it back down, back in. He should say something. Act normal.

'We had cola,' said Ryan, and Lex shrugged his shoulders and looked sheepish, while Mum looked sternly at them both.

'We don't do cola,' she said, but she winked at Ryan anyway. She loaded the washing machine.

'Would you like some coffee?' she said to Lex after she'd put the machine on.

'You know what, I'm gonna say no to that, and take off. Thank you, though. I need a shower and an early night. It's been a great day, Joanna. Thank you for loaning me your son... our... Ryan.'

'You're welcome,' said Mum, her back to them, taking things from the cupboard. She prepared her coffee, then turned, arms crossed again. His parents were looking at each other strangely, like they didn't want to look away, but knew they ought to. Mum softly chewed at her bottom lip.

'So,' said Mum, eventually. 'Will you... w-will we be seeing you again or do you have... other plans?'

'No plans. I told you, I'm sticking around, Joanna. You think I'm going to rent a beautiful house and not live in it? Come on.'

'I see.'

'The house is great,' ventured Ryan. 'It's that posh place with the long drive that you used to say you'd like to live in one day.'

Mum bit her lip harder.

'So, Ryan,' said Lex, 'how about I come get you in a couple of days and we'll go someplace? The movies, maybe? Would that be OK, Joanna?'

'Yes.'

Ryan followed Lex outside and watched him climb onto the bike and secure his helmet. He hoped he really would come back in a day or two and take him "someplace". He didn't care where. He waved goodbye, and Lex was gone, and Ryan stayed outside to listen to the roar of the Harley until it was out of earshot. When he returned to the house, he said little to Mum, who asked lots of questions. Her stammer had stopped now Lex had left. Was she frightened of him? He couldn't see why. There was nothing to be frightened of. Ryan claimed to be tired and he went to bed, leaving Mum downstairs, alone with her coffee. He didn't want to talk to her.

AUGUST 2006

July limped, hot and weary, into August, Ryan's birth month, and with it the weather became a little cooler, but still dry and often sunny, and nobody wanted to do much except laze around in the back garden, drinking Mum's homemade lemonade with the fish-shaped ice cubes. Mum had work to do, but she managed to do most of it outside. She was still working on Mrs Marchant's patchwork quilt. It was almost done, and it was beautiful, the blue and white so striking. All who saw it admired it.

'It's an awesome piece of work, Joanna,' said Lex, when she held it up.

'It's a relief to have it nearly finished,' she said. 'I promised Mrs Marchant that it would be done by the end of this week. I hope she likes it.'

'Is it for her bed?' said Lex, stirring the rapidly melting fish around in his glass with his pen knife. The ice fish made a luxurious clinking noise.

'Yes,' said Mum. 'I think so. But some people hang them on their walls.'

'Like a tapestry, you mean?' said Lex. 'Decorative?'

'Yes. I prefer it if they are used, though. They're supposed to be utilitarian. That's the heritage of patchwork. People can be too precious with it.'

A few years ago, Mum had made a quilt for Ryan, made up of lots of greens and blues and oranges and reds. Not one bit of yellow of course, despite the fact that the pattern was called Sunbeam.

'Could you make a quilt for me?' asked Lex.

During the prolonged silence, Mum seemed to forget that Lex had spoken at all. Ryan and Lex exchanged glances and shrugs. Lex took a long gulp of his lemonade. Ryan took an ice fish in his mouth and held it there, enjoying the sensation of it rapidly melting.

'Maybe,' she said eventually, holding the quilt close to her eyes, scrutinising her stitching.

'Just like this one,' said Lex. 'It's so beautiful.'

'We'll see.'

'What's it called? The pattern?'

'Road to California,' said Ryan.

'Really? So it's perfect,' said Lex. 'Perfect for me, anyways.'

Mum cleared her throat. She carried on with her work, not looking at her son, or at Lex.

'I have to go,' Lex said after a while, and he stood up. 'I'm having some furniture brought over this afternoon. A bed, at last, a dining table and some chairs. Do you think six chairs are enough, Joanna?'

'Why are you asking me?'

'Maybe I'll make it eight.'

Ryan hated it when the tension crept into their conversation. It was always from Mum and he found himself hating her for it. Lex was trying, he was really trying hard, and too often she was just plain rude to him. He was buying dining chairs (eight, not six). For God's sake, didn't that tell her anything? It told him something.

Lex left Ryan and Mum alone in the back garden.

'Why are you so mean to him?' said Ryan, after watching her stitch for a few moments.

'Mean?' she said, not looking up from her work.

'Yes. Mean. He's trying hard to be nice, you know,' said Ryan.

'Nice? Is that what you call it?'

'Sure. That's what I call it.'

'Oh, Ryan, please. You're even starting to sound like him now.'

'Why shouldn't I sound like him?'

'Just forget it, Ryan,' said Mum, as she squinted to thread her needle with fresh cotton.

'Forget what?'

'I'm busy. Let me finish this bit of sewing and then we'll talk.'

'I don't want to talk. Not to you, anyways.'

'What do you mean by that?' Mum put down her work.

'What I mean by that is that you could have been in touch with my dad a long time before you finally bothered to. He told me. He tried to keep in touch with you but you wouldn't let him. He sent you cheques when I was a baby. But you were too proud to spend them. And the only reason you got hold of him in the end is because I was in trouble and you couldn't handle it. You knew I wanted to meet my dad for all those years. I know I didn't talk about it much, but it was obvious, wasn't it? You're not that... stupid, are you? You want everything your own way.'

'Lex said all that?' said Mum, her face contorted in confusion and incomprehension.

'Not all of it,' said Ryan.

'Good. What a load of rubbish.'

'He told me you ignored his letters and phone calls.'

'Of course I did! He ran off and left me alone, twice, all alone with you and I couldn't p-p-pay the rent and had nowhere to go! We ended up in a dump of a hostel and then a delightful council flat with crack addicts for neighbours. Do you understand? I worked hard to get us out of that. So damned hard… I'm sorry, but why should I want to be in touch with a man who treated me and his child in that way?'

'He didn't treat *me* like that. He treated *you* like that. And I don't blame him.'

Ryan stalked, awkward and stiff, into the house.

Ryan refused to leave his bedroom that night for his usual tea of chips and beetroot. It wasn't much of a tea, he sort of knew that, and Mum always tried to persuade him to eat more, or to eat something else. But he liked chips and beetroot. Why couldn't they have pizza more often? He'd eat pizza. Mum said pizzas were unhealthy and expensive and could only be considered a treat. Besides, she didn't have time to make pizzas "from scratch", whatever that meant; and the pizzas you could buy in shops all had tomato sauce that tasted of tin.

But, they both knew that Lex had plenty of money and he could help pay for all sorts of things. He'd offered already to give money regularly, to "help out". Why wouldn't Mum take it? It was as if she had to prove to Lex that she could still manage on her own. Her stupid pride getting in the way, like it always did. So why did she bother to ask him for help at all? What was the point? She wasn't

63

accepting any help, Ryan thought. Not really, apart from small things: Lex bought lunch from time to time. But she would not take cash from him, and cash was what she needed. Ryan thought she wasn't struggling, exactly, not like she had in the past. But money was tight sometimes. The business was going well, but there were only so many hours in the day to create and only so many things that could be made in those hours. Road to California enjoyed a "growing reputation", he had heard her say. She was proud of her achievements. But still, money was limited.

Ryan thought of all the things that Lex could pay for – a car, pizzas, new clothes for Ryan and maybe for Mum too. Ryan hated the smell of charity shops and even though she washed his "new" clothes twice before he wore them, he could always smell the sweet, dusty charity shop smell.

What about brand-new books? She knew how much he loved books, but even they had to come from charity shops, or off the second-hand shelves in the bookshop in town. Everything in their life had once belonged to somebody else. It was crap. And now it was unnecessary.

Ryan sat on his bed, hugging his knees and rocking to and fro, ideas bouncing around in his mind. Later, he heard Mum take her evening shower. He heard her go back downstairs. The rich, choking smell of her coffee wafted under his bedroom door. He heard her open the French windows. She was going out for a smoke; she needn't think he didn't realise. The smell always seeped into his bedroom. He was sensitive to smells. She was pathetic. Ryan wouldn't sleep, despite feeling tired. He was determined to keep awake until Mum went off to bed. He had a plan.

Mum knocked on his door and waited for a reply before she poked her head in and said goodnight.

'You must be hungry?' she said, stroking Ryan's hair. Her hand smelled of the strong hand soap she always kept in the kitchen and the bathroom. But it didn't completely mask the smell of her cigarettes. Talk about hypocritical, with all her talk of "loathsome" big business, her whining about shoddy dealings, sweatshops, tax dodges, the "shameless plundering of the planet's finite resources". Still, it was something to store up for later. A lever. He liked levers.

'I might go down and get a sandwich in a minute,' said Ryan. He didn't look at her.

'OK. There's wholemeal in the bread bin and cheese in the fridge. Help yourself, but for goodness sake don't make a mess. And put the marg back in the fridge. I'm off to bed now. Goodnight, Ryan.' That was another thing: they always had cheap spread, not butter. He loved butter.

She left the room and Ryan listened carefully to her moving around in her bedroom, then fiddling around in the bathroom again, which seemed to take hours. Eventually he heard her bedroom door shut, and the house fell silent. He waited another half hour.

Ryan sat up in bed and flicked on his light.

Now. Do it now. She deserves it!

She wasn't setting her alarm at the moment. She never bothered in the school holidays. That was the beauty of being self-employed: you kept your own hours. Sometimes they were long, arduous, tearful hours. But they were hers, always.

Yet she woke with a start. Something was wrong. She'd

endured an odd dream, full of hidden figures, darkness, corners. Noises half heard, panting and tearing, which in her dream-panic she thought of as an animal being torn apart by hounds. Awake, eyes wide open, straining to listen, smell, *sense*. She got up, put on her dressing gown, opened her bedroom door. Silence. Ryan's door, opposite hers, shut. She glanced into her workroom, the smallest bedroom, next to Ryan's. She screamed.

Fragments, ripped, torn, blue and white, tattered pieces of quilt, were scattered over the workroom floor, on the landing. Joanna pushed open Ryan's door. He sat on his bed, staring at her.

'Oh, thank God…,' she said.

'What's the matter?' said Ryan. Impassive. Cold. He often spoke in that way.

'I think we've had a break-in. I'm going downstairs. You stay here.'

Joanna crept down the stairs. No signs of any damage, of anything being taken. In the lounge her laptop sat on the coffee table where she'd left it last night, her kitsch red telephone on the sideboard. Her TV was still sitting, dusty, in the corner.

In the kitchen-diner her percolator sat on the counter, as beautiful as ever.

A tap at the patio door. Billy. She opened the door.

'How big is it?!'

Billy was used to Joanna's spider-summonses. 'It's not a spider.'

'What's up, then?'

'I think I've been burgled in the night. But nothing's been taken.'

'Uh-huh.'

'Come upstairs.'

Billy followed her.

'Look!' cried Joanna, standing on the landing and picking up scraps of fabric and letting them float to the floor.

'What? What is it?' said Billy.

'It's my qu-qu-quilt. Mrs Marchant's quilt! All that's left of it. The one I promised would be ready by the end of the week. It *was* ready, all but. I was just finishing off the quilting. Look at it! I *must* have been broken into. To think somebody was in my house while we slept. Oh, Billy!'

'Has anything been taken? Have any doors or windows been forced?'

'No. But I might have missed something.'

'You stay here. I'll have a look round,' said Billy. Joanna crumpled up scraps of blue and white fabric, sobbing. When Billy returned, he shrugged.

'No signs of a break-in. I don't get it,' said Billy. 'What was the point?'

'It doesn't make any sense,' said Joanna.

'Ryan OK?'

'I think so. I think I woke him up when I screamed.'

'Let's get you a coffee.'

They went down to the kitchen. Billy made coffee, putting in two spoons of sugar instead of one, because she was trembling.

'Is it repairable?' he asked.

'No.'

'I thought with your needlework skills…'

'No.'

'I'm so sorry, Joanna. You've been working on this for weeks. What sort of mindless thug would—'

'It was Ryan,' said Joanna, quietly.

'Ryan?'

'We had a row yesterday. He called me selfish for not being in touch with Lex before now. He was angry. This is his way of getting back at me.'

'Are you sure?'

'Yes. He went up to his room after our row and didn't come back down again. He was in a huff. How much can a boy hate his own mother?' Joanna's voice cracked as she started to cry again.

'He doesn't hate you!' said Billy. 'He's just angry and confused. His dad has waltzed back into his life and he's trying to work it all out. He's taking his confusion out on you, that's all.'

'That's not much consolation. What am I going to say to Mrs Marchant? "Sorry, Mrs Marchant, but Ryan crept into my workroom in the night and took my scissors to your quilt because he hates me and thinks I'm a selfish cow?"'

'Why not? You've got to tell her something. Tell her the truth. Look, has she paid you already?'

'She's paid half, the other half was due on completion.'

'So pay back the money and apologise and tell her exactly what happened. I would,' said Billy. 'She knows Ryan. She must know what he's capable of. She's seen him in action, after all, the little git. I could strangle him!'

They heard the front door slam shut. Billy and Joanna ran into the hallway and Billy yanked the front door open and they saw an already distant Ryan running along the street. Joanna called after him but it was too late. Ryan had gone.

He stopped running once he had got round the corner at the end of the road. He swung his backpack off his shoulders and trailed it along the ground. He hadn't counted on Billy sticking his oar in. He liked Billy and he didn't want to anger him, or argue with him. When Mum had screamed out like that, Ryan had jumped, sat up, listened. He'd felt... what? Remorse, or pleasure? A bit of both. It was done now, and couldn't be undone, and no, Billy, Mum would not be able to fix this quilt. Stupid question. Mrs Marchant would be disappointed, Ryan thought. It was a new thought, and unwelcome. But it couldn't be helped, not now. Too bad.

At least he knew where he was going, even if he was pretty sure what would happen when he got there. But it was worth a try, and he hoped it wouldn't happen.

A gentle rain began to fall.

Lex unlocked and opened the door.

'Ryan?'

'Can I come in? Please?'

'Sure. I was just thinking about you. What's up? You're soaking wet.'

'I can't say what's up at the moment. I need to come in.'

Lex stood back and held the door open. Ryan entered, head bowed. He felt heavy. Lex closed the front door.

'What in heaven's name is going on?' he said, following Ryan along the passage into the kitchen.

'I ruined Mum's quilt,' Ryan said, heaving his bag onto the kitchen table and turning to face Lex.

'What do you mean, you ruined your mom's quilt?'

'I ripped it. I cut it. I wrecked it. I even stamped on it.'

'Which quilt?' said Lex.

'The one she was making for my old English teacher.'

'Oh, Ryan. Jesus Christ! What the hell were you *thinking*? Don't you know how much work went into that?'

'Yes. That's why I did it.' Ryan stood before him, defiant, his head tilted backwards.

'Shit,' said Lex. 'Why, you really are a—' Lex stood with his arms crossed. He looked angry. It was only to be expected, of course, that he'd stick up for his old girlfriend. They had loved each other once. They probably still did love each other. He probably still wanted to "do her", Ryan thought. And Mum probably still wanted to do him. That was why they acted weird together.

Had he really stamped all over the quilt? All over the tattered bits of quilt, as they floated around and above him, as he threw them around? Like that crazy man from the fairy tale. Rumpelstiltskin? Ryan knew he must have looked stupid. But nobody saw. Nobody would ever see.

'You don't understand,' said Ryan.

'You're damn right I don't.'

'You're angry with me.'

'Not as angry as your mom is, I'm sure. Does she know? Has she seen it? What did she say? When? Why? Eugh! Just tell me what happened, would you?' Lex ran his hands across his hair; he pulled out a chair and, sitting down, he indicated to Ryan that he should do the same. Ryan sat across the table from Lex, who listened in silence while Ryan told him the whole story. When Ryan had finished, Lex let out a long, slow sigh and shook his head.

'OK. OK,' he said, running his hands across his hair again, 'here's what we're going do. I'm going to call your mom and tell her you're safe here with me. Then – after that – I don't know. I don't know, Ryan. You kill me.'

Ryan said nothing. Lex rang Joanna. It was a brief phone call with an occasional terse "yes", "no" and "uh-huh" from him.

'Well, kid,' said Lex after he'd finished on the phone, 'you're staying with me for a while.'

'How long?' said Ryan.

'As long as it takes.'

Lex rode off on his Harley later that morning to Mum's house to collect a few things. Ryan had packed a dozen books in his rucksack and nothing more, not even his toothbrush. 'I'll go get your stuff,' Lex had said. 'Will you be OK here on your own for a while?' Ryan assured him he would be.

The rain had stopped, the sun was out, and the world was evaporating. Ryan wandered around in Lex's garden waiting for him to return. He watched water boatmen skating around on the surface of the overgrown pond. The garden hummed with life and heat, the livid shimmers of summer. The grass needed cutting, the hedges trimming; everything grew a little wild. Out of control.

He would look for nests. There were bound to be some here in all these shrubs and trees and hedges. He tried not to think about Mum. He tried not to think about the quilt, ripped and destroyed, in tatters and shreds. He tried not to picture himself, panting, red-faced, silently crying, as bits of quilt floated around him.

When Lex got back, the two of them cleaned up one of the spare bedrooms, the small room with its own staircase spiralling up from the kitchen. The room was bare, like all Lex's rooms, but it was good enough, with a nice view of the long back garden. Lex had a roll-up camping mattress and a sleeping bag which would have to serve Ryan as his bed, for now. Ryan arranged his books in a neat pile next to the mattress, putting *A Kestrel for a Knave* on top. He then emptied out the bag that Lex had fetched for him. It had been carefully packed by Mum, he could tell, and now he had his toothbrush and toothpaste, a flannel and towel, pyjamas, pants, socks, joggers, a fleece, shorts and T-shirts. At the bottom of the bag was the boy doll with the patchwork clothes and wild woollen hair that Mum had once made for him. It had been her prototype when she started making her ragdolls. Ryan left it at the bottom of the bag. It seemed to him that the doll now belonged to a different age, and to a different boy. And he wasn't a baby. He was thirteen, soon to be fourteen, and fourteen-year-olds don't have any use for dolls. She should know this. God, what the hell was wrong with her? Was she that stupid?

Lex still had few groceries in his fridge and cupboards, so before lunchtime the two of them rode to the local supermarket and bought a few necessities. Lex's idea of necessities – "potato chips", cola, white bread, a frozen pizza – was not quite the same as Mum's. They couldn't fit too much on the bike. Lex said they would have to ride to the store every morning to pick things up. Or, you know, they could walk, he guessed. Did Ryan like to walk?

Ryan felt he was moving through the day in a trance. Nothing seemed real. He ate, he drank, he said little. He hadn't spoken to Mum, and it looked as if she didn't want

72

to speak to him. She must be furious. Deep down, he didn't blame her. He'd done a terrible thing. Beginning to regret his actions, Ryan settled down into Lex's sleeping bag that night with only one comforting thought: the thing he'd thought would happen when he arrived at Lex's house hadn't happened – he *was* being allowed to stay, he *was* under Lex's roof. He hadn't been sent back to Mum to face her anger, her reproach and even worse, her tears of frustration and sadness. Ryan picked up his old and worn hardback copy of *A Kestrel for a Knave*, but after just one page he felt his eyes closing, his mind shutting down on the day.

'So, are you gonna tell me more about why you cut up your mom's quilt?'

They were lying on their stomachs by the pond, studying its depths. A frog plopped in, then out, and back in again. It swam leisurely around the pond, effortlessly propelling itself in the water. Ryan spotted a shadowy newt crawling gracefully across the bottom. Pond skaters raced hither and thither. A grasshopper chirruped in the long grass bordering the other side of the pond. The sun poured down. Ryan didn't like Lex's question, so he ignored it for as long as he could.

'Well?' said Lex, after a while.

'She lied to me,' offered Ryan.

'About what?'

'About you.'

'She did not.'

'She did… too.'

'Kid, she just told it the way she saw it. That's not lying.

It's… perspective.' Lex twirled a piece of grass in his lean brown fingers.

'Grown-ups never lie, do they?' said Ryan. 'Only kids do. Or so adults would like to think. So adults would like to tell us.'

'Well, we both know that's not true, don't we? Hell, adults lie all the time, right? But your mom had… she didn't lie. She had reasons. Everything she told you was true, right? I left. Period.'

'She missed stuff out. That's the same as not telling the truth.'

'It's kind of a grey area.'

'But you tried to help. She told me you didn't. She told me you abandoned her.' Ryan paused. 'Period.'

'Sure, I tried to help. But your mom was proud, she still is proud, you know that, and she was hurt, and she felt she couldn't accept my offers, for what they were worth. What she really wanted was for me to stick around. If you're mad at anyone it should be me, kid, not her. Not your mom. I ran out on you guys. I got up one morning, went out for groceries, and I didn't… I didn't go back. Come back. Whatever. I was gone. It must've hurt your mom like hell. I was a fuckwit.'

'You always stick up for her.' Ryan leaned forward to study a water beetle. The pond teemed with life and purpose. A world within a world, nothing to do with his world. The concerns of the pond were not his concerns. It was oddly reassuring.

'Do I?' said Lex. 'I guess I do.'

'Are you in love with her?'

Lex paused. 'Oh, boy. You sure do ask big questions. Let's just say it's difficult. It's—'

'You're going to say it's "complicated", aren't you?' Ryan looked at Lex. Lex looked doggedly at the pond.

'I was going to,' admitted Lex.

'It's always "complicated" when adults don't want to explain things and they want to hide things. Isn't it?'

'I guess you're right. OK. Here's the deal. I won't say it's complicated.'

'What is it, then?'

'Difficult.'

'But you've already said that.'

'Can you think of anything other than that or the C word?'

Ryan sighed. Lex was annoying. Ryan took off his sun hat and flicked it in Lex's face. Lex laughed, grappled for the hat, yanked it from Ryan's hands, and threw it into the pond. They both contemplated the hat as it slowly submerged.

'I have no idea why I did that,' said Lex. They looked at each other and laughed, rolling over onto their backs and feeling the hot sun on their faces.

'Perfect,' said Lex. 'Isn't it?'

'Yes,' said Ryan.

Lex and Ryan settled down just great, as Ryan overheard Lex tell Mum over the telephone one evening.

They had been living together for two weeks. In that time Lex had bought a proper bed for Ryan's room, with green pillows and sheets and a duvet. He had bought a wardrobe and bookshelves and a desk. All the result of a fun afternoon in Ikea, somewhere Ryan had never been before, because Ikea stuff was *mass-produced*, and his mother naturally disapproved. Ryan had spent ten minutes riding up and down on the escalators. They'd eaten lots of pasta in the restaurant and enjoyed loafing around on all the sofas, and stretching out on the beds.

They had also been to the grocery store and finally got a grip, and bought sensible food – fruit and vegetables, lots of cereals and milk, brown bread, butter, cheese and Marmite. Lex tried some on his toast one morning. He'd not tried it before. He said he thought it was "shitty", and he didn't understand that particular British obsession. He'd organised a weekly online grocery order to be delivered to the cottage. Ryan loved helping to unpack the delivery crates and put all the shopping away.

'You sure like to read,' said Lex one afternoon. They had eaten sandwiches, followed by strawberries. The day was warm, intermittently sunny. Lex had bought some wooden garden furniture and they were sitting out on his patio.

'I love stories,' said Ryan.

'I never read much when I was a kid,' said Lex.

'But you read now?'

'Sure.'

'So where are all your books?'

'In storage. I should really get all my stuff back. Now that I'm settled at last.'

'What does in storage mean?'

… now that he was settled at last…?

'It means all my books and pictures and most of my clothes and all of my music are stashed away in a big metal box in a warehouse someplace. I think I'll get on it. Make this house a home.'

'I thought your old girlfriend took your stuff?' said Ryan.

'She did. But the things in storage were there before I met her. I never got around to taking it all out. Kind of glad I didn't.'

'I think you should take it all out now,' said Ryan.

'Listen, Ryan' – Lex sounded serious – 'I – uh – I'd kind of like to invite your mom over for dinner tomorrow night. It being your birthday and all.'

'Oh,' said Ryan. He had forgotten about his birthday. But of course, it was August. He'd never forgotten his own birthday before. Was he growing up? Did being a grown-up mean you forgot your own birthday?

'You've got to face her sometime, Ryan, right? How about we do it here, you know, a neutral place? It might be too much for you, going over to your mom's house right now.'

'If you like,' said Ryan.

'I'll take that as an OK?'

'OK.'

Joanna took her time in choosing her outfit. It was silly, but she wanted to look *right*. She wanted to look nice. She had not seen Ryan for over a fortnight. Their home was empty and quiet and somehow, it had become an unfriendly place. Children, even troubled teenagers, filled a house with their energies, their voices, their trappings, and that made a house a home. She missed Ryan dreadfully, and it was time for him to come back. But it was the right thing to have undergone, this separation. Ryan needed to learn a big lesson, and in a sense, she did too. Ryan also needed time to bond with his father. He had two parents now. The thought made her tremble. Lex had better stick around after this. She would not forgive him a second – third – time.

She chose her outfit, and examined herself in the mirror. She wasn't certain how she looked these days, which was disconcerting. Nothing much, nothing *obvious* had altered since her twenties: she was a few pounds heavier, although she had dropped some of those pounds over the last fortnight, working flat out on Mrs Marchant's quilt, Mark II. There were a few lines around her eyes and mouth, slowly becoming more marked, and deeper. There were stretch marks across her stomach, but these had faded over the years to become almost invisible. A few grey hairs had been spotted and plucked from her head. She felt there was nothing so far to feel too depressed about. Yet she was a mystery to herself, hard to define. Had it always been so? She wondered. She felt she was on a cusp, balanced, but between what, she could not say.

Joanna arrived at Lex's cottage in a taxi just after seven o'clock. She was excited, and nervous. Never had such a rift grown between her and Ryan, and she feared it was growing wider each minute. It was time to make amends, time to reunite. She paid the taxi driver and as he drove off, she stood at the bottom of the drive, looking at the house she had indeed once dreamed of occupying. She had not yet visited, and she had seen neither Ryan nor Lex since the Ruined Quilt Day. Strictly speaking, she hadn't seen Ryan since the night before the Ruined Quilt Day; but she remembered clearly the bang of the front door as he'd made his escape that morning. She strolled along the drive, the gravel crunching beneath her feet. She tried not to feel impressed or overawed; it was a beautiful property, anybody could see that. Leafy, gravelly, good proportions. This was no "cottage". That was just a silly Lexism, she decided. He was the most blasé person she'd ever known. The king of privileged understatement. She reached the door, smoothed her dress, and rang the bell.

Lex opened the door. He stared at her.

'Hi,' he said. He had a tea towel in his hand and was drying a wine glass. It looked odd, but not displeasing.

He told her to go down the hallway to the kitchen. The floor was tiled, and her feet clip-clipped along it. The hall was cool, quite dark, and smelled of leather, wood, of dogs long dead. It smelled like home.

'Hello, Ryan,' she said, standing awkwardly in the kitchen doorway. 'Happy Birthday!'

'Hello,' said Ryan. He was sitting at the kitchen table. He looked perturbed, even scared.

'You look great,' said Joanna, and she started to cry.

Lex handed Joanna a glass of crisp and cool white wine. 'There you go, honey,' he whispered. She wanted to stop crying. If she didn't... well, it could get messy. She swallowed the wine, one gulp, two gulps. She had to get through this.

'Cheers,' she said. Nobody knew what to say next. 'Lex tells me you have a proper room here now?' said Joanna to Ryan. 'Can I see it, please? Your room?'

'Sure,' said Lex, 'you go right on up and I'll finish dinner. I hope you like pizza and salad?'

'We got beetroot!' said Ryan, and he led the way up the twisting staircase, Joanna following with her wine.

Mum said she liked that Lex's house had two staircases, and how nice that one of them led only to Ryan's bedroom; and how sweet that Ryan's bedroom was small and cosy and overlooked the garden. She could see it was the sort of room he liked. She said nothing about the Ikea furniture. But she said he was in need of his patchwork bedspread. Ryan looked down at the floor. His face burned with shame and guilt.

'Mrs Marchant was thrilled with her quilt,' Mum said, crouching down to look out of the window into the garden.

'Was she?'

'I had to start again, obviously, but I worked like a maniac, day and night, and I finished it yesterday. I had to use the machine more than I wanted, but never mind. Billy helped me, in his own way. He made coffee and sandwiches, which was great. You know what he's like. I owe him. Mrs Marchant came round last night and collected it. She asked after you. We had quite a long talk about you, actually.'

'Oh.' Oh. Ryan did, and did not, want to hear about that conversation. What must Mrs Marchant think of him? That he was a loser, as everybody else thought. Yet he was curious. He liked Mrs Marchant. He hoped she wasn't cross with him. She was a kind person. And she was the only person in that stupid school who had liked him.

'I'll tell you more over dinner,' said Joanna. 'That pizza smells lovely. I'm starving, aren't you? Let's go and badger Lex.'

There was no need to badger Lex, because dinner was ready and laid out on the garden table for them. Mum and Lex had more wine, and Ryan had cola, and the three of them ate, the adults making occasional comments about the weather, the relative cool of summer evenings, the ambience of eating outside in the fading light. Ryan listened carefully. He wanted to understand the mood of this evening. It was strange. Not quite real. Later, Lex lit a few candles. A bat skirted the house, flitting suddenly in unexpected directions. Mum gave Ryan a birthday card with twenty pounds in it. She didn't know what to get him this year, she said. She'd had no time to go shopping. And maybe the best presents weren't things anyway.

'Ryan,' said Mum, after Lex had cleared the plates and returned to the table with another bottle of wine, 'I have an idea and I want to put it to you.'

'Oh,' said Ryan. He knew what was coming – he would have to stay at Lex's for the rest of the holidays. He liked being at Lex's place, because they had a lot of fun, but he was beginning to miss his own bed and the… *softness* of his own home: Mum's home. Lex's house was still stark, it needed more furniture and comfort. It lacked Mum's cushions and rugs and bunting. It lacked her patchwork quilts. It lacked her.

'It's about school,' said Mum.

'Oh. That.' Ryan had forgotten all about school. Meeting Lex, his prolonged stay at Lex's house, and the motorcycle rides, and the deliciously dodgy (but improving) food, all meant school had slipped his mind. The whole idea of it had floated away on a tide long gone out. But now it came flooding back in again. Oh, God. He would have to go shopping for uniform, the worst kind of shopping, and for shoes, and Mum would nag about his hair, she would want to cut it. And he would have to wear ties and blazers and uncomfortable shirts with stiff collars and go into a new school and be as just as friendless as he had been at the last one. He felt dizzy with dread, and that was no way to feel on your birthday. Why had she brought it up now?

'Yes,' said Mum, 'that. Mrs Marchant had an idea. I didn't even know you could do it… but she thought it might suit you.'

'What would suit me?' asked Ryan.

'Not going to school.'

'I have to go to school,' said Ryan. 'At least until I'm sixteen.'

'He has to go to school,' said Lex.

'No, no, he doesn't. He has to get an education, of course, all kids do. But he doesn't have to go to school. I didn't know that either, but Mrs Marchant told me all about it. Her nieces are home educated. She thought… she thought it might work for us. Even if it's temporary.'

'So, what, you get tutors or something?' said Lex.

'We could do that. Or I can teach him myself. He can teach himself, actually, a lot of the time.'

'Is that allowed here?' said Lex.

'Lots of kids learn at home. Some never go to school at all. Imagine that.' Mum winked at Ryan, who stared at her in silence.

'Wow,' said Lex. He took a swig of wine. 'I guess that's cool. The kid in me thinks it's cool, anyways.'

'What do you say, Ryan?' said Mum.

Ryan didn't know what to say. One minute he was drowning in a huge wave of fear and nausea and weariness, and now he had been thrown a life belt. Did she mean it?

Was it another of her half-baked, hare-brained schemes that she occasionally came up with? She must mean it; otherwise she would not have said it. Would she? Not on his birthday. She did often describe school as an *institution breeding obedience and conformity*. She didn't entirely approve of school, he knew. So, maybe she did mean it. Maybe she was being serious.

'Do you really mean it?' said Ryan, his voice small and reedy in the still, twilight-coloured garden. The grasshoppers were quiet. The frog had ceased swimming. The birds were perched in the trees, silenced. The world was hushed, waiting.

'I mean it, Ryan, of course I do. You loathe school. You have nightmares about it. I hear you at night, calling out and saying such odd… well, never mind. The fact is I should have done something about this long before now. And then maybe you wouldn't have ended up thumping people and… and destroying things. We can't go on with you beating kids up and vandalising other people's property. It's not worth it, Ryan. There might be a simpler way. I'm willing to try if you are. Shall we give it a go?'

'We can… try,' said Ryan. Try? *Try*? He was incredulous. But better not let Mum and Lex see that. What if he messed up again? What if he lost his temper at home and punched Mum like he'd punched Clarissa Cooper? Surely he wouldn't do that? Of course he wouldn't. Mum wouldn't flick yellow bits of rubber in his hair. Mum wouldn't call him a loser or a freak, or a wanker, even though he was all of those things, and more.

Mum was right, the best presents were sometimes not things. This had turned out to be his best ever birthday.

83

And of course, there was Lex too. Lex had missed twelve of Ryan's birthdays. Ryan had worked it out. Lex with his strong body and his Harley-Davidson and his large cottage. Lex with his stuff coming out of storage. Lex with his white T-shirts, his black jeans, his red scarf, his handsome smiling face, his soft-spoken American accent. And now Mum with her idea... Mrs Marchant's idea... it was all too much. Ryan could not hide his smile behind his can of cola.

But – was it against The Rules? So what if it was? It must be one of the rules that could be broken. But was Mum *sure* it wasn't against The Rules? She'd said so. But she could be silly and rebellious at times. Ryan felt he couldn't always trust her judgement or her knowledge. But Mrs Marchant had said so. Mrs Marchant would know. Mrs Marchant knew The Rules.

'Do you think he's pleased?' said Lex.

'Oh, yes, I think so,' said Mum, and they laughed and clinked glasses. Somewhere in the woods an owl hooted. An aeroplane, a long way up, flew over them, a bright blinking light, going somewhere, anywhere, who knew where, with people unseen, people unknown. Ryan wondered if the passengers on the aeroplane felt like him, whether their hearts were beating like his, beating to the rhythm of expectation and possibility and hope, as they journeyed on through the dark to their own destinations.

Later, after Ryan had said goodnight and retreated to his bedroom, Lex and Joanna sat in the garden until the early hours of the following day. They opened a third bottle of wine.

'Thank you for coming back,' said Joanna, tapping her fingers delicately against her wine glass.

'Don't thank me, Joanna,' said Lex. 'You should be furious with me right now.'

'Oh, I am. Rather, I was. All these years of having Ryan all to myself, though… it's had its advantages.'

'You should have accepted my money. I know it was hard for you, and I know I was a mean bastard running out on you both like I did… but the money would have helped, right?'

'I didn't want your money, Lex. I wanted you.'

'I'm sorry,' he said simply, and shrugged. 'There's really not much else for me to say. I'm not going to insult you and trot out excuses.'

'Are you truly back to stay? In Ryan's life?'

'You want me to be?'

'For now, at least.'

'Do *you* mean it?'

'Yes.'

'Then I'll stay. I can't lie to you. When you called me in Greece I'd met… a woman. A waitress. We kinda had a good thing going—'

'Do I need to hear this?!'

'Yes. You do. Hear me out. She was cute, she was fun, but she… she wasn't you.'

'Oh, please…'

'I mean it, Joanna. This past year I've been thinking about you, about Ryan, realising I've missed out. And wondering how you were doing. I thought of getting in touch, but I haven't forgotten that last call. When was it, ninety-five? You were so angry and bitter and I couldn't make it better for you by then, could I? You told me to leave you alone for ever.'

'I told you to fuck off, Lex.'

'You sure did. So I did fuck off.'

'Yes.'

'Until now.'

'I wanted you to come and help with Ryan. That is all.'

'I know. But I still lo—'

'No! Lex, just no.' No! No, he would not say that. She did not want or need to hear such nonsense. He had no right to think such thoughts, let alone give a voice to them. He was stupid, stupid… he always had to play the romantic hero. Well, not with her he wouldn't. Never again. Just a few weeks ago he was having it off with a Greek waitress. He would never change, not ever.

'Don't let our son down again,' she said. 'That's all I ask of you.'

Joanna felt chilly, so Lex brought a blanket out from the house for her, and he wrapped it around her shoulders. He stroked her hair. He crouched before her, and stroked her face and told her she was still beautiful, she was more beautiful than ever, and Ryan was not the only thing he had missed out on, damn it. What a prick he'd been! Her head swam.

'Has there… I know it's not my business and all, but… has there been anyone else? Not that it matters to me.'

'Obviously it does matter or you wouldn't be asking, would you?' Joanna took a sip of wine, put her glass back on the table and looked at Lex with a small smile.

'No, I guess not. I'm just curious.' He rested his hand lightly on her knees to steady himself. Wine always made him giddy. But Joanna hated beer, so he drank what she drank. He was… he could be thoughtful like that.

'There has been nobody else,' she told him. 'Nobody of any importance, anyway.'

'Oh God, what does that mean?'

'It means I dated a couple of blokes a few years ago. Nothing serious.'

'Right. OK, then. How many years ago?'

'A few. After I moved next door to Billy. It was his idea. He offered to babysit Ryan.'

'Great.'

'You do remember how I felt about you, don't you?"

He looked away from her.

'That forgettable, was it?' Joanna said, sudden tears rising.

'I remember everything, Joanna,' said Lex, quietly. 'It's just I'm so ashamed of myself.' He looked at her, half smiled, half grimaced. She reached out her hand and, snaking it around his head, she pulled him towards her.

They kissed for a long time. Eventually Lex drew back from her and they studied each other in the candlelight.

'There hasn't been anyone else, has there, recently?' he said eventually. 'I can tell by the way you kissed me.'

'What do you mean?'

'You're out of practice.'

'I am not!'

'So there has been somebody recently?'

'No! You're teasing me.'

'A little, maybe. I'm sorry.'

'You should be sorry. Come here.' Joanna pulled him to her again and they kissed some more. She wasn't sure what she was doing. He had no right to question her about lovers, when he'd had lots of them, and one of them until very recently. He was a hypocrite. A wave of misgiving rose up and through her and drifted away, fleeing the scene. Her love remained. She was enlivened. They rose together, the blanket slipping from her shoulders to the ground, unnoticed. Lex had good hands, warm and strong. He kissed nicely, and for years she'd thought she would never kiss anybody again, let alone him.

'Let's go in,' murmured Joanna as she felt Lex's hands plunge through her hair.

'Whatever you say,' said Lex.

They stumbled into the house.

SEPTEMBER 2006

The nights were longer, the late August days slowly becoming cool and brisk. After another week at Lex's place, Ryan returned home. Lex rode him back on the Harley. But from now on Ryan was going to spend a couple of nights a week with Lex. Before the ride home, Ryan dutifully hung his clothes neatly in his new wardrobe, he made his bed, and packed his books away tidily on his new shelves. He placed *A Kestrel for a Knave* on his bedside table. He wouldn't miss it back at home because he had several editions. Mum was making a pair of curtains for his room at Lex's cottage. It all felt so permanent. Yet it wasn't, because here he was, going back to Mum's home to carry on living with her like he always had. It was confusing, having one and a half homes.

There were new ground rules. Firstly, and absolutely, there could be no more vandalising of Mum's work. If it happened again, Ryan would be out for good. Lex agreed.

'That's right,' he said, 'you mess up again and you live with me. Only there'll be no cola, no potato chips, no late nights. No motorbike rides. Do you understand?'

Ryan was to talk things through, with his mum or with his – with Lex. *The drifter*, as Mum had called him at the Melsham House Vintage and Craft Fair. Ryan hadn't forgotten, and he wasn't sure what it could mean, but it seemed to fit. Lex was cool and… and *breezy,* and relaxed, about most things. He didn't seem that aware, Ryan observed, of problems. But that would surely work to Ryan's advantage.

As Ryan was no longer going to be in school, he would have to work hard at home.

'You can start by finishing that pile of books in your room,' Mum said. 'Read something other than Kes, please!'

'A Kestrel for a Knave,' corrected Ryan. 'The film was called Kes.'

Mum rolled her eyes. 'Whatever,' she said. 'We'll go shopping and get you some maths workbooks. And if you like we'll go out to museums and such from time to time. As often as we can, at any rate.'

Visiting museums and reading books sounded great. Doing maths did not. Mum spoke of meeting new people, making new friends. She was not going to allow him to become a recluse, she said, Lex nodding in yet more vigorous agreement. This new adventure would not be undertaken in isolation. Ryan pulled a face. There was a group she had been in touch with, Mum said. They held regular meetings and events, most Mondays. It sounded fun.

'And no, it isn't school, Ryan, don't panic! – I promise it's not school. It's a group of like-minded people. It will be fun. I want to meet new friends, even if you don't.'

Zephyr was thirteen years old, and his sister, Clover, was ten. Neither of them had ever been to school. Ryan thought them the luckiest children alive. They stood before him, frank and curious. Not judging, or sneering. The hall was noisy, with sharp echoes that hurt Ryan's ears. He didn't like it.

'D'you want to go out on the swings?' said Zephyr.

Ryan liked swings, he liked the soaring power, the air hurtling over and around him. It was a bit like being on Lex's motorbike, only not as exciting.

Ryan decided he liked Zephyr. He guessed he would not flick yellow rubber in his hair.

'What's it like?' said Zephyr. 'School?' He wore a chunky fluffy jumper in rainbow stripes and he had scruffy hair. He smelled a little odd, but not unpleasant. Like cut grass.

'It's shit,' said Ryan, and he shrugged. 'The one I was at was shit, anyways.'

'So you're glad to have left, then?' said Zephyr. Ryan couldn't tell if Zephyr's skin was tanned, or dirty. He looked like he spent a lot of time out of doors. His fingernails were definitely dirty.

Ryan swung higher. Zephyr kept up with him.

'You bet,' said Ryan.

'Are you American?' asked Zephyr.

'No,' said Ryan. 'But Lex is. He's really cool. He rides a Harley.'

'Who's Lex?'

'He's my mum's boyfriend.'

Zephyr and Clover's mum, Sharon, took Joanna under her wing. Mum and Ryan arrived at their first meeting, not knowing what to expect. A group of kids had been running around in the playground outside, screaming, shouting, playing a game that appeared to be Cowboys and Indians. Inside the hall, some children were playing, others painting, and another group were sewing, which Mum was drawn to. She looked at their work, and offered to help. Ryan sat beside her, mute. He wanted to go home. Then Sharon sent Zephyr and Clover over.

Sharon organised the group. She was small and efficient. She had messy bright red hair and a ring through her nose. She smelled a little odd too.

The meetings were weekly, and Mum had a ball. She took her ragbag and her sewing kit along and talked to Sharon and a couple of the other parents about setting up a regular sewing club. She could even bring along a sewing machine (the "old" one). She would be happy to allow the group to make use of it. She thought it might be nice to take along the Singer, too, to show the kids how it worked.

Ryan was less keen, as the meet was so noisy, but it was OK when he went outside with Zephyr, who was cool, even if he did have a silly name and crap taste in jumpers. Clover was all right, too; she was quiet, which Ryan approved of. She didn't play with dolls. She didn't have any, she said. She also wore rainbow jumpers, and jeans, never dresses or skirts. And Ryan liked to see Mum making new friends and laughing and smiling. It was good for her, even he could see that, and she still had time to do all her work for Road to California and Ryan still had time to do maths and read and it was all going to be just fine.

Mum and Lex frequently glowed red in the face when looking at each other, and Ryan caught the two of them looking at each other on many occasions. It was fun, it was funny. Mum had melted into her unpredictable mode, a rare occurrence, and Ryan loved her when she was like this, light and zinging and crazy. It was like she fizzed, if a person could fizz. Mum spent more and more time at Lex's house, along with Ryan. They both began to stay overnight two or three times a week, usually over the weekends. Lex had another spare room, smaller than Ryan's, and this he kitted out for Mum. These weekend sleepovers were the best times; time for him, Mum and Lex to be together. Ryan felt that he was beginning to belong to something like a proper family. They were in love, he thought, Mum and Lex, despite everything. But they weren't... well, they just weren't. Yet Mum didn't always use her bedroom.

Ryan read a lot, he wrote a journal, of sorts, and he wrote stories and poems, or tried to. Mostly they were no good, and Ryan didn't really know what he was doing. He thought he was probably being too self-critical. Mrs Marchant had told him once at school that he judged his own work too harshly, and that he shouldn't, because it would stifle him. She said there was a time to just write, and a time afterwards to analyse. He wasn't sure what she meant at the time, but now he was beginning to understand.

The time to read was a luxury, and he relished it. He had his new friends, and he looked forward to seeing them every week. There was talk of arranging a sleepover at Sharon's house, a huge chaotic slumber party for the group's teens and pre-teens. Ryan wasn't sure he liked the sound of it. He preferred it when it was just him and Zephyr hanging out, on the swings, talking, or hunting for birds' nests. He was getting Zephyr into nest hunting, although Ryan knew his new friend's heart wasn't really in it.

All of Lex's things came out of storage, and Ryan and Mum spent a long, dusty weekend together helping Lex arrange his house. Lex had a large box of books and Ryan was allowed to place them on the bookshelves as he saw fit. He revelled in the responsibility. He looked through some of the more interesting books, about motorbikes, about travelling, about America, about mountaineering and hiking, and about music and musicians and bands. The books smelled so good: that mix of dust and must and ink and paper. There were pictures too, some framed, many in cardboard tubes. Places I've been, Lex said. Ryan was allowed to look at them all, and he took them from their tubes, carefully unfurling the prints. He was drawn to a picture of a large lake, surrounded by mountains, and blue and green and grey, grass and water and rocks and sky.

'Where is this?' asked Ryan.

'That is the most beautiful place in this country of yours,' said Lex, taking the print from Ryan and holding it against the wall above the fireplace. 'I'm going to get it framed and put it right here.'

'Where is it?'

'It's Loch Coruisk, in Scotland. I went there a few summers ago. It blew me away. The most peaceful place I've ever visited. I didn't want to leave.'

'I've never been there.'

'It's on the Isle of Skye. Which parts of Scotland have you been to?'

'I haven't been to Scotland.'

'Oh! But hasn't your mom...? I guess not. I'm sorry,

kid. I'll take you there, one weekend, you and me. We'll check it out together. OK? We'll scoot up there on the Harley in no time at all. We'll camp out. You'll love it.'

Later, after Ryan showed her the poster, and Lex was cooking dinner, Mum said of course they hadn't been to Scotland. She had no car, remember? And she could never afford the expensive rail fares. There was never any money for holidays. Lex! You have to understand what our life is… was… is like.

And Mum, in tears, ran from the kitchen into the garden. Lex looked at Ryan, and Ryan looked back, unsure of what to say or do. It wasn't like Mum to run off crying. She wasn't usually so… theatrical.

'I'm sorry, Ryan,' said Lex. 'I'm being a little careless.' He put down the knife he was using to chop onions. 'I shouldn't have… I'll go talk to your mom. Don't worry. She'll be cool.'

The following day Lex took the Loch Coruisk print into town. He got it framed, and a couple of days later he hung it above the fireplace in the living room, as he'd said he would.

'We'll go, Ryan. You and me. I promise.'

OCTOBER 2006

No more meals were taken outside, there was no more lazing around in deck chairs reading under the warm sun, not even wrapped in a blanket; at least, not for the adults. Ryan loved nothing more than being outside, in chilled air, reading, listening to birds. But the sun was feeble now. Rides on the Harley were colder, and Ryan was thankful when Lex bought him some thick leather gloves like his.

'Are you all right, Mum?' Ryan asked one Saturday morning, after he and Lex had returned from the supermarket with milk, fresh bread, cheese, apples and oranges.

Mum sat at Lex's large kitchen table, making a patchwork cushion: a website order. It needed to be made and sent as soon as possible. Mum was struggling to keep up with orders. Road to California meant the world to her, and she was nothing if not a hard worker. So, determined, she was working. Even though she was feeling pretty awful, and had been for a week or two. She hoped it would right itself. She was working too hard, maybe. She was always susceptible to colds at this time of year, at the turn of the season, she said. She was worrying too much; about Ryan, about the business.

'I'm fine, Ryan, thanks.' But she didn't look fine. She was pale and she looked tired.

'You want some fresh air? A hot lemon with honey?' said Lex, putting the shopping away. 'A cup of coffee?'

'No, thanks. I just need to get on with this cushion. I think I might go home to finish it. I wanted to hand-sew some of this, but I'll get it done so much quicker on the machine. Needs must and all that.'

'OK,' said Lex, 'I'll give you a ride back.'

'No, I'll ring Billy and see if he could pick me up. I feel a bit dizzy for the bike.' She had been on it once. It had frightened her. She didn't trust it.

'Are you OK, honey?' said Lex, crouching down next to Mum. He eased a strand of hair from her face and tucked it behind her ear. Ryan looked away.

'I'm just a bit under the weather. Nothing to worry about. Could you keep Ryan here until tomorrow, please? I think I need some peace and quiet. Then I'll be all right. You know?'

'Yeah, I know. No problem, Joanna,' said Lex. 'It's OK.'

Only, it wasn't OK. A week later, she couldn't get out of bed, not without feeling dizzy and being sick. She and Ryan missed the group's weekly meet-up. Joanna felt bad about it because she had been planning to start on a Christmas stocking project with the small but enthusiastic sewing group. She rang Sharon, who said no problem, the sewing group could do their own thing this week. And next if needed. Joanna was not to fret. She was to rest and get well. What was wrong?

Joanna stayed in bed for three days and she couldn't

work. Ryan started a project on World War Two. He liked history. He took glasses of iced water to her. But in the end, even these made her sick.

Billy called round one Friday evening, popped upstairs to see her, and after taking one look, helped her out of bed, down the stairs, and into his car. Ryan climbed into the back, and they set off for the hospital.

'For God's sake, Joanna,' said Billy, 'why didn't you let me know you were feeling so rough? You look horrible, woman, just horrible! You can barely stand up! What's Lex playing at? You've lost weight, any fool can see that. This one can, at least.'

'I've lost over a stone,' mumbled Mum, as she opened the window and poked out her head for fresh air. 'I can't seem to keep anything down.'

'It shows. You look haggard,' said Billy. A little bluntly, Ryan thought. 'Hasn't Lex noticed?'

'Don't bring Lex into this,' whispered Joanna. 'It's not his fault.'

'I suppose you've been stubborn, as usual? Have you seen a doctor? This is no bug, woman.'

At the hospital, Mum was seen by a nurse, and she was taken off to lie down on a bed. Billy bought Ryan and himself some chocolate from the vending machine. He telephoned Lex, who arrived a few minutes later, carrying his black helmet. He looked worried. He ruffled Ryan's hair, and told him to be patient. He went in to see Mum, and stayed with her a long time. Billy bought Ryan more chocolate. When Lex eventually came back out, he looked shocked and tired. He might even have been trembling,

Ryan thought. He did not look like Lex, who was always so sure of himself.

'What's happening?' asked Billy, standing up.

'They're keeping her in,' said Lex. 'She's got to go on a drip. She's totally dehydrated. Why didn't I realise? I'm so dumb! Listen, can you take Ryan home? Keep him with you for the night? I know it's a lot to ask, but I'd sure appreciate it. I'm going to hang around here for a while yet.'

'I want to see Mum!' cried Ryan.

'Whoa, kid, not tonight,' said Lex, grabbing Ryan as he attempted to push past him. 'Your mom needs to rest. Actually, she's asleep right now. I'm sure you can see her in the morning, OK?'

'Come on, Ryan!' said Billy. 'Let's get home. I'll make you some supper! How does mushroom stroganoff sound? You know how much you like that.'

Ryan knew that the people in the waiting room were watching him, listening in. He supposed they must be bored, and he was entertaining them. Calm. He must be calm. This wasn't school and nobody here had it in for him. Simmer down, he told himself. Mum will be OK. She's asleep. She's in hospital with doctors and nurses. They'll look after her. She needs to sleep. Mushroom stroganoff. Billy's excellent cooking, better even than Mum's. Billy was kind. Ryan trusted him, and yes, he would go back to his house with him. He knew he didn't really have a choice.

'Can I bring her some flowers in the morning?' said Ryan. He hated hospitals, he realised. They smelled bad, so bad, even the waiting rooms. Flowers were fresh and clean.

'Sure, you can bring your mom flowers,' said Lex, taking his wallet from his jeans pocket. 'Take this. Get her the biggest bunch you can find. She'll appreciate it, kid.'

Ryan took the twenty-pound note. He turned to Billy, and together they made for the exit.

'I'll give your mom your love, OK?' Lex called after them.

In the morning, Lex, who had "gotten home late", collected Ryan from Billy's house and they rode to the hospital. Ryan tucked the bunch of flowers inside his jacket. He held on tight to Lex and hoped the flowers would remain intact. 'Ride slow,' he told Lex, and Lex did.

Mum had eventually been sent down to "G" ward the night before, Lex explained, as he and Ryan navigated the endless hospital corridors. He'd hung around until she was settled, and hooked up on a drip. He was pretty tired this morning. He couldn't sleep at all. It had been a long night.

Ryan and Lex followed the signs for "G" ward, which was near the canteen. Ryan tried to ignore the peculiar-to-hospitals smells of cabbage, chips and disinfectant.

'Hospitals suck!' Lex whispered as they finally arrived at the ward, and Ryan had to agree. And Mum had been stuck in here all night. Ryan felt sorry for her. There was no visiting until ten o'clock, but Ryan had been up and waiting for Lex to pick him up since half past six. He too had spent a fitful, sleepless night, on Billy's sofa. But he'd had poached eggs on toast for breakfast, which he quite liked, as well as the promised mushroom stroganoff the evening before.

Lex and Ryan rubbed the alcohol gel from the dispenser

into their hands, opened the heavy wooden doors, and found themselves in the rarefied world of "G" Ward; it was autonomous and orderly, busy. Nurses flitted about hither and thither, a telephone rang continuously, a couple of young women in white coats chatted earnestly by the desk, and lots of patients lolled around in, or on, their beds, some reading magazines, some chatting to fellow patients, some sleeping. Lex asked a nurse if they could see Joanna Jones. Yes, they could, but her curtains were drawn. She was probably asleep. She was tired. The nurse smiled sweetly at Lex.

Lex and Ryan poked their heads around the curtain, but Mum wasn't sleeping. She was propped up on her pillows, staring at nothing, and she seemed to Ryan to be covered in tubes. Her hair was a mess and she looked paler than ever.

'Knock, knock,' said Lex.

'Ryan!' she cried.

'Hello, Mum,' said Ryan, moving slowly towards the bed that contained this ghostlike wired-up woman who was still his mother.

'Sit down, love,' she said.

Ryan sat down and offered up his large bunch of flowers. He had chosen them at the supermarket on the way to Billy's house the evening before. They were mostly pink, and smelled sweet and fresh and earthy. Billy had put them in the fridge overnight and they were cold, a little stiff. Only one flower had snapped off during the journey. Ryan put it in his pocket.

'Oh, they're lovely, sweetheart,' said Mum. Lex leaned over the bed and kissed her on the lips. Ryan looked away.

When he looked back, he stared at Mum's hand, which appeared to have a tube sprouting from it. This tube was long and connected to a bag of clear liquid which was suspended from a tall stand next to her bed. It looked terrifying, and gruesome. A sudden dread flooded through him, a certainty, and he felt heavy tears pool.

'Are you going to die?'

'What?' said Mum and Lex together, staring at him.

'Are you going to die? Are you seriously ill? Is it… cancer?' Ryan's bottom lip trembled. He made a big effort to stop it, but he couldn't.

'No, no, oh, Ryan, no, no, no…,' said Mum, and her voice faded away, and she started to cry too. Ryan, wiping his eyes on his sleeve, waited for somebody to tell him what was going on.

'Your mom isn't going to die, Ryan,' said Lex, handing them each a tissue from the box next to the bed. Mum cried softly, silently, tears creeping down her cheeks. She wiped them away, and tried to smile.

'I don't have cancer. I can promise you that.'

'What's wrong, then?' said Ryan. He dabbed politely at his eyes. He hated to cry, or make a fuss.

There was a long silence around the bed, punctuated by the noises of a busy ward going about its business. Mum looked at Lex, and raised her eyebrows. Lex shrugged, and nodded.

'It's the opposite of death, Ryan,' said Mum at last, smiling at him through her tears and reaching out to hold his hand. 'I'm – Lex and me – we're going to have a baby.'

Ryan looked at Mum, then at Lex, then back at Mum again. He lowered himself onto the edge of the bed.

'A baby?' he said.

'Yeah, a baby,' said Lex.

'A baby,' said Ryan. 'Oh.'

'We weren't going to tell you just yet, you see,' said Mum. 'But I can't leave you worrying. Cancer indeed!' she sniffed, and winked at him, and he stared back, unmoved. He no longer felt like crying.

'Your mom's going to be feeling nauseous for a while yet, so we thought it was probably right to tell you. She's been worried that you would worry. I can see why: is she going to die! Ryan, come on, kid. Get it together!'

Lex laughed, Mum smiled weakly, and Ryan frowned.

'Is this a joke? Do you mean it? I'm going to have a brother?'

'Or a sister,' said Mum.

'A brother. A real little baby brother. But I don't get it. Why are you feeling so ill?'

'Because sometimes you can be horribly ill when you are pregnant,' said Mum. 'Worse luck!'

'Mrs Marchant was sick. She kept having days off school,' said Ryan.

'That's right, she did. She told me about that when she collected her quilt. And she's feeling better now, no more sickness. It should pass for me too, just not for a while yet. I'm going to take some tablets to make me feel better. I shouldn't be sick from now on, fingers crossed! Ryan, the thing is... the thing is, I'm going to need your help. I'm pretty weak and tired. I'm only just nine weeks into the pregnancy, you see, and it's early days.'

'Have you told Billy?' said Ryan.

'No,' said Mum. 'We're not telling anyone else just yet.

Our secret, eh? Just for the three of us to know about. It's exciting, isn't it?'

Was it? Ryan wasn't sure. It might be nice to have a baby brother. Babies were cute, he thought. And if Mum and Lex had decided to have a baby, then it must mean that Lex was intending to stay. It would make Lex "stick around". Wouldn't it? If he was intending to leave, why would he decide to have another baby?

And where had Mum's trust come from, all of a sudden? Surely she could remember what had happened last time they'd had a baby together? Ryan felt more tears prickle the back of his eyes. People who had babies were in love and they were together and intending to stay together. Sometimes, they were married. They were families. Or they should be, he thought. He knew he should feel happy, and glad. But he didn't. He just didn't. Something… something was wrong.

Joanna was sent home the following day. Billy drove to the hospital to pick her up after he finished work. She was waiting for him, sitting alone and quiet on a threadbare chair just inside the ward. Lex had taken Ryan out for tea somewhere, she said. Probably they were at Pizza Hut. It was just as well. She couldn't see how she was going to prepare food. Everything made her feel sick. Really it might be easier to stay in hospital…

'… but they needed my bed,' she said, as Billy held open the heavy swinging doors for her to pass through. They walked along the corridor towards the exit.

'When's it due?' Billy asked.

'You've guessed,' Joanna said. She carried on walking, slowly. Billy offered her his arm.

'Of course I've bloody well guessed. I'm not stupid.'

'Well, nobody else is to know just yet. It's supposed to be a secret.'

'Let's get you home.' Billy slowed to her pace. 'Knocked up once again by the American hunk. Deary me. Whatever next?'

'Billy!'

'Well… I'm sorry. It was just a joke. I can't blame you for… you know. I mean, I would.' Then: 'How does Lex feel about it?'

'Fine. He's fine. He seems pretty excited.'

'Have you told Ryan?'

'Had to. He thought I had cancer.'

'Oh, the poor lad.'

'We had to put his mind at rest.'

'Of course you did.'

'I got the feeling he wasn't impressed.'

'You can't blame him, can you?'

'I suppose not.'

Billy took her home.

NOVEMBER 2006

'Joanna! Be reasonable, honey, please. Think about it at least, will you?'

Mum and Lex were having another argument. They had been having a lot of arguments recently. At least it meant she was getting better and getting her energy back, as Lex pointed out. Ryan was fed up with her lounging on the sofa watching daytime TV and complaining about feeling sick. The tablets the doctors had given her worked in one way – she no longer threw up, just as she'd hoped – but they didn't stop her *feeling* sick, and Ryan and Lex and even Billy had heard more than enough about it. They'd given up asking her how she felt; there really was no need.

'Lex!' said Mum, pushing herself up from reclining on the sofa. 'Just shut up, please.'

'You can't work. When's the last time you produced anything? You're beat. It's all you can do to get out of bed and struggle to the sofa in the morning. Joanna. Let me do this. Let me help you. Please.'

'I don't want or need your charity,' said Mum, pointedly turning the volume up a notch on the TV. 'And anyway I'm feeling a little better. I'm eleven weeks today. Don't you remember what the midwife said? It should start to fade soon. It's certainly not going to get any worse.

I'll be back on my feet and working as hard as I ever did. You'll see.'

'OK. I hear you, honey, and it's great that you're feeling so optimistic and positive. But what I'm offering… it's not charity, Joanna. That's kind of an insult, when you think about it. You're having my baby. We're lovers. I want to help you. You need my help, right?'

'I do not.' Mum slumped back on the sofa, arms crossed.

'So, when was the last time you made anything?' said Lex. 'You must have orders backing up on your website… '

Mum said nothing. Ryan looked at her, waiting. He raised his eyebrows; she grimaced, shook her head. She mouthed, 'No!'

'Mum shut down her website,' Ryan said, and poked his tongue out at his mum.

'She did?' said Lex. 'Right there, Joanna.'

'It's only temporary, just for a week or two. And I haven't shut it down, for heaven's sake. Ryan's exaggerating.' Mum glared at him. 'I've just suspended it while I catch up. Then I'll be up and running again. As you rightfully say, orders are backing up and I can't take any, just for a while. There's nothing to worry about.'

'There is something to worry about,' said Lex. 'It's the future of your business, for Christ's sake. Swallow your pride, get real and take my money. Just for now, until you're up and running again. Better still, come live with me. Pack your bags, leave this cramped little house, and move in with me. If we're doing this thing, let's do it properly. I'm pissed off with this half-assed situation. It doesn't help any of us.'

Joanna looked at Lex, and she looked at Ryan, who looked like a puppy dog who'd just got wind of a box of biscuits.

'No. Thank you,' said Joanna. Just no, Lex. Not now, not yet. This is too much, too much right now, and how the hell do I know you mean it, you... you *twerp*. Stop getting Ryan's hopes up! Stop getting my hopes up, damn it. If it was half-assed, their life, their arrangements, it was half-assed for a reason, and what the hell did he expect? Lex heard her, somehow. He was silent, staring at her. He'd always had that ability to get to the heart of her, to read her. Despite everything, it was thrilling to be so in tune with another human being.

'Mum!' said Ryan.

'No, Ryan, love, I'm sorry. This is our home. We're staying put.'

'Joanna,' said Lex, sitting beside her and taking her hand. 'I mean it, honey, really I do. You guys have practically moved in already, right? I'm just saying. I know none of this is easy for you, believe me, I get it. I don't exactly have the best of track records, right? I do know that.'

He was persuasive. The self-deprecation hit just the right note. She felt herself melt. It was all so *tempting*.

'Do you really, truly mean it?' said Joanna.

'I mean it,' said Lex. 'And I mean it about loaning you some money to tide your business over too.'

Joanna thought for a long time. 'OK,' she said in the end, and the word hung in the air, a plum not quite ripe enough to drop.

'OK to what?' said Lex, in the end.

'OK to the loan. Thank you. But Ryan and I are staying put. I'm not giving up my home for anything or anyone.'

She turned up the volume on the TV another notch. Lex grimaced at Ryan. They both sighed, and shook their heads.

Ryan had grown in recent weeks and his ankles and wrists were sticking out of the ends of his trousers and sleeves. His shoes were getting tight and his socks and underwear were becoming worn through.

'Let's go shopping, kid,' said Lex one Saturday morning. Mum was snoozing on Lex's brand-new red sofa. Mum and Ryan had, of course, more or less moved in permanently with Lex, despite her protestations. They stayed over four or five nights, sometimes more. It was just easier, and it was the obvious thing to do. And Mum had not had to suffer the "shame" of agreeing to Lex's invitation to move in with him; there was still a pretence, a show of her refusing his "charity". Ryan couldn't decide if this pride of his mother's was wonderful or terrible. It was silly, often. But Mum was tired… the pregnancy was taking its toll, she said. So he couldn't be too hard on her. She was worried about his education. He was supposed to be getting one, and she had "done nothing with him for weeks". Lex suggested school. Ryan said No Way. Mum wondered if school might be the answer, now that she was having another baby. Ryan tried not to listen to his parents as they talked about him. They talked about him often. Mum was normally pretty good at asking him for his thoughts and opinions. Maybe they forgot, he reasoned, or maybe his opinion wasn't important. Either way, it didn't matter, he was not going back to school. So what if it was a private school? Which is what Lex thought might work. Hell, he could pay for it, no problem, he said.

So what if they would hunt around for the "best"? It was still school. And he'd heard stuff, weird things, about private schools. You had to be posh to go there. Or at least rich. He knew Lex was rich but… it wasn't the right kind of rich, he thought. And he would still have to wear stiff collars and stupid ties and he would still be called a freak. Posh kids, he felt sure, would be just as unkind as un-posh ones.

'What do we need to go shopping for?' asked Ryan, although he knew exactly what for.

Billy was keeping his eye on Mum's house. She was thinking about letting it, she often said. But she was only thinking about it. It was hard to ignore what Lex had done when Ryan was a baby. Ryan couldn't blame her, but he did think she needed to learn to trust Lex at some point. That little nut of anger that had blossomed in him a few months ago had subsided, and nowadays he often felt a great deal of tenderness for Mum. It was, after all, thanks to her he didn't have to go to school, which was a big deal, a real biggie, as Lex would say. It made such a difference to his life. Ryan took himself off to the weekly home education meet-ups, and sometimes called on Zephyr to hang out, and "study". Mum and Lex argued, a lot. But it was never mean or hostile. They seemed to enjoy a frank and thorough exchange of views, which was odd, because they agreed on almost everything, deep down. What did they find to argue about?

'You need new stuff, kid,' said Lex, and he threw Ryan his coat. 'Get your ass in gear.'

Lex didn't wake Mum, but he scribbled a note for her and propped it on the coffee table. They walked into town, as neither of them wanted to carry their helmets around all morning. They were too cumbersome, Lex said. Ryan liked that word. Cumbersome. He would add it to his favourite words list in his notebook.

'I really should think about getting a car,' said Lex, as they paced into town. Ryan struggled to keep up, but he managed. 'I keep saying it, don't I? With a new baby we're sure as hell going to need one.'

The day was dry and not too cold; a soft wind.

'What kind of car should we get?' said Lex. Ryan shrugged. He'd never been into cars. He didn't know one make from another.

When they arrived in town, Ryan entered his mum's favourite charity shop, followed by a bewildered Lex.

'What is this, a thrift store?' he said. He screwed up his nose and looked around doubtfully.

'It's a charity shop. I get nearly all my clothes in charity shops,' said Ryan.

'You do?'

'Yes. And Mum gets most of her clothes here too. She says it's Environmentally Friendly to buy second-hand clothes. And they are better quality. And it helps charities to make money and it's a lot cheaper than buying brand new. And it doesn't line the pockets of Capitalist Pigs. And it's "integral to the ethos of Road to California" to use second-hand things and she likes to practice what she preaches.'

'Wow. And she can preach, right?' said Lex. 'Listen, I don't doubt any of those things are true, kid, but how about we go get you some brand new stuff? Let's get the hell out of here. I don't like the smell.'

Ryan's feet had grown by one size. They spent a long time looking at shoes and trying them on. None of them felt comfortable. Lex, patient as he was, began to sigh and scratch his head and hint that he needed coffee. But Ryan didn't take hints. He knew when somebody was hinting: it was like they had an itch. But he wasn't prepared to scratch it. If somebody wanted something, they should come out and say it.

They weren't going to find shoes. New shoes were unbearably uncomfortable. His existing ones were uncomfortable too, now they were too small. And Ryan had a feeling Lex was thinking about getting new socks. He had a pair of socks. They were fine. Why couldn't they leave it at that? What was the problem? His feet smelled, he knew. But it didn't bother him, so why did it bother other people? He was wearing his favourite socks, every day, and Mum said she "didn't have the energy to wash and dry them overnight."

'Ryan?'

Ryan and Lex turned from the rack of trainers.

'Beau,' said Ryan.

Beau Stirling stood in front of them, smiling. The real Beau Stirling. A little taller. His voice now a man's voice, no vestige left of the child voice. How could somebody shake off their childhood in just a few months? Ryan knew his own voice was beginning to become a man's, but it was lagging behind Beau's. Ryan continued to stare at his foe in fear and curiosity and, he realised, even a bit of envy. Why...?

'What are you up to these days?' said Beau. 'We haven't seen you around.'

And bloody hell, he wanted to chat, like grown-ups do, about small things. Was this really Beau Stirling?

'I don't go school,' said Ryan. 'I don't go to school at all.' And who exactly was *we*? *We* haven't seen you around? Ryan didn't want to be standing in a busy sports shop on a Saturday morning wearing nothing on his feet but smelly, worn through (but extremely comfortable) socks, chatting to Beau Stirling about nothing much. Beau Stirling hated him. Why was he even bothering to say hello? Why was he pretending to be so friendly?

Ryan thought about socks. He knew he would have to get new ones, he would have to give in on this. They would find soft ones. They would have to. Seamless soft socks. He wouldn't accept anything else, and Lex would have to understand that. Beau was still there, standing in front of him, smiling.

'You don't go to school?' said Beau, incredulous. 'I knew you got kicked out of ours. I thought you went to a different school,' said Beau. 'Or the… what do you call it… you know, the unit. Thing. Whatever.'

'The Pupil Referral Unit,' said Ryan.

'That's it.'

Ryan, motionless and blank, said nothing. He would let this idiot Beau feel like a gimp. He deserved it. Lex prodded Ryan in the back. 'No,' said Ryan, fidgeting from foot to smelly foot. 'I don't go there or to school. I really don't go to school at all.' *Go away, go away…*

'Oh. Right. Weird. I mean, great. And weird. Who teaches you, then?'

'My mum.' And Ryan knew he sounded babyish. 'Actually, I teach myself, mostly.' *Fuck off, fuck off…*

'What do you do all day?'

Lex cleared his throat. Ryan glanced at him, looking for reassurance. There was none. He was expected to keep up this conversation, to be polite. The world was full of stupid rules. This was definitely one of them.

What did Ryan do all day? Lately, a lot of washing up, a lot of fetching and carrying drinks and making wholemeal toast with crunchy peanut butter for Mum. She "craved" it. Reading, of course, whenever he got the chance, always reading. But he hadn't done any maths. And they were yet to visit a museum. Sometimes they got to the weekly meet, sometimes they didn't. If he felt like it, he'd go by himself. He didn't always feel like it. It all depended on how Mum was in the morning, how she felt. She said, soon, Ryan, we'll get back into the swing of things, properly.

'I do all sorts,' said Ryan. 'Pretty much anything I want, actually. I started my Maths GCSE in September.'

Lex cleared his throat again. Beau turned to him and looked him up and down, but in a friendly fashion.

'Hi,' said Lex, offering his hand. 'You gonna introduce me to your friend, Ryan?'

'This is my… this is Lex,' said Ryan. 'This is *Beau*.'

'All right?' said Beau.

'Hi, Beau. It's good to meet you. Say, aren't you the kid—'

'Yes, he is,' said Ryan.

'Right. Well, Ryan's real sorry about what happened, aren't you, Ryan? Hitting a girl and all… it was a genuine mistake. Ryan thought he was gonna hit you.'

Beau stared at Lex. Then Beau laughed. He shrugged. Lex laughed too, and Ryan looked from one to the other. None of this was funny.

'Clarissa's OK, anyway,' said Beau. 'She got over it. She's my girlfriend now. We go out together.'

'Great,' said Lex, 'and I'm Ryan's mom's boyfriend. At least, I hope I am. We "go out" together too. But probably it would be more accurate to say we stay in together.'

'Cool,' said Beau, nodding. Ryan stood mute, as the conversation carried on around him. It was like one of his dreams, but it was no dream. It might have been a nightmare. He looked down at his feet. His socks were a disgrace, he realised. Mum was right. He shut his eyes and visualised Beau wandering off, and when he opened them again, that was exactly what Beau was doing.

'See yer, Ryan!' Beau called over his shoulder. He raised his hand. Lex did the same.

'See… you!' called Ryan after him.

'He seemed like an OK kid,' said Lex.

'He's all right,' Ryan had to admit, 'for a bully.'

'Hey. I have an idea… Beau?!'

'You bumped into Beau Stirling?' said Mum.

'We chatted,' said Ryan.

'He's an OK kid,' said Lex, pulling Ryan's new clothes and trainers from the carrier bags. 'Good manners. He was nice as pie to Ryan. I gave him my address, is all. And yours. Told him to come visit, if he wants to. I thought… well, I just thought. You know? Check this out, Joanna. We got some really cool new stuff today. I guess you could say it was Goodwill on my part.' And Lex winked at Ryan, who stared back blankly. 'Never mind,' said Lex, and he continued unpacking the shopping.

Mum cast a disapproving eye over the new trainers, the

trousers, the T-shirts, the stripy green jumper, the new (soft, seamless, with in-built odour-control) socks, as Lex emptied out the crinkly, bright plastic bags.

'We usually get our clothes from the charity shops in town,' said Mum, and she turned away from the crisp, new, yet-to-be-worn clothes, with their stiff chemical smell. 'And I take my own shoppers when I go shopping. We don't do carrier bags if we can help it.'

'Sure,' said Lex, in his most conciliatory tone. 'I forgot, is all. Give the kid a break, would ya? We all need brand-new things from time to time. It won't hurt.'

'No. I suppose not.' Mum looked at the clothes, picking them up, smelling them, rubbing the fabrics between her fingers. 'That's a lovely jumper. Beautiful colours. It will suit you, Ryan. And keep you warm in the winter.'

'Lex thought it was my kind of thing,' said Ryan.

'You've always liked green. Just make sure you wear it. Get your money's worth from it. And new socks I see! Thank goodness for that. Do wear them, Ryan, please. Now, can we talk about Beau? Your sworn enemy who is apparently going to come visiting. Is it a good idea?'

'It'll be fine, Joanna,' said Lex. 'Trust me, OK?'

Beau called round to Mum's house the following Monday afternoon. Ryan heard the doorbell ring. Mum was upstairs in her workroom, making bunting. She was getting back into the swing of working every day. Lex was taking a shower. He'd been out running. *Man, am I outta practice!* Mum called to Ryan to get the door. Ryan didn't often get the door. Slowly he approached it. The doorbell rang again. And there Beau stood. Ryan thought he just wanted to have a nose around that freak Ryan Jones's house, and report back to all the kids in school.

Beau smiled and said, 'All right?' He was polite and charming to Mum, who gave them both a cola. They went upstairs to Ryan's room to "hang".

In Ryan's bedroom, they somehow ended up playing Top Trumps, lounging on the bedroom floor. Beau spotted Ryan's games and said he hadn't played Top Trumps for ages. Ryan had many sets, so they played with a different one for each game.

'You're still skiving school, then?' said Ryan, analysing his card.

'Fucking French this afternoon. Fucking hate French.'

Ryan nodded.

'Is Mrs Marchant still there?'

'Yeah.'

'She knows my mum.'

'Yeah.'

'She told my mum to home educate me.'

'I don't see much education going on.'

'That makes two of us, then.'

'At least I go to school sometimes. You fucking skive all the time.'

'Whatever.'

'Strength… 2050,' said Beau. Then: 'Lex seems OK.'

'Lex? He is OK,' said Ryan, staring at his feeble card. He sighed and handed it to Beau.

'Is that his motorbike out the front?'

'Yeah.'

'It's cool,' said Beau.

'Yeah. He takes me out on it sometimes. It goes fast.'

'You're lucky. Bet you're glad he's your mum's boyfriend. Speed, 150 KPH.'

'He's my dad too.'

'Thought he might be.'

'He's from California. He's going to take me there one day. His mum was a hippy, or something. But she's dead now and she left Lex all her money. A lot of money, I've heard. Speed, 200 KPH.'

Beau whistled. He handed over his card. 'Rich hippy.'

'Lex is very rich,' Ryan said, 'very rich indeed. "Filthy rich."'

Beau nodded slowly.

Ryan told Beau all he knew about Lex. Beau was an attentive listener.

'Aren't you scared that he'll run off again? Now that your mum's having another baby?' asked Beau, as he took Ryan's last card in a fifth straight victory.

'No,' said Ryan.

'He might. He's got form, that's what my mum would say,' said Beau.

'No. He won't,' said Ryan. 'He's too involved now. And another baby is coming, so he wouldn't dare, not this time.'

DECEMBER 2006

Winter crept on, slowly at first, with crisp, fresh mornings hinting at much colder mornings to come. Light flurries of snow swirled around, dusting Lex's garden. Trees and bushes were bare, with grey ghostlike birds fluttering among the branches, searching for food and shelter. Ryan put out seeds and biscuits, and fat balls that he'd made at the weekly meet. He'd led the activity, showing the younger kids how to make them. He'd really enjoyed it, and even laughed when Sharon had said, 'Looks like you kids are having a ball.' He liked it when he got jokes.

Skies were grey and white and heavy, yellow-tinged and loaded, ready to fall and deluge the world with winter. The sun, when it shone, was low and cold in the pale blue sky, dazzling but not warming. Ryan shivered. They all shivered.

When the early snow turned heavier and fell in long, silent bursts, Lex and Ryan fashioned a snow cave at the bottom of Lex's garden under the drooping willow tree branches. Mum watched from the patio, taking photographs and laughing. She didn't like snow, and rarely ventured out in it, unless she had to.

Beau continued to visit, mostly during school hours. Ryan overheard Mum say to Lex, 'You can't blame the poor lad, not really. Why wouldn't he bunk off? I did it enough in my time. As long as they're doing something constructive, I don't mind.' Ryan thought Mum's definition of constructive was broad. The "stupid fight" between Ryan and Beau was long forgotten. Most of the time they played Top Trumps, their mutual childhood interest in the game rejuvenated. Or they watched DVDs. The Clarissa incident was not discussed.

Lex took Ryan and Mum shopping and bought them each a brand-new winter coat. Mum's clothes were all too small for her now, as her stomach grew ever bigger. And not only her stomach, she complained. She said she felt "elephantine", and it was crap. She had forgotten how bloody uncomfortable it was to be pregnant. Lex told her she looked gorgeous, and anyways she'd get her "fig-yure" back in no time; she'd just spring back into shape without even trying. He was sure of it. And if she didn't, if it took a little longer, or a lot longer, or even if it never did, so what? It didn't signify.

What was important, was Road to California. Lex's "loan", gratefully accepted in the end by Mum, was tiding the business over. The website was up and running again, and Christmas orders were still coming in. Mum talked about hiring somebody to help, perhaps a long-term employee. She would want some time off to look after the baby and just be a mum for a while. But there was no urgency. She would think about it. Thanks to Lex, the business was no longer in trouble.

In mid-December, on a cold, bright Sunday afternoon, Billy called round to Lex's cottage. He had a new friend with him.

'This is David,' he said, and David smiled and shook everyone's hand. David was a mature student and he was studying to become a midwife, Billy proudly announced.

'Wow,' said Lex, and Ryan thought Lex was bemused; perhaps a little embarrassed.

'Really?' said Mum. 'Did we… haven't I…? I think we met at my last appointment?'

Billy looked sheepish.

'You were shadowing the community midwife, I think?' continued Mum.

'That's right,' said David. 'I was.'

'Lex, do you remember David?' said Mum.

'No, I… I don't think so,' said Lex.

'Then it must have been the appointment you drove me to, Billy. Was it?'

'It was,' said Billy. He blushed.

'Ah,' said Mum, 'I see.'

'I left a note for him at Reception,' said Billy. 'Luckily he didn't think I was a perverted weirdo.'

'You've got some nerve, Billy, I'll give you that.'

'Have you seen a baby being born?' asked Ryan, genuinely intrigued.

'I have seen a baby being born,' said David. 'I've helped lots of mothers to give birth. I'm in my final year of training now.'

'What's it like?' asked Ryan.

'Childbirth? It's, oh, it's noisy and messy and beautiful and a bit crazy. Childbirth is the most amazing thing in the world.'

'That's one way of looking at it,' said Mum.

'But is there much blood and stuff?' said Ryan.

'Buckets of blood! And stuff,' said David.

Billy advised Mum to keep the central heating on at her house, otherwise the pipes could burst in the cold weather. Mum and Billy moved all her work stuff over to Lex's cottage, and Lex set up a new workroom for her, using yet another "spare" room. Mum's house felt cold and sad and empty. Lex fiddled with the thermostat.

'I think I should let the place,' Mum said sadly, for the umpteenth time, 'if… if…'

'Sell it,' said Lex. 'Really. Why the hell not? Sell it, honey. I mean it.' Lex sounded convinced. Mum was less so, as usual. She told Ryan, when Lex wasn't around, that she liked the security of having her own home, the home she had worked so hard for, and eventually managed to secure a mortgage on. One of the proudest days of her life had been moving-in day. She would not sell it; not yet. She would let it.

A couple with a brand-new baby came to look at the house and liked it, because of the long back garden, Ryan guessed. He was going to miss that hedge at the bottom of the garden, but not too badly, because Lex's garden was surrounded by thick hedges and Ryan had discovered several nests. The nests were all empty now, of course, but he couldn't wait for the spring. It wouldn't be a disaster not to be living at Mum's house anymore, as long as he could live at Lex's.

They started to clear things from the old house, and they threw lots of things away, and gave things to charity shops. Mum called it a "life laundry" and she said it made her feel "free and uncluttered in mind and body." It was a little alien to her, she admitted, but refreshing all the same. She sorted through her bookshelves, and after careful consideration of each book, she eventually had a box ready to take to The Old and New Bookshop, where she and Ryan loved to browse. She had less and less time to read these days, she complained. But she still kept a large boxful of her very favourite reads, and another, larger, box which housed her numerous craft and sewing books. Ryan just felt sad to see some of his things, his old toys and his old books, being given away. He tried to resist, but Mum insisted, and at times like these there was just no point in arguing with her. Besides, Ryan could see the sense in it, despite his unease. You had to grow up, and you had to grow out of things. It was the way of the world.

'They're too dog-eared to keep,' Mum said. Ryan thought his books and toys looked nothing like dog's ears. But the books were torn and scribbled in, the pages were brittle and yellow, missing altogether in places, and many of his toys were faded, dirty and broken. Which is what she must have meant, he thought. He was learning. *Dog-eared*. He wouldn't forget.

This morning, while Mum and Ryan were sorting through Ryan's bedroom, the doorbell rang. It was probably Beau, but Ryan inched nervously down the stairs to answer it. He didn't like answering doors any more than he enjoyed picking up ringing telephones, but he knew he had to help Mum because she was pregnant and tired. Lex had stressed this to him many times: 'You have to help. I won't always be around.' And indeed, this morning, he wasn't. He'd popped to the shops to pick up lunch. Ryan knew what Lex meant, of course, when he said, "I won't always be around" – although Ryan had wondered, to begin with, if Lex was making it clear to him that he would be taking off at some point. Was he suggesting the possibility? Was he warning him? No. He couldn't be. He had to stop fretting. Ryan shuffled to the front door, and he opened it. It was a woman. She wore a dull grey suit and deep red lipstick. She looked official. Probably, it was somebody from the letting agent. Ryan looked at her charily. She attempted a smile.

'Hello,' she said.

'Mum!' called Ryan, turning away from the door. He didn't want to deal with this woman. He didn't like her, already.

'Who is it?' And Mum lumbered down the stairs, hanging on to the banister. She had funny balance at the moment, because of the baby, she said. And funny breathing. The baby was big, and she was big, as she complained daily. She was bigger than she had been with Ryan at the same stage, much bigger, and she was never, ever going to get her "fig-yure" back, no matter what Lex said. She was done for.

'Ah, good afternoon,' said Official Woman. 'Miss… Jones?'

'Is it, already? Afternoon?' Mum glanced at her watch. 'So it is, just. I'm Miss Jones, yes.' Mum leaned on the door frame, breathless.

'Ah, hello. My name's Rita Bone. I'm the Education Welfare Officer. I've been looking into your son Ryan's case. Is this Ryan?'

'Yes, this is Ryan. What do you mean, you've been looking into his "case"?' Mum was alert all of a sudden, and standing straight. She was, miraculously, no longer breathless.

'You withdrew your son from school back in... September?'

'No, not exactly. I didn't withdraw him. He was excluded from his school at the end of the summer term, and over the summer break I made the decision to take on his education myself. I did write to your... office. Department. Whatever you call it.'

'Yes, you're quite right, you did. And we wrote back to confirm receipt of your letter and we requested information from you regarding your proposals to educate your son. But so far we have received no information from you despite several telephone calls and a further letter.'

'Oh. I see. Well, I haven't been here much,' Mum said. 'We're in the process of moving. I'm going to rent this property out. There's a pile of letters on the side in the kitchen. I haven't had time to go through them yet. And I'm pregnant, so... but hang on, what do you mean, "proposals"? I've informed you that I *am* educating my son. I'm not "proposing" anything.'

'Well,' said Rita Bone. 'If it's all right with you I'd like to come in and have a chat with Ryan and maybe see some of his work. Do you follow a timetable?'

'A timetable? Of course we don't. Ryan ... er ... Ryan does his own thing. He learns... organically. Especially lately as I'm expecting a baby and I've been pretty ill, unfortunately. Yuck!' Mum flashed the woman her winning smile. But Rita Bone remained stony-faced, obviously irritated. She couldn't give a toss, Ryan decided, if Mum was pregnant or if she had six heads, or the body of a whale; which she did these days, by her own estimation.

'So, Ryan,' said Mum. 'Would you like to chat with this lady?'

Ryan looked at the red lipstick, the (he thought) sneering face, the grey eyes that were as dull as the grey suit.

'No,' he whispered.

'I thought as much,' said Mum. She smiled at him, reassuringly. It was the smile that said, "I'll handle this". She turned to Rita Bone. 'Look, you've caught us on the hop, rather. As I said, we are in the process of moving. How about I get in touch with you after we have moved out and I can fill you in then? Ryan doesn't do work in the conventional sense, nothing like he did in school anyway. He reads mostly, and just learns through life. Biology, for instance' – Mum pointed at her belly – 'Ryan's learning about reproduction in a hands-on way. It's right in front of him. It's right in front of everyone, come to think of it.'

It was increasingly apparent that Rita Bone was a person with no sense of humour. Mum cleared her throat. 'He's coming to my scan next week. Aren't you, Ryan?' Mum poked him in his back. His parents were forever poking him in the back these days.

'Yes,' Ryan heard himself reply.

'I see,' said Rita Bone. 'I expect we can put your file on hold for a month. But after that I would need to see some evidence that Ryan is receiving a full-time education. You are aware of your responsibilities in this regard?'

'Yes, I am,' said Mum. But – was she? Ryan wondered. Had she rushed headlong into this lifestyle? She hated "authority"; specifically, "authority figures", in suits of drab colours, or no colour, wearing shirts and ties

126

and carrying clipboards. Figures who had no "authority" over her at all, as she told Ryan often: merely the appearance of it. Teachers, bank managers, doctors, nurses, solicitors, accountants; even chefs, for heaven's sake. Always she felt bridled by them, by the uniform; ready for a fight, to defend herself, to keep these people in their place, and to keep herself in hers. It was a matter of balance; of seeing through people. She had taught Ryan this. He bridled too.

'And I'm also aware of my rights,' Mum continued, her eyes narrowing. *Just so you know, Ms Bone.* 'And unless I'm mistaken, I believe I'm under no obligation to allow you entry to my home, nor do I have to allow you to talk with my son. Actually, I think it's common courtesy to arrange these things in advance. Mutually.'

Rita Bone coloured. She stammered a sort of apology, a sort of defence… no reply to letters… initial enquiries… couldn't make an appointment.

'So if you could, as I say, give us a few weeks…,' said Mum, a little more politely this time, Ryan thought. Which was probably a good thing. She could "get people's backs up", as Billy had once said. Ryan didn't want her to make an enemy of this Rita Bone woman. There was too much at stake. Surely she knew that?

'Fine,' said Rita Bone, briskly, unmoved. Perhaps she was used to such confrontations? 'I'll leave you my card. Mrs…' She consulted her clipboard. '*Miss* Jones. Please understand I'm not here to judge or to interfere. I think we share a common concern for the educational welfare of your child. That's all.' Rita Bone retrieved a card from under the clip on her board and handed it to Mum. 'Good luck with the move,' she said, not unkindly. Then: 'Could I just make a note of your new address…?'

Mum laughed. 'No,' she said. 'As I said, I'll be in touch.'

'Good. Thank you. It might be a mistake not to get in touch. In the long run.'

Rita Bone turned and left them. Mum slammed the door after her. Ryan hoped Ms Bone hadn't noticed. The woman hadn't been rude; in fact, she'd been quite understanding, in the circumstances.

'Am I really going to your scan?' Ryan asked.

'If you want to.'

'Will I have to go back to school?'

'Again, only if you want to,' said Mum.

'Never!'

Later, Joanna dug out the unopened letter from Rita Bone from the pile of correspondence in the kitchen. She rang Sharon.

'Ignore her,' said Sharon. 'Actually, she's not that bad, I've had dealings with her a few times. She's just one of life's disapprovers. You know the type. If you don't eat meat and two veg and don't live in a neat little semi with three bedrooms and two cars on the drive and you don't watch The X-Factor *and* you don't send your kids to school, you're a menace to society. You could simply ignore her if you wanted, or you could do something just to get her off your back. It's up to you. Just remember, you're the boss, not her. Reports work quite well. Add photos, they always help. I expect it will become an annual thing, so if you're going to accommodate her, you need to get used to it. But don't worry. If you do find yourself feeling intimidated, just imagine her sitting on the lavatory. It always works for me.'

Joanna wrote up a report that evening, dressing up what Ryan had actually been doing in educational language. But there were no photos. She'd hardly taken any. There was no written work to photocopy and send in, Ryan refusing to share his writings. *Next time, next year,* thought Joanna, *once this baby is born and we're all settled, I'll add photos.* She decided to put Lex's address at the top of her letter. It was only fair, she thought. There was no need to be petty. This was her decision. She remained in control. They'd probably track them down anyway. And Ryan had looked so fearful. She must remember to remain sensible, not to allow this woman to get under her skin.

'How many pages have you done in your maths workbook?' asked Joanna, looking up from her letter. Lex was in the kitchen doing the dishes. Ryan was reading. He looked at her over his book.

'Do you want an estimate or an exact answer?' said Ryan.

'Estimate, please.'

'Seventy-two?'

'And the exact answer?'

'Zero.'

'Right.'

Ryan resumed his reading. Joanna wrote a little more, frowning and biting her pen in between.

'And if you were still in school you'd be gearing up for GCSEs now, wouldn't you?' she said after a while. Ryan looked up again from his book.

'Suppose so,' he said.

From now on, he was to do two full pages in his maths workbook every day: every day, without fail, because this is what Mum put in her letter. Mum reckoned if they could show that Ryan was getting a good grounding in literacy and numeracy, it would satisfy Rita Bone. It would have to, for now. Soon they would start on GCSEs, properly. Mum would feel strong and energised, once the baby was born, after a few weeks, and things would get back on track for them all. He wouldn't be able to faff about playing Top Trumps forever. Did he understand?

They posted off the report. Ryan worried. What if Rita Bone decided his education wasn't good enough? She could make him return to school. She had the power to do that, didn't she?

'She'll have to get past me first,' said Mum. Her confidence was infectious, and Ryan soon forgot about it.

The scan was incredible, Ryan thought. He could see his tiny brother, arms and legs snaking around, his little heart jumping. Lex cried. Ryan had never seen a grown man cry before. Ryan privately thought it was wrong, and he pretended not to notice.

'Wow,' said Lex, wiping his eyes. 'Wow.'

They didn't find out the sex of the baby. 'We want a surprise when she's born,' Mum said, and she winked at Ryan. Ryan looked and looked and thought he saw some proof the baby was a boy. It had to be a boy. It was a boy.

They got pictures of the baby: unearthly, chalky shapes and hints on a dark background. Meaningless images, Ryan secretly thought, and the photographs were pinned up on the corkboard in Lex's kitchen for all to see and admire.

There was talk of names. There was name disagreement. Ryan would have liked his brother to be called Tom, or Bob, or Ted, because those names were plain and simple and boyish. He didn't like fancy names. But his parents didn't ask him what he thought, so he said nothing, and instead he listened to them argue over the merits, or otherwise, of Sian, Liberty, Rock – "You have got to be joking, Lex?!" – Roper, Hubbard.

Ryan couldn't sleep. In the dark, hushed bedroom that was his, and now, at last, felt like his, he lay awake, fidgety. Lex's "cottage" had become his home. It was warm and comfortable, and full of both his parents' furniture and books and pictures. Mum's makes now decorated the house: the curtains she had made for his room, her cushions and throws on the sofa and chairs and beds. Their old house was going to be rented out, but it was there "to fall back on", as Mum had quietly told him.

Ryan wondered how late it was, or how early, and he saw that it was half past three. So it was neither late nor early, but that strange time where nothing had meaning, where nothing felt real, where dreams and thoughts ran wild. He quite liked it, that feeling of being between two days, being in a darkened, hushed limbo where nothing really "was".

But, he heard a noise in the kitchen. It "was". Definitely, a small noise. A knock? A door closing, or opening? He wasn't sure.

It could be Seamus, their new cat, jumping onto the table or knocking something over. He was a clumsy cat. He was a friendly cat. He wasn't strictly their cat. Nobody knew who he belonged to, but he had taken up residence, entering the cat flap in the kitchen whenever he liked. Lex had said to it: Have you no shame? – and the name stuck. Ryan didn't mind Seamus, which was surprising to him: on account of birds, Ryan hated all cats, or so he'd thought. But Seamus was all right. He wore a noisy little bell, to warn the birds he was on the prowl. He hadn't yet brought into the house any dead animals, or living ones. He was black and fluffy, fat and affectionate, especially with Ryan. Ryan was undoubtedly his favourite.

It *must* be Seamus making the noise. There was nobody else who would be up and about at this time.

He heard another noise. It was definitely a door opening. Seamus, although clever, could not open doors. Was it Mum? She was complaining of waking up in the night feeling hungry, her stomach rumbling. The noise could be the fridge. He knew it was the fridge. It was obvious. So, it was Mum. But he felt he ought to check.

Ryan got up and pulled his dressing gown tightly around him. He put on his Scooby Doo slippers. Quietly, slowly, he crept down the spiral stairs. Halfway down, the thought occurred to him that there might be an intruder in the house and what exactly would he, Ryan, weak and helpless in his dressing gown and slippers, be able to do about it? But he couldn't go back up the stairs now. That would be pathetic.

Ryan bowed his head and peered into the kitchen. A glow radiated from the fridge, casting a pool of light up onto the face of the person standing before it, who was quickly, quietly, taking things out.

'What are you doing?' said Ryan, descending the rest of

the stairs. He saw Lex's rucksack on the table, his helmet next to it. Lex was wearing his leather trousers, his leather jacket, his bright red scarf. *Oh my God*, Ryan thought. *This can't be happening. He can't seriously—no!* It was a nightmare, wasn't it? He was actually tucked up in bed dreaming this, wasn't he?

'What are you doing?' repeated Ryan.

'I'm – er – I'm just getting some... er... food from the... the ... refrigerator,' said Lex. 'Actually, it's a fridge, isn't it? You guys say fridge.'

It was no dream, no nightmare. It was much worse. Even in the dim light, Ryan could see that his father's face was as bright red as his scarf. He looked shameful, and Ryan knew he'd caught him, red-handed, whatever that meant, another of those silly expressions. Even so, this is what it was.

'What do you need food for?' said Ryan. 'You do know the time, right?'

Lex looked at the floor. He ran his hands over his dark hair. Seamus jumped up onto the table, but neither of them took any notice. Mum would have shooed him away.

Ryan knew why Lex was taking food from the refrigerator. The certain knowledge flooded over and through him. He felt sick. It was happening again; history was repeating itself. "He's got form," as Beau's mum might say. It looked like she was right. Ryan should never have stopped believing in Lex's unreliability. He'd been a fool, a stupid little kid. This was always going to happen, always. It was inevitable. Mum was right, he could not be trusted, not an inch. Stupid, stupid...

No!

'I'm not letting you go!' cried Ryan, rushing at Lex, and throwing his arms around him. It felt weird. He didn't like hugging people, or even touching them, or being touched. But he felt he ought to do something, something big and obvious, to make Lex understand.

'But I'm scared,' said Lex, standing motionless in Ryan's arms.

'What are you scared of?' said Ryan, his voice muffled as he buried his head into Lex's chest.

'All of it. The whole shebang. Fatherhood and responsibility and domestic stuff. It's all so foreign to me Ryan, you got to understand that. Seeing my baby at the ultrasound today… it was awesome but… I don't know if I can—if I can…'

'You can,' said Ryan, drawing back from Lex. 'Of course you can. And this time you have to.'

'Who says I have to?'

'Me.'

'OK. It's just I'm used to obeying my own rules, you know?'

'So what? It's not just you anymore, is it? You're not free and single. Really and truly, you haven't been since I was born, have you? You've just acted like you were.'

Lex looked transfixed. Like he was really, really taking notice. Ryan thought of something else to say. He felt he ought to keep talking, to keep Lex here, in the kitchen, listening to him.

'You can't let Mum down again. Nor my baby brother. You can't do to him what you did to me. Do you know why?'

Lex shook his head.

'Because you would never forgive yourself. I know what it's like to hurt somebody really badly and then feel terrible about it. You know how that feels too, don't you? It – sucks. You have to stay. Please.'

'No.' Lex shook his head, and took a step back from Ryan. 'I don't have to stay. I don't have to do anything. Don't you get that?'

Ryan stared at his father in disbelief. How could this person, who he idolised, in a quiet, voiceless way, how could he be so...*fucking* selfish?

'Stop being a selfish fucker,' he said. 'Please, Dad. Stop it.'

Lex sat down heavily at the kitchen table. Ryan sat down too, opposite him. Lex drummed his fingers on the table. Seamus jumped down and slunk away through the cat flap. Ryan couldn't tear his eyes from the anguished man before him. There was a long silence before Lex stopped drumming his fingers and finally spoke.

'You called me Dad. That's the first time,' he said.

'I know,' said Ryan. 'I called you a selfish fucker too.'

'Say it again.'

'Selfish fucker.'

'No. Not that.'

'You mean "Dad"?'

'Mm-hmm.'

'Did you like it?'

'I think so. Say it again, please.'

'Dad.'

'Again. More.'

'Dad. Dad. You're my dad. I don't want you to go. If you leave again I'll be broken-hearted and so will Mum.

We're good people, but we'd never forgive you. Please stay. Dad.'

'I really am your dad, aren't I?' said Lex, but more to himself than to Ryan. Ryan said nothing; he didn't move. He fixed his eyes on Lex, who started to cry, for the second time in less than twenty-four hours. Ryan looked away. Men shouldn't cry, he thought, and dads certainly shouldn't.

'Oh, Ryan!' said Lex, after getting up from the table and blowing his nose loudly on a piece of kitchen towel, 'I don't deserve you and your mom. I'm a fool, a damn stupid fool. Thank God you came down the stairs when you did... thank God for it.'

Lex took off his jacket.

'Get back to bed, kid,' he said. 'I'm going to unpack my shit – my stuff – and get back to bed myself. Can this be our secret? I mean, man-to-man stuff? Your mom doesn't need to know I was going to run out on her. Especially now that I'm not running out on her, and never will. Please, kid?'

'OK,' said Ryan.

'Thanks. Get back to bed now. I'm sorry. This won't happen again. I promise.'

'You really promise?'

'A solemn promise, Ryan. I had a moment of weakness back there, is all, but you saved me. No more weakness. No more selfish fucker. I promise. Goodnight, kid.'

'Goodnight, Dad.' Ryan backed away towards the spiral staircase, watching Lex.

Lex's eyes sparkled in the fridge light as he put back the food he had taken out just a few minutes before. He then stood and watched Ryan as he wound his way back up the stairs to his room. Lex flashed him a reassuring smile as Ryan took a last look at him. Lex put up his hand in what could only be perceived as a salute. Ryan didn't know what to do back, so he did nothing. He continued up the staircase.

Ryan returned to bed with the strangely ecstatic feeling that he had single-handedly, and narrowly, prevented a disaster. He felt vivid and alert. Yet something troubled him. Had it been too easy? Had Lex backed down too readily? Had he been stalling? Once, he'd just popped to the shops and had not returned. Mum had told him about it, bitterly, many times. Ryan almost felt like he remembered it; he felt Mum's sense of betrayal. But he had been so young, and could not recall his early life with his dad in it.

So he'd caught Lex this time... but what about next time? There would be a next time, he was certain. He felt energised, and he was cold; he didn't trust the euphoria which was creeping away from him, stealthy, silent, like Seamus slinking out through the cat flap. Ryan had a strange feeling, a bad feeling, and he didn't sleep for a long time, not until the sun began to rise.

It was Christmas Day. Billy was cooking. They were going to be eating (free-range, organic) turkey, carrots, beans, Brussels sprouts, Yorkshire puddings, stuffing and roast potatoes; and Christmas pudding for dessert. With ice cream, brandy butter, or cream. Billy was in charge, beating the Yorkshire pudding batter and splooshing it everywhere. He was a messy cook, but nobody complained. His food was great. Mum sat at the kitchen table, pretending to help.

Lex opened bottles of cava and served the drinks. The wine sparkled in the glasses. The day was warm and cosy in so many ways, just like Christmas Day ought to be. Outside, a smattering of snow lay frozen on the earth, and the small, beleaguered garden birds hopped optimistically from twig to twig, seeking out Ryan's never-ending supplies of food. Seamus perched on the windowsill looking in silent fascination at the garden. Like Mum, he hated snow.

After lunch they pulled crackers and Ryan read out the awful jokes. Everyone moaned and groaned and laughed and put on their brightly coloured hats. Lex opened and poured champagne for himself, Billy and David. They were all getting giggly and red-faced.

Lex stood up, and cleared his throat. Ryan wondered what he was going to say. He looked as though he meant business. What was it? Ryan felt the hands of fear run up his spine and finger his neck. Was he going to announce his imminent departure? Was he going to dump Mum? No. For Christ's sake…! This was Christmas. They had guests. They were having a nice time. Lex might be… he might be a "drifter" and he might "have form", but he was not into humiliating people, especially people he loved. It was impossible.

'Lady and gentlemen,' Lex said, tapping his champagne glass. 'Can I have your attention, please!'

'Shhh!' said Billy.

'Thank you,' said Lex. 'I have a few things to say on this special Christmas Day. I'll keep it brief, of course. First, can we have a toast to my incredible son, Ryan. Thank you, Ryan, for accepting me into your life in the way you have. It hasn't always been easy for you, or me, or Joanna. I…

138

I… am so humbled by your acceptance and your willingness to befriend and even like me. I'm proud to be your dad.'

Ryan felt his face burning as he looked down at his plate. Did his father have to be quite so… *American*? Mum reached over and stroked his hand. David took a sip of champagne and raised his eyebrows. Billy said, 'Ahh!'

'Secondly,' continued Lex, 'I would like to thank this beautiful woman here, Joanna, for inviting me back into her life and accepting me with such open, generous arms. Joanna, you are an inspiration, and I don't deserve you.' Lex's face clouded over; he seemed to be looking inwards, at himself, at memories that only he and Mum shared. 'We went through a lot together when we first met and we had some great times,' he said, looking hard at Mum. 'Do you remember?'

Mum nodded, glowing as red as Ryan.

'And we had some less than good times too, right? I… I ran out on you when you needed me most. I'm not going to deny it. I was an idiot. A coward. And I am more sorry about that stuff than I can ever say.' Nobody ate. Nobody drank. 'But here I am, here we are, with a second chance,' continued Lex. 'Joanna, you're having another of my children and…' Lex gulped. He frowned, and looked at Ryan. 'And I'm going to get it right this time,' said Lex.

Lex put down his glass of champagne and lowered himself down in front of Mum, on one knee, and cupped her hands in his. He wasn't going to—oh no, he wasn't! Yes, he was. Ryan heard Mum gasp; he sensed Billy and David leaning forward in their seats, hardly daring to breath.

'Marry me, Joanna,' said Lex.

If she knew the goings-on of that night, just a few nights ago... if she could peer into Lex's heart, would she find something ugly?

But Lex had stayed. He had changed his mind. Or, Ryan had changed it for him. So maybe Lex meant this, maybe it wasn't just a... gesture. Ryan tried to push away the image of Lex, his bag and helmet and scarf on the table, taking food from the fridge, readying himself to leave.

'Marry you?' said Mum, shaking her head slowly from side to side.

'Marry me,' said Lex, refusing to look at anybody, especially *me*, thought Ryan, but that was hardly surprising, given their little secret. But really it was up to Mum. She would have to be the one to do all the trusting. She wasn't good at trusting, Ryan knew. But it would be a good thing if his parents were to get married. It would be proper. It would make Lex stay.

'Marry *you*?' said Joanna.

'I'd like it very much if you would do me that honour,' said Lex. He smiled encouragingly at her. He stayed on his one knee, holding onto her hands. Nobody else dared speak.

Mum looked at Ryan. He looked back at her, willing his eyes to communicate how he felt. But he wasn't sure how he felt. He wasn't sure what she might see in his eyes.

She'd only seen fictional marriage proposals, on TV dramas, in films; and famously real but disastrous ones on YouTube where the woman (usually a woman) said an emphatic *no* and everybody was shocked and embarrassed, and the man (usually a man) was left humiliated. And now this: Lex before her, lap level, down on one bloody knee, exposing himself to the sort of ridicule she avoided, at all costs, for herself. She was thirty-eight years old and here it was – her first proposal. And this one seemed pretty romantic, as they go. Ryan, Billy and David looking on, silenced, waiting for her reply. She looked at Ryan, and thought she saw hope in his eyes. This wasn't YouTube. This was real, and unexpected, so unexpected, because Lex was not a man to propose marriage. Marriage was not his thing. Yet here he was, proposing, in front of their son, and what could she say, truly, now, to make it right?

'Yes,' she said. 'OK. I can't believe I'm saying this, but yes. I'll marry you.' And Lex smiled his huge, expansive smile that showed off his TV-show teeth and David and Ryan sighed, no doubt with relief, and Billy whooped and Lex hugged and kissed Joanna and then he poured more champagne for everybody, even for Ryan, and a tiny token amount for Joanna. They toasted.

They were going to be a family, Joanna thought. It was her only thought, and she knew that her acceptance had been for Ryan and for her unborn daughter as much as, more than, for herself. But, she loved Lex; and that was the only test, surely? She loved him. She always had loved him. She would always love him. And getting married was a big deal for him, more than for her in many ways. He drifted in and out of women's lives; of people's lives, his relationships and friendships coming and going. And now here he was, proposing to her, proposing to stick around, in her life, forever. But she wasn't just anybody. Neither was he. He was the father of her children. That meant

141

something to both of them, to all of them. It would be all right; they would work it out; and Ryan, dear Ryan, how good it was to see him smiling so broadly, unabashed, clearly delighted that his mum and his dad were to be united at last.

JANUARY 2007

L ex had another surprise. In the New Year, he bought his rented cottage. He'd rung the owners back in November, he said, and asked if they would be willing to sell. Although reluctant at first, they'd agreed in the end, probably because Lex was persuasive, Ryan thought, and most importantly, he was rich. Lex had offered them a generous amount of money to buy it: several thousand pounds "over the market value", whatever that meant. But, whatever it meant, Ryan didn't care. The house was now Lex's and Mum's, and Ryan's bedroom under the eaves at the back of the house with its own spiral staircase would be his for a long time; for as long as he needed it, Lex said. Ryan had a home, a home with a mum, and a dad, and himself, and a brother on the way.

It was all so perfect.

Joanna studied her growing bump in the mirror one morning in mid-January, as though for the first time. She looked at it, of course, often, in dismay, every single day: but today she seemed to have a revelation. It was tinged with fear; it was a fear. She couldn't ignore or deny the discomfiture that settled over her when she woke this day. The baby, the house which was now hers and Lex's, the out-of-the-blue marriage proposal on Christmas Day. Just a few months ago she had been a single mum, working hard for herself and her son, living her own life, self-contained, imperfect, but hers. And now she found herself among all these new things, this new life.

She hadn't expected it. She hadn't expected any of it. It was so out of character for Lex, and she feared it was out of character for her too. Did she really want to be married, to anyone? She had resigned herself to never marrying; she had decided to make a point of never marrying. When she had summonsed Lex in those dark summer-filled days, mere months ago, she had not done so with any designs on him. She had been more than prepared to continue "loathing" Lex, but simultaneously allow Ryan to form a relationship with him, for Ryan's benefit only. But it had gone beyond that, way beyond, almost to the point of no return. Almost. And it had happened so quickly. Too quickly?

Was Lex husband material? It seemed he was, now. *For now*, her mind whispered spitefully, as though mocking her, the part of her that "knew" Lex only too well, daring the certainty to rise up and acknowledge itself. From the outside, it must all look so sparkling and palatial: a handsome American man with pots of money was her man; he was also the father of both her children, and he enthusiastically intended being her husband. Surely she would be a fool to pass all this up, especially as it meant so much to Ryan? It had perhaps been wrong of her to refuse Lex's help for so many years. Lex did make an effort of sorts in those early days, she admitted to herself; and she did turn him down, turn him away, no doubt about it, every time, until he gave up. And why wouldn't he have given up? Anybody would have done, surely?

Oh, she was too proud, too opinionated! She had to learn to relax, and trust, and accept the new life unfolding around her. There was nothing to fear, nothing at all, and everything to look forward to. She must pull herself together. She would not let Ryan down, and she would not let Lex down. She would play fair, be an adult, and form this family. She turned from the mirror; she gently rubbed her belly. Her baby girl kicked her. What was she saying? Do it, do it, do it? Or no, no, no?

'Your mum and dad don't hang about, do they?' said Zephyr. It was a freezing cold Saturday in late January, and Debenhams was noisy and overheated. They were looking at suits for Lex and Ryan. The wedding was to take place on St Valentine's Day, the second wedding of the day: the only remaining slot.

Mum had her outfit, but it hadn't come from Debenhams. She had a long dark green velvet dress that fitted neatly over her bump, the bump which, although growing, wasn't *so* big, she reasoned (but she couldn't seem to make up her mind about this, and Ryan secretly thought her belly was huge). She'd found a black velvet shrug to wear with it. Both of these things she'd found in charity shops. She wasn't going to do much with her hair or buy expensive shoes. She wouldn't get into ridiculously high heels anyway, with her puffed up ankles and wonky balance. She'd found a "beautiful vintage" pair of black lace-up boots on eBay, for £15, and she said they were "perfect" for her winter wedding outfit. Lex asked her repeatedly if second-hand clothing was appropriate, was it good enough for her; good enough for his bride? She was adamant she wanted second-hand, it was her style, it was her way. OK, he conceded. But they were not skimping on the flowers.

'In that case,' Mum had asked breathlessly, 'can I have black roses and black tulips, please? They'll go so well with the shrug and my boots. I adore black flowers.'

Black flowers, Lex had agreed. Black roses, black tulips.

'Mum wanted to get married before the baby gets born,' Ryan explained to Zephyr as they sat alongside each other on the floor next to the changing rooms. 'But she didn't want to look like a beached whale in the photos, so they chose St Valentine's Day. She's gone all weird.'

'Oh,' said Zephyr. And, 'You should say "is born". Not "gets born". That doesn't sound right.'

Ryan shrugged. He said nothing. He knew it didn't sound right, really, and if he was ever going to make it as a writer one day, he wouldn't use it. He'd decided, secretly, finally, that he would be a writer. Not a vet.

'I'm bored,' said Zephyr.

'Me too,' said Ryan.

'Shut up, you lot,' said Mum, holding up a jacket in front of Ryan. 'Lex is the one who wanted to get married on St Valentine's Day, not me. Well, not so much. I would have happily waited until next summer. Summer weddings are just so gorgeous. And this baby would be out by then. And I'd look like a bride should look. I ask you, St Valentine's Day…? It makes me feel even more nauseous than this flipping pregnancy does.'

'You do know that changing rooms have ears, right?'

said Lex. 'It's romantic to get married on the patron saint of lovers' day. Get over it.' Seconds later, when Lex stepped out of the changing room, Ryan didn't recognise him. He looked extraordinarily handsome, with his closely-cropped black hair, and the dark grey suit sitting sleekly on his strong body.

'Oh! You look lovely!' said Mum. She smiled proudly at her fiancé.

Lex, looking over his shoulder at himself in the mirror, said, 'Does my butt look big in this?'

Of course, it didn't, so Lex bought the suit, and a slightly smaller version for Ryan. Joanna couldn't believe how much Ryan had grown. He was growing ever taller, and filling out, just a little. His arms were thicker, his legs just that little bit sturdier. She studied him as he tried on his suit. Her boy was rapidly turning into a man.

It was comforting, in many ways. His childhood had been difficult, so often. Hers had been difficult too. She remembered how welcome her eighteenth birthday had been to her. She'd celebrated it with her friends. There had been alcohol, lots of it, and punchy bursts of amyl nitrate in the toilets of the seedy club she frequented. More alcohol. A spliff, or two. Vodka jelly. A hushed, cold bedroom at the top of a house. A young man whose name she'd never caught, good looking, tattooed. She blushed at the recollections, not recognising herself. Her headlong race into adulthood had been frantic, chaotic, her parents banished.

It was a habit, she thought, banishing people from her life. People who hurt her. Yet she had not once looked back, nor longed for her childhood days. Adults had all the freedoms, all the choices. And Ryan would have those choices too, he would have those freedoms, soon. Would her son cope with being an adult? He'd have to. That was life. She would be there to help him, and so would Lex.

The only guests at the wedding would be Ryan, Billy and David, and Sharon, Zephyr and Clover. Lex and Joanna, although they had lots of old friends between them from their travelling days, their partying days, their festival days, decided they could not invite one set of friends without another, and the guest list would get out of control, and what the hell do you do about divorced couples? And ex-girl-and-boyfriends? Joanna said she didn't have that problem. Not on Lex's scale, anyway.

And they wanted a small, intimate wedding. Lex had no immediate family to invite; he had cousins in Salinas, California, he said, but he hadn't seen them in years. He'd send photographs.

'What about your folks?' said Lex to Mum when they were home and hanging the new suits in their wardrobe next to the green frock and the black velvet shrug. Ryan was sitting on their bed, playing with Seamus.

'What about them?' said Mum. Her voice sounded… crippled. Oh God. This was a bad choice of subject, Lex. *Dad*. Really bad. Ryan hoped the conversation would end there. But Lex had other ideas. He seemed oblivious.

'Shouldn't they be invited?' he asked. It sounded innocent. But you could never tell with Lex. He knew which buttons to press, always. No doubt about it. And sometimes he didn't hesitate to press them.

Ryan heard his mother's quick little intake of breath. Oh, be careful, Lex, choose your words carefully. Ryan wanted to cry out to his dad to warn him.

'No,' said Mum. From her point of view, that was the end of the conversation, Ryan could tell, but Lex either wasn't aware (unlikely) or he was determined to persist. It would end in a row. Ryan sighed. He raised his eyebrows at Seamus, who stared back blankly.

'Why not?' said Lex. He folded his arms across his chest. He tilted his head to one side. Battle mode.

Mum slowly closed the wardrobe door. 'I must remember to sprinkle lavender in there. We don't want moths eating our wedding gear. Maybe I should get hold of some mothballs?'

'Don't worry about it. We're getting married in a couple of weeks, honey. Why shouldn't we invite your folks?' Lex was persistent. It was probably unwise, thought Ryan, if he didn't want another row. Maybe he did? Was he winding Mum up?

'Because, as you know, they're not in my life,' said Mum, quietly.

'You're their only child, right? Their one and only beautiful daughter. And you're getting married.'

'And?'

'And it's the "done thing" to invite your folks to your wedding. I sure wish I could invite my mom.'

Despite her obviously rising anger, Mum's face softened. That was a good sign, Ryan thought. Keep her sympathy, Lex, hold on to it. That was good, that was safe. It was difficult to be sympathetic and furious at the same time.

'I know,' said Mum. 'She would have been thrilled, wouldn't she? But, Lex, you should know by now that I don't do the "done thing". Anyway, my parents wouldn't turn up. There's little point in even discussing it, let alone inviting them. I haven't spoken to either of them for years. You know that.'

'Do they know you're having another baby?' said Lex.

Seamus stretched out across Ryan's lap as he continued to stroke the cat's soft fur. He felt his face burning in humiliation and anger. The little nut inside him started to grow again. So, it had not gone away, like he'd thought it had. And why should he say nothing? She shouldn't always be allowed to get away with her... nonsense.

'They don't even know about me,' he said. He buried his face in Seamus's fur, avoiding Mum's cool stare. Lex looked at his son in disbelief.

'Oh my freaking God!' said Lex. 'Joanna. You kill me.'

'Can we talk about this another time, please?' said Mum, indicating Ryan. He got up from the bed and sloped from the room, Seamus going with him, haughtily. A walkout. Mum deserved it. He didn't mind that he had never met his grandparents. It was just the way it had always been. He had never given it much thought. But, of course, it might be *nice* to have grandparents. And Lex was an open-minded person, Ryan knew; nothing much surprised him. But even he looked shocked that Mum had not told her parents she had a son. And why was he such a secret? Was he something to be ashamed of? Sometimes, too often, he didn't understand his mum. Sometimes he didn't want to understand her.

'So, well done, honey. Great.'

'Fuck off, Lex. Please.'

'No. I won't fuck off. That poor kid… can't you see what—'

'I can see everything perfectly, thank you.' Joanna, hands on hips, tried hard not to cry. OK, so Ryan again, missing out, because of her. But not entirely because of her. Her parents "disapproved" of their daughter, and they had done so since her announcement at thirteen that she would be a vegetarian from then on (she was a vegetarian for five years before changing her mind). After that, nothing she did made any sense to them. They were conservative, Conservative, and they were nothing but "pathetic reactionaries!" as Joanna had shrieked at them one morning, two days short of her seventeenth birthday. She'd stomped from their house that afternoon in her Doc Marten boots, carrying her Army Surplus holdall rammed with clothes, toiletries, make-up and hairspray.

She still hadn't been back. There had been occasional phone calls and birthday cards, all done in a strange spirit, as though she were a niece not often seen but sometimes remembered. Joanna finally stopped believing in them, as they must have stopped believing in her. The cards ceased, the stilted phone calls too. The relationship was over and Joanna wasn't sure it had ever really begun. And she was not going to attempt to resurrect it now. It was impossible.

FEBRUARY 2007

Mum developed a hankering for jam doughnuts. The hankering became an obsession. They had to be "proper" jam doughnuts although she would accept apple doughnuts at a push. Custard doughnuts if absolutely nothing else was to be had. They had to be smothered in crystally, crunchy sugar, and plenty of it. She couldn't get enough of them. At any time, day or night, doughnuts had to be in the house, ready for her to stuff herself with. She was getting fat. Ryan wondered if the dress would still fit on the wedding day. But she didn't seem to care; she was going to get fatter and fatter anyway, she said. She'd never had a huge appetite; she had always been slim, sometimes thin; she thought this desire was her body's way of ensuring she took in enough calories. Ryan was doubtful, but conceded to himself that he didn't know enough about the ins and outs of pregnancy to judge, and Mum did. Lex said it was cool, honey, you got to do what you got to do. He kept the supplies in. The doughnuts from the supermarket were acceptable, but Mum's favourites were the doughnuts from the little bakery in town. It was a narrow, cosy shop, tucked in between Boots on the one side and a Clarks shoe shop on the other. The window was always stuffed with cakes, and breads, and delicate little biscuits with pink and yellow icing. Ryan liked the look of the hedgehog-shaped cakes best, with chocolate buttons as spikes. He never bought one, of course, not these days; they were far too babyish, but he liked to look at them all the same.

Lex and Ryan were dispatched one chilly Monday afternoon, a few days before the wedding, to pick up doughnuts from the bakery and some stretch mark cream from Boots. If Mum saw the irony of this, she didn't say so. Lex said nothing either, even when Ryan raised his eyebrows at him. Lex just shook his head. He and Ryan hopped on the Harley and headed into town.

'You get the cream, I'll get the cakes,' said Lex, outside the bakery. He gave Ryan a ten-pound note.

Ryan wandered around in Boots looking for the cream. Then he spotted Beau, standing by the make-up, looking bored. Ryan was about to call his name and wave hello, when Beau spotted him, and his face froze. He seemed to look right through Ryan as though he wasn't there. Then Ryan noticed Clarissa Cooper, uglier than ever, as she stood up and said something to Beau. She didn't see Ryan. Hurriedly, Beau pulled Clarissa away from the make-up aisle. Away from Ryan.

Ryan didn't know how to feel or react. Most probably he should just buy the cream and not worry about it. He'd already guessed that Beau didn't tell anyone he was occasionally hanging out with that freak Ryan Jones. Why would he? Why would he admit to that? Ryan was widely regarded as weird, and he had smashed his fist into Beau's girlfriend's face. Ryan, in Beau's position, might have kept their friendship quiet too. Schoolkids were ruthless. He got it.

Ryan found the stretch mark cream and went to the counter to pay.

'No school today?' said the assistant as she served him. She had too much powder on her face. She wore bright red lipstick that was seeping into the skin around her mouth, like little scarlet rivers on a pale map. She had grey hair and wore huge round glasses which Ryan didn't like. She reminded him of Rita Bone. It was the lipstick; or the general air of disapproval and suspicion.

'I don't go to school,' replied Ryan, looking over his shoulder. He saw Beau and Clarissa, hand in hand, leaving the shop, Beau pulling her along, and looking over his shoulder, nervously. They made brief eye contact. Then Beau was gone. Ryan looked back at the assistant.

'You don't go to school?'

'No. I learn at home. Or in other places.'

'Oh. Oh well, good for you. Why not, eh?'

Ryan could tell the assistant thought he was weird, or lying. He decided he'd give her something to really disapprove of.

'I beat up a girl because I didn't like the way she chewed gum. That cham cham cham noise. I got kicked out of school. Other schools won't take me. Not even the Pupil Referral Unit. That's where the really bad-assed kids go. So I'm doing what the… what the fuck I want all day and I don't give a shit.' The assistant stared at him. She handed him his change and the receipt. She didn't smile, or say anything else. Ryan fancied she looked scared.

He left the shop.

Why did he do that? Should he go back in and apologise? Mum would have a fit if she knew how he'd

154

spoken. The woman would never want to see him again. He didn't blame her. There was no point in attempting an apology.

'OK, kid?' said Lex when Ryan met him outside Boots. 'I just saw your buddy. But he was in kind of a hurry. Was that his girlfriend with him?'

'Yes. That was Clarissa. I saw them too.'

'That's the girl you—?'

'Yeah.'

'Right. How did it go saying hi to her? A little awkward, I guess?'

'It wasn't awkward at all.'

'We can't afford a honeymoon,' said Mum, eating her second jam doughnut. Ryan sat in the rocking chair in the corner of the kitchen and Seamus purred loudly on his lap, squinting smugly as Ryan stroked his fluffy black fur. Joanna licked sugar from her lips, from her fingers.

Lex was making coffee for himself, decaffeinated for Mum. 'But my question was,' continued Lex, 'where would you like to go for our honeymoon? I didn't mention money.'

Mum popped the last of the doughnut into her mouth. She chewed slowly, closing her eyes. God, thought Ryan. She really did like them. She looked entranced.

'OK, so what exactly do you mean, we can't *afford* a honeymoon?' said Lex, shouting to be heard over the sound of the kettle beginning to boil.

'Maybe that's not strictly true,' said Mum. Her eyes were still closed. '*I* can't afford a honeymoon. And that's academic, actually, because I don't want a honeymoon.

How's that?' said Mum, snapping open her eyes and raising her voice, just a little louder than was necessary.

'You do too. Stop lying. And you know good and damn well that *we* can afford it. Stop being so obtuse.'

Ryan shrugged. The kettle flicked off, the sound of boiling subsiding gradually. But Mum was beginning to boil too.

'It's too late in my pregnancy for me to fly,' she said, rustling the bag of doughnuts and peering inside. 'Did you get apple ones too?' Her voice was normal again. Ryan felt something like relief.

'Yeah. Thought I'd cover all the posts. Why the hell are you being so fu—stop being so… *lame*, would you? It is not too late for you to fly. I checked on the internet last night. What are you now, six months? Or damn near. You can fly anywhere right now. I want to take you to California. What do you say, Joanna?' He placed a mug of the "vile" decaff on the table before her.

'No, thank you,' said Mum, examining the doughnuts. 'But thanks for the coffee.'

Ryan stopped stroking Seamus and looked at Mum. She started nibbling at her third doughnut. She was concentrating on it, as though working out a complicated mathematical conundrum. *It's actually simple, Mum.* When she looked up she saw all of them, Lex, Ryan and Seamus, looking at her. She swallowed.

'What?' she said. 'It's against my principles to fly. I want to keep my carbon footprint as low as possible.'

'Oh, please. Your what?' said Lex.

'You heard.'

Ryan laughed to himself. *Carbon footprint?* That wasn't

the reason. Ryan decided enough was enough. Unlucky, Mum. Again.

'Mum's too scared to fly,' said Ryan, earning himself a glare from her, and a wide-eyed look of surprise from Lex.

'Scared?' said Lex, pulling out a chair from the table and sitting alongside Joanna. 'Joanna Jones is *scared* of flying? Oh, my God! Joanna? What is this? Is this true?' He nudged her.

'You're laughing at me!' snapped Mum, poking her tongue out at Ryan. 'I am not scared of flying. I choose not to fly. There is a difference. By the way, is this fair trade decaff?'

'Oh yeah. Quit being obnoxious, would ya? You know it is. I've learned my lesson there, right?'

'It's not a crime to care, Lex,' said Mum.

'Yeah, you say that. And you're right, honey. But can we get back to our discussion, please? Now that I think about it, we never did fly anywhere, did we? We always took the ferry. D'you recall that shitty trip to Amsterdam…? Look, Joanna, can't you make an exception? It's our honeymoon, and I want you to see where I grew up, where I spent my time as a kid. It's beautiful there, Joanna, the sea is warm and blue and the beaches are soft and the sky is oh so pretty. We can hike. We can rent a car. And the mountains… you'd love it. I can drive you around and show you where I lived with my mom. We can go to Disneyland even, if you'd like to. You know, I'm sure the planet will forgive you for a once-in-a-lifetime trip to the west coast. What do you say?'

'Hike? In my condition? Anyway, I don't have a passport,' said Mum. She seemed to have finally had enough of the doughnuts and put her third, half-eaten one back in the bag.

157

'We'll get you one,' said Lex. 'God, you really are scared, aren't you?'

'No! But there's no time to get a passport. We're getting married in just a few days. Be practical, damn you.'

'So we'll go along to the passport office and apply for one in person. It's not a big deal. Come on. Let's do this before our baby comes along and our life becomes nothing but diapers and puke. And, OK, no hiking. But we can do everything else, right?'

'I'm not going on an aeroplane,' Mum said quietly, 'and you mean *nappies* and puke.'

Lex sighed. He shook his head, and sipped his coffee.

'I'll go to California with you,' said Ryan.

'OK, kid. I'll take you there, someday. That's a promise. You'll love it.' Lex winked at his son.

'I promise to go on the plane and not be scared,' said Ryan, looking at Mum triumphantly. She ignored him, got up from the table, and put the bag of doughnuts in the fridge. There would be no more honeymoon talk.

The morning of the wedding was bright and sunny and cold. Ryan woke up early, feeling excited, but at first he couldn't remember why. Then he remembered, and as he sat up in bed, Lex gave him a knock and told him to get a shower first because his mother was, without doubt, going to hog the bathroom for the next two hours.

The wedding was to take place at the Register Office at ten o'clock. At a quarter past nine, Mum was ready. She grabbed a brush and went to work on Ryan's hair, trying to shape it into something resembling a style, without much success. But you look handsome, Ryan, she said. Lex took pictures, unobtrusively, snapping all the intimate, small moments which he said made an occasion memorable. He might do a photography course, he said. Get some good equipment and go for it. He'd want to get some beautiful pictures of the baby.

Lex really did look handsome in his grey suit. Anybody could see that. Ryan knew he would never match up to his dad's looks. Lex had shaved off most of his stubble and he looked incredibly young, far younger than his forty-two years. Mum pinned a black rose onto Lex's jacket, she kissed him, and they were all three ready.

Billy and David bounced into the kitchen, Billy in a red suit, David in a more subdued blue. They kissed everyone, told Mum she looked beautiful, and told Ryan he was handsome, just like his dad. They heard the friendly growl of Sharon's camper van – 'Here come the hippies,' said Billy – and when they entered the increasingly crowded kitchen, Sharon looked decidedly unhippy-like in a chic red woollen dress, heeled boots, a cloche hat, and silk scarf. Even Clover wore a frock and a pretty cardigan.

Lipstick was touched up, ties straightened, corsages pinned. Billy was driving Mum and Lex. Everyone else was going in Sharon's camper van.

Although there was a lot of traffic in town, they were in plenty of time for the wedding. They sat in their vehicles and watched the wedding party before them come out, and have their photographs taken. The bride and groom were happy and smiling and confetti floated all over them. Ryan turned in horror to David.

'We don't have any confetti!'

'Oh, yes, we do! I got some this morning. Here you are, have this box. I have rice too.'

'Rice?'

'It's a symbol of fertility. It's traditional to throw it over couples when they get married. It's supposed to ensure they have lots of babies.'

'Oh.'

David winked at Sharon.

'Do you like being a midwife?' asked Ryan, as he carefully stowed the box of confetti in his jacket pocket.

'Like it? I absolutely love it. It's an amazing job. I can't wait to qualify.'

'Isn't it a job for women, though?' said Zephyr.

'There's nothing to stop a man doing it, not in this day and age. You get the same training. Some of the dads can get a bit sniffy sometimes. But I just tell them I'm gay and that seems to make a difference.'

'What made you want to do it?' said Ryan.

'Well, about four years ago my sister was pregnant and she went into labour, and I ended up in the hospital with her and I was basically her birth partner. Long story. Anyway, I mopped her brow and rubbed her legs, you know.'

Ryan didn't know. It sounded revolting.

'Are there really buckets of blood?' said Ryan.

'Oh my God…!' muttered Zephyr.

'There's blood,' said Sharon.

'There is blood, of course there is,' said David. 'It wouldn't be natural otherwise, would it?'

As Ryan and Zephyr pondered this, they saw Lex leap out of Billy's car and open Mum's door for her.

'Let's go, kids!' said David, and he grabbed his camera.

The wedding was almost over before it started. It was disappointing. After a long-winded speech from a woman (dressed in a suit which was, of course, grey) about the solemn nature of the occasion, Lex and Mum said a few words, and then they signed the register, and that was that. Lex and Mum were husband and wife. Ryan and Zephyr were bored throughout the service, but they were wise enough not to show it.

Afterwards, they all went outside, and David took some photos. Lex handed his camera to a passer-by and asked her to photograph the whole wedding party. The passer-by seemed delighted; she took a few photos and wished Lex and Mum good luck. Snowflakes began to twirl and twist, mingling with the rice and confetti. Lex and Mum kissed and shivered.

'Come along, Mrs Nicholson,' said Lex. 'Let's go get warm and let's eat. Let's go home. Come on, everybody!'

Back at the cottage, Billy uncovered plates of sandwiches, Lex opened champagne and later Mum and Lex cut the wedding cake, picked up the day before from their favourite bakery. The cake was delicious, a light sponge with white icing and black sugar flowers arranged on top. Billy opened up some packets of posh crisps and they ate cheese and crackers, grapes and biscuits. There were quiches and pizzas, and slices of (organic, free range) chicken and ham. There was also a large plate laden with jam doughnuts; nobody quite knew if that was a joke, or not. Lex put the plate in the middle of the table with a flourish. They all laughed, even Mum.

'This is the simplest wedding I have ever been to!' declared Billy, and David agreed.

'But it's perfect, right?' said Lex, and he squeezed Mum's hand. Mum looked happy. Ryan watched her, looking for signs of doubt, or regret, or fear.

'It's totally Lex and Joanna,' said Billy.

They opened the cards. They were mostly from a few old friends whom Lex had contacted to let them know he and Mum were marrying; and one from Mrs Marchant.

Ryan was in bed, stuffed with cake and crisps and pizza and doughnuts. Sharon had taken Zephyr and Clover home, and Lex and Mum had gone off to a hotel for the night. It wasn't in California, of course. But Lex didn't seem to mind. Whatever Mum did or said or wanted was always all right with Lex in the end, it seemed. Was that marriage? Ryan wondered. He wasn't sure if he'd like to be married. Ryan listened to the muffled chatter of the TV from downstairs. Billy and David were staying over for the night. Billy was going to do a cooked breakfast in the morning. Ryan was looking forward to poached eggs on toast again.

It was snowing hard outside, and Mum had fretted about making it to the hotel, but Billy had driven them there and got back to the cottage with no problems. It was a Country Hotel, he said. Posh. Must have cost an arm and a leg.

Ryan lay in bed and looked out at a dark, heavy sky, orange and luminous with snow. His mum had married Lex. They were married, his *parents*. It seemed incredible to Ryan that any of this could have happened, and so quickly. He wasn't used to it yet, but he was looking forward to getting used to it. He wondered when Lex would take him to California. He wondered if Mum would let him fly. Surely she would with Lex? She let him ride on the Harley and that was far more dangerous, even though Lex was sensible when Ryan was on board.

Ryan wondered what Mum and Lex might be up to. Then he realised with a private blush that he shouldn't wonder, and when he turned out his light, he closed his eyes and slept deeply.

A few days after the wedding, a letter arrived for Mum. She read it, swore under her breath, and tried to hide it from Ryan.

'It's from that Rita Bone woman, isn't it?' Ryan said. 'I knew she'd be trouble. Let me see it, please, Mum.'

Mum handed Ryan the letter, and he read:

'16th February 2007

Dear Miss Jones,

Thank you for your letter of 5th December 2006 regarding your proposals for your son Ryan's Elective Home Education. I do apologise for not responding until now, but I have been away from work with flu' – 'Good!' said Ryan – 'for some time, and I was away over Christmas, and I am now in the process of catching up with my work.

It would appear that on the balance of probabilities that your son Ryan is not receiving an education suitable to his age, aptitude and ability. I am sorry to respond negatively, but I am not convinced that a reasonable person would be satisfied that a suitable education is taking place. While your provision for numeracy and literacy is a start, it falls a little short of satisfactory for a child of fifteen years of age' – 'She can't even get my age right!' – 'and you failed to give any details regarding your provision in other subjects, for instance, Science, Modern Foreign Languages, Art, PE, History, Geography. This list is not exhaustive.

It is my policy to give you two weeks from the date of this letter to provide further information illustrating your provision for Ryan. Failure to do so will result in my beginning proceedings to ensure Ryan enters full-time education. This may mean that, ultimately, a School Attendance Order is issued for him. However, I sincerely hope that this can be avoided, as I am aware that this would be against your wishes and would be likely to cause both you and your son considerable distress.

I look forward to hearing from you within two weeks from the date of this letter.

Yours Sincerely,

Rita Bone'

'What can we do?' said Ryan, handing the letter back to Mum. 'She wants me to go back to school.'

'Maybe you should, Ryan,' said Mum.

'Do you want me to?'

'Yes and no.'

'I'm never going back! Never!' Ryan bolted from the kitchen, knocking over his glass of orange juice as he ran.

Later, Lex took one look at the letter from Rita Bone and laughed.

'Don't worry about it, kid,' he said. 'You're not going to

let an officious person like that get under your skin, are you? Beat her at her own game.'

'How?' asked Mum and Ryan.

'Well, we need a plan here. Ryan, you've actually done some math, right?'

'Two pages in my workbook every day, like Mum said.'

'Good. Didn't Sharon say something about sending copies of work to prove you're actually working? We can photocopy some of those, can't we? And send them to this Rita. What about English?'

'I read,' said Ryan.

'Boy, do you read. But you need to do more. Let's get you started on your GESC or whatever it's called. What about science? Shall we get you a chemistry set or something? What do you say?'

'GCSE. Sharon and her friends are setting up a weekly science club,' said Ryan. 'Zephyr told me. One of the mums used to be a science teacher and she's going to run it. She's going to do GCSE stuff.'

'Cool. So make sure you go. It's in town, right?'

'Yes. At the science teacher's house, I think. I can go with Zephyr if Mum's not up to it.'

'Great. You've… we've got to make an effort, OK? If you don't want to go back to school, we have to work at it.'

They had a lovely afternoon, Lex and Ryan, poring over books in The Old and New Bookshop and in the library, and looking at science kits in the toyshop. Ryan came home staggering under a pile of workbooks and reference books, including a new dictionary and thesaurus, and mountains of pens, pencils, paper and exercise books. Ryan politely refused paints and paintbrushes. 'I hate drawing and I hate painting and I'm no good at either of them,' he said. 'Rita Bone will just have to accept that I don't do Art.'

'That's fair enough, kid. Make sure you paint with words instead,' said Lex.

In the evening, Lex and Ryan sat up until late checking out useful websites on the internet. There were so many, and Ryan couldn't see where he might begin. It was overwhelming.

'Don't sweat it, kid,' said Lex, switching off the computer. 'Just spend an hour or so a day on the net, do some math, some English, do some experiments with your kits. Get your ass to the weekly meets and that science club you told me about. Get a project going, why don't you? What are you really into? Think about it, settle on something, and then concentrate on that when you're on the net. History, maybe? You began work on a history project, didn't you?'

'It fizzled out,' said Ryan.

'Well, fizzle it back in. I'll compose a reply to this Rita woman. It's all gonna be fine and dandy.'

'February 22nd 2007

Dear Ms Bone,

Thank you for your letter regarding my son Ryan's education. I am sorry that the previous report from my wife did not fully explain where we are at. But my wife is pregnant, and she recently moved in with me and married me, so her life has been kind of hectic.

Please find enclosed some copies of Ryan's work. As you can see, we are focusing on English and Math. A

166

good grounding in these subjects opens doors to all the others, in my opinion. Ryan is particularly fond of, and good at, English. Please see the attached list of books he has read in the past six months or so. Ryan is soon going to be working his way through an English GCSE course, through distance learning. In the Spring, we're going to start with his Math GCSE. He continues with his Math workbook for now. He doesn't find the subject easy but he gets help from myself, his mom, and his friend who is in school and has agreed to come over and work with Ryan from time to time.' (Lex had collared Beau when he'd called round one afternoon, gently suggesting Beau should no longer skive off from school; he also suggested he and Ryan could actually, you know, do some schoolwork together? *After* school?) 'Ryan also attends a weekly science club for older kids, run by a former science teacher, and he regularly attends a weekly meet-up for, and organised by, other families who are also not in the school system. They do regular activities and organize trips and have visitors. A couple of weeks ago a guy took some real bats along to the meet, which fascinated Ryan.

Ryan has started a project on American culture. I am from the States myself, and he is keen to learn about where I come from. This project is set to encompass history, geography, religion, science, literature, art, media, computer skills. You name it, this project will cover it.

I sure hope this letter and the attached work of Ryan's is now enough to convince a reasonable person that a suitable education is taking place. Ryan is flourishing learning at home, and is determined not to return to school. Whatever your take on that, his wishes need to be responded to and that's what his mom and I are working hard at doing.

Yours,

Alexander Nicholson (Ryan's father)'

Ryan's father.

It sounded good, it looked good. It was good. But it was weird, and Ryan wasn't yet used to calling him Dad. Around other people, he was Lex, always Lex, and nobody seemed to mind. When alone, Ryan still called him Lex most of the time; occasionally he used Dad, but mostly as an afterthought, and because he felt it was expected. Since the Running Away Night, Ryan had found it difficult to say 'Dad'. It was as though Lex was a big secret that Ryan had to keep, even though everybody knew that Lex was his father, and nobody would have found it strange that Ryan called him Dad.

'He'll fig-yure it out in his own time,' Lex said to Mum the morning after he'd composed and posted his letter to Rita Bone. Lex and Mum were in the kitchen drinking coffee and Ryan was listening to them from the lounge, as he often did. He'd read that writers have to be nosy, so it was all right.

'I'm sure he wants to call you Dad. It's just shyness, I think,' said Mum. 'He's not used to you yet. The idea of you. Shall I talk to him about it? Is it upsetting you?'

'No, I'm not upset. Let him be coy about it. Besides, I'm not sure that I'm ready to be called Dad just yet. It's kind of embarrassing. I need to earn it, you know? There's

168

a world of difference between a father and a dad, right? You know what I'm saying?'

'Hmm-hm,' said Mum.

'There's a long ways to go. Leave it Joanna, don't push it, whatever you do. It'll work itself out.'

There was a pause. Ryan listened keenly.

'Lex?' said Mum.

'Yeah?'

'Would you be really sweet and fetch something for me?'

'Sure. Let me guess. Doughnuts?'

'Doughnuts, yes. I'm so sorry.'

'Girl, you are going to explode!'

'Go on, Lex. I really, really fancy some.'

'Some?'

'All right, then, one. For now.'

Ryan heard Lex get off the sofa and walk over to the large bay window.

'Looks cold out there!' he said.

'Oh no, don't bother, then. I could have a go at making some...'

'Joanna, I will hop on my bike and go get your doughnuts. Are you sure your name isn't Homer Simpson?'

Ryan wandered into the kitchen.

'Morning, kid,' said Lex. 'I'm heading out for doughnuts.'

'Can I go with you?' said Ryan.

'Nah, too cold. Stay here and eat toast or something.'

Lex briskly shook his head back and forth as he always did before putting on his helmet. He put it on, carefully doing up the strap. He mounted the Harley, pushing it off its stand. Ryan stood at the front door.

'Lex!' called Ryan. 'Lex!'

Lex looked up.

'Can't I come with you?'

'No! I'll be twenty minutes, max. Go on inside. Look after your mom, OK?' Did Ryan imagine it, or did his dad linger on looking at him? Was there something… was there… No. It was just his imagination. Stupid. His dad was going to the shops to pick up doughnuts for Mum. That was all. Just that. He had to let go of this stupid fear that Lex would disappear again. If Mum could trust him, so could he. They had to trust him. They had no choice; that was the truth.

Ryan waved, Lex waved back. He kick-started the Harley and rode off slowly along the gravel drive. Ryan retreated back into the warmth of the house, closing the door firmly.

After a quick breakfast, Ryan worked on his project at the kitchen table. The glow of the Aga gave off a comforting warmth that filled the kitchen, and it had become his favourite place to work. He was enjoying learning about the United States of America, especially Lex's home state of California, which was huge, bigger than Britain. It had a space centre and lots of oranges and bears, and Disneyland. And the beaches were soft; and the skies were blue, just as Lex had described.

'Where's Lex got to?' said Joanna, as she finished

washing up the breakfast things. 'He's been gone half an hour. He should be back by now.'

Another twenty minutes passed, and Lex did not return. 'Do you think he's all right?' said Joanna, looking at Ryan. 'I'll try his mobile.'

Lex didn't respond to Mum's call. So she texted, and waited for a reply that did not come.

Oh no, no, no. Ryan looked at Mum, but he couldn't tell what she was thinking. She knew nothing about Running Away Night. Was this Running Away Day? Had Lex decided to return to Greece? Was he planning to abscond to France... or Australia... or California? Or had he just taken off, "gotten away", with no destination in mind? He was capable of all of these things, Ryan knew. He remembered the look of pure fear on Lex's face when Ryan had found him that early morning in December, taking food from the fridge, preparing to leave them all over again. Had he done it now? Would they see him again? Oh, God. He'd gone. Ryan knew it. He'd said goodbye all matter-of-factly and all the time he was plotting and planning to leave them. He'd been waiting for this moment where he could casually ride off, and never return. That's how he'd left him and Mum all those years ago, wasn't it?

How could he? Ryan felt sick. His parents should not have bothered getting married. It was all too much for Lex to handle. Why hadn't Ryan persuaded them not to marry, but to stay as they were, girlfriend and boyfriend, having a baby, but having fun together, arguing about the smallest of things, as they so often did, but not really arguing, just discussing really in their silly, heated way. He should have done more to dissuade them. It had all been a horrible mistake. And now he and Mum would have to face the consequences.

Mum suggested Ryan might like to get some fresh air.

'Will you be all right indoors by yourself?' said Ryan.

'Of course,' said Mum.

'I've got to take care of you,' explained Ryan. He felt a lump in his throat. He swallowed.

'Oh,' said Mum, bemused. 'Right.' She didn't seem overly concerned, but maybe that was for his benefit.

Ryan tried to ignore his worries, and they were only worries, he told himself (he worried all the time and far too much). Of course Lex hadn't left. Ryan was being melodramatic. He put on his coat, boots, gloves, hat, scarf. He went outside. He fed the birds, replenished the bird table, the feeders, he put out fresh water. It was difficult for birds to survive in the winter. He really should make some more fat balls.

Lex could be unpredictable sometimes. It was just the way it was. He'd probably gone to another store on the hunt for doughnuts. Or maybe a spin along the "freeway" as he liked to do sometimes.

Ryan put aside his worries. Lex wouldn't have run away, of course, not now. Too much had happened and he had promised. *Promised.* He knew that Lex wouldn't let them down again. He wouldn't let down his new baby. He and Mum were married now. That must mean something. It did mean something. Ryan had faith. It would work out, and they would all be OK. It was time to stop being silly, he chided himself.

Ryan's hands and feet were cold, but he didn't mind. He sang Christmas songs, songs he loved because he loved

Christmas and even though it was February now, it felt like Christmas this icy morning, and he lost himself, he lost track of time.

Which passed, silent and white.

Ryan heard the back door being yanked open, and he heard Seamus's protests as he was thrown out of the kitchen.

Mum knew Seamus hated the ice. Why was she throwing him out in it?

Ryan saw Mum's face, and he saw an expression that chilled him far more than the weather ever could. He didn't understand. He noticed then the police officers standing in the kitchen, looking at him sadly through the window. As he slowly approached the house, he heard a police radio crackle into life, a strange tinny voice saying something, the male police officer bowing his head to speak into it.

Ryan entered the kitchen. He looked from face to face. He was only dimly aware of his frozen feet, his cold hands, the tight shivers along his spine. He removed his hat, his gloves, unwound his scarf.

'What's up?' said Ryan quietly.

'Ryan. Come here,' said Mum, and she beckoned to him and as he reached her, she pulled him tightly to her. 'There's been a… an accident. Involving Lex.'

So that's why he's late. He's fallen off the Harley in the ice. Lex had been right not to let Ryan go with him. Lex was always right about stuff like that. And he hadn't left them. What a relief! He could feel Mum's heart beating fast, and he pulled gently away. But no: why was he feeling relief? These were police officers, and Mum was crying and she

173

was white and trembling and her heart was beating "like the clappers", as Billy would say, and there was no place for any sense of *relief*. Why was he being so stupid?

'He's been knocked off his bike, Ryan,' said Mum, her voice wavering between crying and squeaking. 'Do you understand so far?' She suppressed a sob.

The female police officer rested her hand on Mum's shoulder. The male officer stood by the Aga, warming himself, Ryan thought. He looked close to tears too. If he was close to tears, what on earth had happened? Ryan felt sick.

'I understand,' croaked Ryan. 'But why are you crying? He's come off his bike before. You told me. He'll be OK, won't he?'

Mum looked at the police officers. 'He fell off his bike years ago and broke his ankle,' she explained. 'That was in France. He rides too fast, you see. He always has done.' The woman police officer nodded sympathetically.

Silence, broken only by the muffled miaows of Seamus at the door, begging to be allowed back in. Lex had blocked up the cat flap, because Mum complained of the draught. Ryan drifted towards the door, preparing to let Seamus in.

'Is Lex in hospital?' asked Ryan. He opened the door and the cold cat slinked in, throwing Mum a dirty look.

The front door opened. Somebody was making their way down the hall in to the kitchen.

'He's here!' cried Ryan.

Billy. He was pale. He had never looked like this before. He looked terrified. Mum cried his name as Billy charged towards her and took her in his arms. And now Billy cried. Ryan stood mute and silent by the kitchen door, looking from adult to helpless adult. Suddenly, he was furious. What weren't they telling him? What did they know?

'Tell me!' he thought he cried.

'Ryan,' Mum said, holding on to Billy with a tight grip. 'Come back over here.'

Ryan joined Mum as the police officers looked awkwardly on. He stood between her and Billy. It was bad, he knew. This could be nothing but bad. He might have already guessed how bad it was, but he couldn't contemplate it. He wanted to stop up his ears now because he knew what was coming, he just knew, and he wanted these last few seconds of not knowing, before a harsh and cruel inevitability took over his life and changed him forever.

'Lex is not exactly in the hospital,' said Mum. She made a huge effort and pulled Ryan in to her, like she wanted to shield him from attack. 'You see... oh, Billy, help me!'

'Just tell him, Joanna, there's no other way,' said Billy quietly. 'I'm sorry. He's not a baby.' The female police officer murmured in agreement.

'You're right,' said Mum. She looked deeply and surely into Ryan's eyes, just as surely as he avoided looking into hers. 'Lex died, Ryan. He was in a bad accident. Lex died this morning.'

2

THE ROAD TO LOCH CORUISK

MARCH 2007

His dreams were becoming more frequent, night by night, as the days, cold and uncaring, marched on from that snow-covered February morning. He supposed they were nightmares, rather than dreams, but that only became apparent after the waking up, after the assimilation of the dream with the light of day, with the stretching of thoughts. At first the glimpses were fleeting: Dad shooting past on his Harley, Dad running along a beach, Dad kissing Mum. Then the dreams became longer, louder, more vivid. Ryan spoke to Dad, he laughed with Dad, he reached out for him when he faded away. Every dream faded away, every cry of Ryan's to *'Come back!'* was ignored. Dad left him, over and over again. And then the terrible waking up. The suffocating reality. The recollection of the truth, the new rules, learned anew each day, binding him to his waking hours. The rules that governed, that could not be broken.

Ryan's First, and hardest, Rule of Grief: The Dead Do Not Come Back.

There was a police investigation into Dad's death. There had to be. The car driver was not to blame. Ryan thought this should have made things that tiny bit more bearable, but it didn't.

Lex, it seemed, after buying the doughnuts, had decided to give the Harley a spin. He'd taken it out onto the dual carriageway. He must have been going fast. Witnesses said he was going fast. There was a slip, a collision, it wasn't clear… witnesses weren't clear… it happened so fast and nobody really saw all of it. Later, they learned there had been debris on the road, gravel, stones, and this is what Lex's bike had slipped on. Lex had slipped, he'd lost control. He'd hit a car. The car driver was OK. Lex was dead "'at the scene", which meant he "did not suffer", as everyone reassured Ryan. There was no ice. The road had been treated. It was just recklessness and bad luck that had killed Lex, and it had almost certainly been his own fault, if it was anybody's. Speed had definitely been a factor; that was made clear. It was death by misadventure. That was all.

Ryan imagined the scene over and over. Dad, in the road, a crumpled heap, stilled and quiet, unconscious already, *dead* already, not knowing anything about it, and doughnuts strewn all over, squashed, misshapen, with dirt, oil, petrol sticking to them: inedible. And shocked motorists pulling over and somebody calling an ambulance and perhaps a woman crying, in shock, because there was always a woman crying in shock when these things happened; he'd seen it on television. What had happened to the doughnuts, Ryan wondered? Nobody said. They were not mentioned. The bike was recovered and Joanna and Ryan had not seen it, and they never would now. Probably it was a "write-off", an odd term that Ryan didn't fully understand. There was so much he didn't understand. He decided that "write-off"' probably meant the bike was damaged, destroyed, unable to be fixed. Like Dad.

The one comfort: Dad had bought the doughnuts. If his spin along the dual carriageway had been a bid for escape, he would not have bought the doughnuts first. That was common sense. So he had not been in the act of leaving. And Ryan remembered clearly, the words spun around in his mind, those words from just a few weeks ago, "I won't always be around". Had Dad somehow known? That he was going to die soon? Because those words, they were prophetic. They had come true. Had it been a premonition?

No. Of course not. Dad wasn't into "that shit". Yet he had left. And it had been his fault. An accident, caused by him. So, not an accident. An incident. He had left, however you looked at it. Ryan recalled, over and over, that night in December, which seemed like years ago, when he'd prevented Dad from absconding. Ryan remembered the unease he'd felt afterwards, lying awake and cold in bed, not entirely trusting his dad, not fully understanding what it was he'd averted. Had *he* had a premonition? No, of course not. He didn't believe in that shit either. Ryan didn't believe in anything and he never would again.

The funeral took place three weeks after the death. The snow had melted, the day was bright and sunny. Mum said it was "fitting", but Ryan felt it should be raining and thundering and blowing a gale, a gale of protest, he thought, the phrase coming to him from somewhere, he didn't know where. There were few people at the funeral; and not because Dad was a Jay Gatsby type (Dad had recommended *The Great Gatsby* to Ryan, who had read it and enjoyed it, and thought wistfully how nice it might be to write like that, and how impossible), but because Mum had preferred it that way. She wanted a quiet funeral. She told few people that Dad had died, until afterwards. Billy and David were there, of course, and Sharon. Zephyr came along to "keep Ryan company". Ryan was glad the funeral was a quiet affair, even though Mum hadn't asked him what he thought of the plan. He didn't want to be stared at by strangers who would pity him. The funeral was short and not sweet and Dad's coffin sat there, it just sat there, and when Ryan walked past he couldn't look at it, he had to look the other way. On top were flowers, and a photo of Dad.

Mum thought a simple service, and a cremation, were what Dad probably would have chosen for himself, but she didn't know for sure. They had not discussed dying. They had not discussed funerals. They had not discussed the merits of burial or cremation. They had never felt the need. They hadn't got that far. But she had to choose, so cremation it was.

Mum disappeared. She didn't speak, she didn't laugh, she didn't even cry. She behaved like a robot, doing all the things a mum does, but doing them with no heart, no feeling. Breakfast was on the table every morning for Ryan, she told him to brush his teeth, she made him his lunch. She served up chips and beetroot for his tea, she reminded him to shower, and she ordered him to go to bed at ten o'clock every night. You would almost think nothing had happened, but the utter blankness of their lives gave it away. It was Mum but it wasn't Mum; it was life but it wasn't life.

A letter came addressed to Dad, from Rita Bone. Mum read it, impassive, unmoved, and passed it to Ryan. Rita Bone wrote that it now appeared that Ryan was receiving an education suitable to his blah, blah, blah.

Dad had done it. He'd got the authorities off their backs. But he wasn't here to see it and it didn't matter anymore. Ryan almost (*almost*) wanted to return to school. At least there he would get away from Mum. He didn't care where he went, or what he did. It was best to curl up in a tight ball in his bed and do nothing, say nothing, especially to her.

His Second Rule of Grief: Nothing Else Matters.

Snowdrops flourished around the garden, and ranks of daffodils. The pond was a thick, cloudy green again, free of ice. It was the time of year for new growth, new beginnings, new life. Ryan felt he'd finally grasped a sense of irony. He found Mum clearing Dad's things from the bathroom.

'Don't do that,' Ryan said, standing in the doorway.

'We have to, Ryan,' said Mum.

'No. We don't have to. Stop. Leave it all as he left it,' said Ryan. 'This is my dad's house and these are his things.'

'Ryan, keeping Lex's stuff... it won't bring him back.'

'Just like sending him out for doughnuts won't bring him back,' said Ryan, a frightening new cruelty infesting his heart. He liked it. He felt powerful. Mum stared at him; fear, confusion, painting her face ugly. She was ugly.

'Don't you think I know that?' said Mum quietly, looking at the bathroom floor. Ashamed, as she should be.

'I don't care what you know,' said Ryan, '*I* know. If it

hadn't been for you and your greed for stupid doughnuts, I'd still have my dad.'

'I'm sorry, Ryan. Can we talk about it?'

'No.' Ryan left the bathroom.

Beau came to visit. He talked a bit about school and he played with Seamus, who didn't seem to notice that Lex had gone. The cat behaved as he'd ever behaved. Mrs Marchant had given birth to her baby, and she was going to go back to school to teach for three days a week, but not until September. She had brought her baby, a boy named Sean, into school for a visit. He was cute, Beau said; if you liked babies.

'It's not your mum's fault,' said Beau, after a while. They were in Ryan's bedroom, playing Top Trumps, even though they both knew the fad was over. It had become a habit, the thing they did. Ryan said nothing. Clarissa thought she might be pregnant, said Beau. It was a bit scary. Her friend was going with her to the doctor's later. She wouldn't allow him to go with her. Beau didn't know what to do. He thought they had been careful.

Ryan didn't hear him.

Beau tried again: 'It's really not your mum's fault, Ryan, you know?' he said, staring hard at his Top Trumps card.

Ryan looked right through Beau as though he wasn't there.

The Third Rule of Grief: Somebody Is To Blame.

Ryan couldn't find the doughnuts. He had been up and down every aisle in Boots at least six times. He knew they were here, they were just hiding from him. He looked behind shelves, under shelves, he threw soap and tissues and shampoo and tampons and diapers out of his way in his quest for doughnuts. Something was wrong but he didn't know what. Where were they? An assistant in a grey suit with huge, bright red lips looked disapprovingly at him. Then, thank God, there was Lex, standing by the make-up aisle. He would know where to find the doughnuts. Ryan waved and was about to shout out, when Lex saw him and froze. Lex leaned down and pulled someone up from the floor, and it was Mum, chewing gum. Lex said something to her and they ran from the shop, Lex throwing a glance back at Ryan, shrugging his shoulders. Ryan called, 'Come back! Dad!' and when Ryan finally stopped shouting he was standing in a dark and empty shop, no shelves, no bottles, no tampons, no diapers, no make-up, no red-lipped assistants, just Ryan's calls echoing off the grey, cold walls.

The Fourth Rule of Grief: You Are On Your Own.

Joanna moved from one hour to the next mechanically. Lex had left her life again and in a way it felt natural. He'd left before. There was no real difference, apart from this time, Lex would not return. She could not believe he was dead, she could not fathom it. It was easier and it made more sense to imagine him simply absconded. She could cope with that, because she had coped before. She'd never stopped loving him, she knew that now, and could admit it to herself. She wished she'd told Lex that. Had she told him? She couldn't remember.

It was a miracle to Joanna that he'd ever returned. Her call to him that long ago day last summer... mere months, in reality… she'd had hope, but nothing more, that he would return, that he might be able to help her with her – their – troubled son. And Lex had come, and he had helped, he had done so much, and she had fallen in love and lust with him all over again. Everything had been rekindled. That was all. The spark had never quite gone out.

They had been married for nine days. It would be her only marriage, she felt sure.

Ryan; almost she was too scared to think about him. He would not let her in. He wouldn't share. She was on the outside. She had no idea how she would ever get in again. She had not realised life could be so cruel. She could not help her son. And the last time this had happened, Lex had swooped in, picked up the pieces of their lives, and put them back together again. And now she would have to do this, just her, and she didn't know where to begin. Her feelings were overwhelming and she wondered how her body held on to the baby, she felt as though she would slide out from her, like Lex had slid away, oh so literally, a slide into death, so easy, and losing the baby would be another failure to complete her impressive set of failures. But her body did hang on, and her daughter tumbled round inside her as though nothing was wrong.

Joanna sat down with Ryan one evening in mid-March and explained to him their financial position. Lex had left a will, drawn up between the wedding and his death. He had been surprisingly efficient, which was fortunate, she said, because it saved a lot of work. And then she wished she hadn't said these things, because they sounded heartless and mercenary, and she was neither. The house, everything in it, and all of Lex's money, was now hers, she told Ryan. There was a lot of money, more than Ryan could imagine, more than she could imagine, and some of it was going into a trust for Ryan to use when he was an adult. Lex had *stipulated* it in the will. There was money for Ryan's education. Lex had thought of everything: college, university, Ryan's first home. Sums set aside. Ryan looked blankly at her as she spoke.

'We don't have to worry about money ever again,' Joanna said. 'But I've decided to carry on with my work. I want to make more quilts and toys. I think having something to do, something to focus on… will help.'

'Help what?' said Ryan.

'Help me to get over losing Lex,' said Joanna.

'How will it help? It won't bring him back.'

'I know it won't bring him back, Ryan. But that's why it will help. This awful thing that's happened, and these terrible feelings, well, it helps to have something to do to stop you thinking about it.'

'Why would you want to stop thinking about your dead husband?' said Ryan.

'I don't want to stop thinking about him, Ryan. I want to stop thinking about the fact that he died.'

'But he has died.'

'I know.'

'You want to assuage your guilt,' said Ryan.

'What kind of word is that to use?'

'Assuage? It means to make better or—'

'Guilt. I meant the word *guilt*. You're so angry with me.'

'You're so guilty. You always will be. You can make all

187

the patchwork quilts you like but you can't change the fact that you sent my dad out for doughnuts and he never came back.'

'It's a what-if situation, Ryan. What-ifs can go on forever and ever. They're meaningless too, because what happened, happened. It can't be altered. There are no other possibilities. I didn't kill him, Ryan. He was killed in an accident—'

'Incident.'

'Incident. Accident. Whichever. He came off his bike by accident and hit a car by accident and he was badly hurt and he died. It's that simple, and nobody else is to blame. The inquest made that clear, don't you remember?'

Silence.

'Why don't you try making something? I could teach you to sew, or knit. Using your hands… it's soothing. It's healing.'

'I don't need to be healed.' Ryan glared at her, aghast. 'I don't want to be soothed either. I don't want to learn to fucking *knit*.'

'Think about it, though, please?' Joanna started to cry. 'We could get the rag bag out and you could do a collage or s-s-something. For Lex, a c-c-collage to remember him by. It might help you to get your emotions out that way.' She cried properly then, big splashy tears. Ryan told her to pull her fucking self together. He stood up, and left her.

She'd really lost it this time, thought Ryan, as he climbed the spiral stairs to his bedroom. And now she was counting out her dead husband's money and urging her fourteen-year-old son to knit. Ryan hated the red, pinched-up face, framed by the scruffy blond hair, and the snot and tears pouring down her face. She used to be pretty, but she would never be pretty again. Ugly, ugly… bitch. He called out the word, loudly: '*Bitch!*' He hoped she heard.

Billy tried to help, and came around nearly every day. He brought groceries, and wouldn't take any money for them, and had long chats in the kitchen with Mum. Ryan caught snatches of their conversations: '… he's cut himself off from me… I can't help him… he blames me… lonely…' and '… give him time… he'll be all right in the end… of course he loves you…'

But did he love her? How could he love her any more, after all that had happened? That day, the quilt destroying day, he'd felt anger then, he'd thought. But he hadn't, not at all. *Now* he felt anger, overwhelming, burning, self-hating, world-hating, and it threatened to incinerate him from the inside out and reduce him to a pile of smouldering ashes. The little nut inside him had exploded, and it could no longer be ignored or contained. It was destroying him. But he felt powerless.

'Give him time, Joanna,' said Billy, as Ryan lingered at the top of his spiral staircase, listening in. (It was sensibly said, of course. But Billy knew nothing, and Ryan smirked.) 'Give yourself time, too. You can't rush healing, you know? It will go at its own pace. So what if he calls you a bitch? Let him. It's only a word.'

A different day: a quiet knock at the front door and Ryan, who was in the kitchen feeding Seamus, shuffled along the hallway. He opened the door. He was surprised to see Mrs Marchant with a bunch of white and yellow flowers in her hand. The flowers looked a little faded, sad.

But everything did now. Mrs Marchant looked cold. He'd better ask her to come in, he thought, although he hated to have visitors. Even if they were his former and favourite teacher.

'Hello, Ryan,' she said. 'I heard about your father. Beau Stirling told me. I'm sorry. I wanted to pop in to see if there's anything I can do to help. Is your mum in?'

Joanna was in bed. She got up and Mrs Marchant helped her to make coffee. After that, the two women sat at the kitchen table. Ryan wasn't sure if he should join them, or not. He hovered. He refused a biscuit. He sat down. He stood up. Sat down. Listened. Took a biscuit, but couldn't eat it. He let Seamus lick it.

'I lost my first husband,' said Mrs Marchant, quite casually, as if she was talking about a lost dog. Ryan pretended not to listen. He left the table and sat in the rocking chair. He stroked Seamus who circled his lap as usual, before settling down and licking his paws. Ryan liked to sit in the rocking chair in the corner of the kitchen. He supposed it was "healing", the gentle, easy rocking. It was at least comforting; not quite the same thing as healing. Seamus purred loudly. He still didn't appear to miss Dad.

'I'm sorry to hear that,' said Mum.

'Oh, it was years ago,' said Mrs Marchant. 'It does get easier, I know you probably don't believe that now, but believe me, it does. You learn to live with it and this raw pain, this shock, it will fade. It will become muted somehow, but it will flare up occasionally. Like an old injury. You must expect that.'

They sipped coffee in silence for a while. Ryan stroked Seamus.

'So, Ryan,' said Mrs Marchant, turning to him. 'You're still being educated at home, are you? How's that going?'

'It's not,' said Ryan.

'Oh?'

'Since Lex d—since we lost Lex, Ryan hasn't been up to doing much in the way of work,' said Joanna.

'That's understandable,' said Mrs Marchant. 'But really, Ryan, you need to work, you need your education. Can I help at all? I hate to think your talents are going to waste. Have you thought about doing any writing lately? It may help with your feelings. Poetry, for example, is a fantastic way to get things out. Why don't you give it a go?'

'Poetry?' said Ryan. Why the fucking hell did these… *ridiculous* people think he should all of a sudden start making things, writing things?

'Don't worry about making it rhyme or anything like that. Just try to put down on paper how you are feeling. Some of the most beautiful poems have been written in response to great tragedy, you know. And you don't have to show anybody your writing. It can be for your eyes only. Write it all down.'

Ryan shrugged.

'Think about it. You have great ability, Ryan, don't forget that.' Mrs Marchant turned to Joanna. 'He has something very special.'

'I know,' said Joanna, smiling. 'You've said that before.'

… *paint with words, instead*… Dad had once told him. Is this what he'd meant?

F. Scott Fitzgerald could paint with words. Could he do it too?

He thought about it.

Beau brought his homework round to the house after school sometimes, and he and Ryan worked together. They were quiet and diligent, and Joanna was grateful for it. Beau helped Ryan with his maths, and Ryan helped Beau with his English. It was mechanical, but somehow it worked. Beau seemed keen to work. Beau wanted to do something, he said, with his life. He wanted to achieve something; he didn't know what. But his education seemed the right place to start, even it was boring most of the time. Clarissa wasn't pregnant, and Joanna expressed her relief. They were both far too young to become parents, she said.

It was springtime, the snowdrops had been and gone, and now the buds and young leaves on the hedges were growing and the daffodils were fading and all the ice had finally melted away. The garden felt clean, as though a huge hand had wiped away all the grime and slush and dead things.

Ryan spent a lot of time outdoors, huddled in the green jumper Lex had bought for him. He drank hot chocolate and read books. Joanna watched him from the kitchen window. He looked like an old man, she thought, and she cried as she watched him, every day.

'At least he is reading,' she said to Mrs Marchant, who became a regular visitor, popping round once a week to encourage Ryan with his reading and writing, and to look at his GCSE work with him. Mum had ordered some correspondence course materials for Ryan to work through, on the advice of Mrs Marchant.

'He's so alone,' Joanna said. 'Lex became such a companion to him in those few months they knew each other. He won't talk to me. He still blames me for Lex's death. He always will.'

'He'll get over it. He doesn't really blame you. He's angry with everyone and everything at the moment.'

'Oh, Mrs Marchant, it's all such a mess.'

'Call me Liz, won't you?'

'All right, then. Thank you, Liz. You're being a great help. Ryan does look forward to your visits, even if he does sit outside in the cold most of the time.'

'I don't mind in the least. It gives us a chance to talk. And he'll turn back to you, when he's ready. Probably you won't even notice, it will just happen bit by bit.'

'Oh, Liz, I wish I could believe that.'

'Who else has he got?'

APRIL 2007

Ryan laughed and laughed as Dad tickled him, rolled him over, hoisted him onto his strong shoulders, spun around, 'Scream if you wanna go faaaasssterrr…!!' Breathless, he put Ryan down and they contemplated each other. Ryan was two years old again, but he was also fourteen, and Dad was playing with him, laughing with him, and he had never left, he'd not travelled all over Europe nor chickened out of fatherhood nor had other girlfriends. 'Ryan!' gasped Dad, as Ryan charged at him and leaped into his arms. 'Slow down, kid! You're going to get hurt. I wasn't ready for you! Let's go find your mom.' They walked into the house, hand in hand, and there was Mum, enormous, sitting at the kitchen table, hidden behind a mountain of doughnuts, and she opened her mouth to speak and it was full of chewed-up doughnuts, and bright red jam tricked down her chin. Ryan turned away in disgust and Dad ran out, ran away.

'Come back! Come back…!'

Ryan heard a strange noise. What was it? It sounded like an animal in pain, a low moaning, a sound from the stomach, not from the throat. Was it Seamus? Ryan crept to his bedroom door, but all was silent. Ryan crept back to bed and listened again for the noise.

There it was.

Was it Mum? It was coming from her room. Ryan got up once more, and tiptoed along the landing to the room Mum had shared with Dad. The door was slightly open, and Ryan peered in. She wasn't in bed. She wasn't in her room at all. He looked round and saw a strip of light under the bathroom door. He went to the door and listened, and the sound came again. What was she doing? Being sick? She'd eaten no doughnuts since... Dad. She'd never eat doughnuts again, she'd said, several times. Ryan always smirked at her, his lip curled so nastily he knew he looked ugly and cruel. She just looked away from him, crying, of course. Always, always crying.

So what was making her sick? Had she spotted herself in the mirror? She sure wasn't pretty.

Ryan didn't know where the nasty thoughts came from. Sometimes he couldn't believe they were even his thoughts. But they kept on coming.

'Are you OK?' Ryan said. He felt he ought to say something, although really he could quite happily go back to bed and let her get on with whatever it was she was doing. He didn't care. Really, he didn't. What would Dad do? Ryan flushed.

He tried the door. Something was blocking it.

'Are you OK?' Ryan said again, louder.

'Ryan? Let me move. I'm... behind... door.' Mum's voice was strained and strangled, as if the effort to speak was too much. Ryan pushed open the door, fearful of what he might find behind it.

She was hunched up on the floor on her knees, rocking to and fro. She looked up, and Ryan saw fear and pain in her face. Fuck, had she tried to kill herself or something?

'What's wrong with you?' he said, staring down at her.

'Pain.'

'What kind of pain?'

Surely it couldn't be the baby. He wasn't due for another month. He hadn't really given much thought to the baby recently. In fact, he'd all but forgotten there was a baby.

'I think it's—the baby. Call—amb—'

'Is he going to get born?' said Ryan.

'I—don't know. Hope not yet. Not sure Ry—just—call—ambula—plea—'

Ryan ran downstairs to the hallway and dialled 999 on the kitsch red telephone. Dad had loved the phone as much as Mum did. He'd said it was "cool". Ryan's hand shook, his head flooding with hot thick blood, chemicals popping all over his body. He'd never dialled 999 before. He'd never dialled any number before, apart from Mum's mobile. He felt a small thrill of excitement. So this is what it felt like!

'Which service do you require?' said a woman with a funny voice. Ryan wondered if she was in fact a computer. It would be easier if she was a computer, he decided.

'Ambulance, please,' said Ryan, and his voice came out all squeaky and silly. He still didn't have a broken voice like Beau's.

'Connecting you now,' said the Computer Voice who, Ryan knew, was a real human.

Ryan waited and waited; he heard Mum's long, low moan again.

'You're through to the ambulance service. Can you tell me the telephone number you are calling from?' It was a new voice, Scottish this time, Ryan thought. He could hear her breathing. She could probably hear his breathing too. This was weird. What if he burped or something? That would be horrible. What if Scottish Voice burped? That would be even worse.

Ryan gave the number and then the address.

'And what is the problem?'

'My mum's in pain. She's on the bathroom floor. She's wearing her pink and white pyjamas.'

'Are there any other adults in the house?'

'No. I'm nearly an adult. I'm fourteen. But there's just me. My—my dad would have been here but he died a few weeks ago. He was knocked off his motorbike. It was icy and snowy but that wasn't the reason. It… it wasn't anyone else's fault. He was just going too fast. It wasn't anyone's fault. At all.' Ryan felt he was floating above words, above death, above the world, and all was before him, everything, in sharp detail, and this clarity of thought was a new discovery, like a new land mass, green and lush, that he alone had just discovered. 'My mum can't speak very well,' he added. 'She needs help.'

'OK, love. I'm dispatching an ambulance now. They should be with you within twenty minutes. I'm sorry to hear about your dad. It must be hard for you. But can you tell me more about your mum now? Has she been sick?'

'I don't think so,' said Ryan.

'Does she have an illness or a disability or anything like that?'

'No. She's expecting a baby, that's all,' said Ryan.

'Do you know when the baby is due?'

'In May. But it's only April.'

'OK. Are you with your mum now?'

'No. She's in the bathroom upstairs. I'm in the hallway, talking to you on the red telephone.'

'What's your name?'

'Ryan.'

'Ryan, here's what I need you to do. Unlock all outer doors so the paramedics can enter your house. Shut any dogs you may have in a separate room. That's very important.'

'We don't have a dog. Only a cat. His name is Seamus.'

'Fine, I don't think we need to worry about Seamus. Can you go back to your mum? Do you have a mobile telephone I can ring you on?'

'My mum has a mobile.'

'Do you know the number?'

Did he? He hadn't dialled it in ages. He couldn't remember it.

'No.'

'Fine. Unlock those doors for me now, would you? I'll stay on the line and when you have unlocked them, I want you to come back and tell me you have done that.'

Ryan carefully put down the receiver, opened the front door and left it ajar, then ran along the passage to the kitchen and unlocked the back door too. He ran back into the hallway.

'I have done that,' Ryan said to Scottish Voice. He wondered if she had ever been to Loch Coruisk. He felt he should ask her, but now was not the time.

'Great. Now, I want you to run upstairs for me and

check on your mum. I'll get off the line, as the paramedics will be with you soon. You're doing really well, Ryan. If you need to, ring back on your mum's mobile. You just dial 999 like you did on your landline, OK?'

'OK,' said Ryan and he put the phone down.

He ran back up the stairs two at a time to find Mum leaning back against the bath, panting and gasping, looking like she couldn't breathe.

'I've phoned the ambulance,' said Ryan, 'they'll be here in a few minutes.'

'Thanks. That's great, love – I think the baby is coming. I'm having pains. They're called contractions and when I have one I'm probably going to scream and make a fuss. Just ignore all that. Here we go, it's coming—'

Mum sat forward and breathed hard. She reached out for Ryan's hand and he offered it. Her grip was strong and Ryan winced. Mum didn't scream but she did gasp and pant and rock and open her eyes wide in shock and surprise. And then she eased her grip and she could talk again.

'Get some towels please, love, as many as you can find. They're in the airing cupboard. And I'm going to take my pyjamas off and have a feel to see if this baby is on its way. Don't panic. Ryan, whatever you do, don't panic. If you panic, I'm done for.'

Ryan fetched the towels and when he got back to the bathroom, Mum was laughing, a laughter of pain and panic rather than amusement.

'Oh, Ryan! This baby isn't waiting. I can feel the head. I think—oh! Oh!'

Ryan crouched down and put his hand on Mum's

shoulder. He looked down and yes, sure enough, he could see the top of the baby's head. A gush of liquid flowed out, all onto the floor, a strange-looking, strange-smelling fluid. Ryan tried not to notice it. He wondered if Mum had wet herself. But this must be "her waters", that he'd heard her talk about. Where was the blood? David said there would be buckets of blood. David. *David.*

'Where's your phone?' Ryan asked.

'Handbag. Bedroom.'

'I'm going to ring David.'

'He'll be… at Billy's house. Ring—Billy.'

Ryan ran to his mum's room and found her handbag on the floor next to her bed. He tipped it up, and scrabbled his shaking hands around among the tissues and make-up and keys and diary and pen and the sticky bottle of lavender oil and the little purple pouch that he knew contained her cigarettes, and he wondered, fleetingly, if she had been smoking again; she'd given up on account of the baby, so why was the pouch still in her bag? It would have to wait, and it was too late now, his baby brother was on his way. He found her mobile phone and he grasped it, trembling, and he found Billy's number. It seemed to ring forever, but in the end Billy answered.

'Hello?'

'It's Ryan.'

'Ryan, are you OK?' said Billy. 'You do know it's two o'clock in the chuffing morning?'

'Mum's having the baby. I can see its head coming out. I rang for an ambulance but they're not here yet. Can David come over?'

'Oh my God! David! Wake up! We're on our way, Ryan.

Stay there. Stay with your mum. Get her hot towels or something.'

'I've done that,' said Ryan.

'Good man. See you in a minute. Don't go anywhere!'

Ryan rushed back to the bathroom.

He knelt down in front of Mum. She was breathing deeply, her eyes shut tight.

'David and Billy are coming over,' said Ryan. Mum opened her eyes and smiled weakly at her son.

'You've done good, Ryan,' she said. Then: 'Where the hell is that ambulance?!'

'I don't know. The Scottish lady said they'd be here soon.'

'I think this baby will come with the next contrac—here we go—Ry—an—catch her!'

Ryan picked up a towel, leaned forward and watched as Mum pushed, and then the baby's head was out, and Ryan squeezed a towel underneath it, and Mum panted, panted, laughed, panted, and then out poured a baby, out poured the promised buckets of blood. Ryan stared at the mess, shocked, not believing his eyes, his ears, his nose. Mum leaned down and pulled the baby up onto her stomach, and Ryan placed towels over them, and then sat next to Mum, and she cried. But these were happy tears, Ryan could tell.

'Hello?' said a woman's voice after a minute or so. Ryan wiped his eyes, his face.

'We're up here!' he called, and a lady paramedic, dressed all in green, followed by a man paramedic, filled the bathroom.

'You're too late,' said Mum, and she smiled up at them. It was a smile that Ryan had feared he would never see

201

again. But here it was, wide and generous. It almost made him want to smile too.

'So I see,' said the lady paramedic. 'Let's have a look then, Mum. Wow, what a beautiful baby. A whopper too! How are you feeling?'

'I'm all right. I'm fine, thanks to my son,' said Mum, smiling proudly at him.

'Your baby looks grand anyway. A good healthy colour. We'll get you ready and take you both to hospital. How many weeks is the baby?'

'Thirty-six, plus a day or two,' said Joanna.

'A bit early, then. But a good size.'

'He was due in May,' said Ryan, but nobody seemed to hear. They were too busy with the baby. The paramedics fussed around, and made sure Mum wasn't bleeding too much, which she wasn't, even though Ryan thought there was a lot of blood. Buckets, in fact.

'Joanna?!' David poked his head round the door.

'You're a bit late too!' said Mum.

'Is this Dad?' said the lady paramedic. She was injecting Mum with something to make the placenta come away, she said.

'Er, no,' said David. 'I'm a friend. I'm a student midwife. I'm just about to qualify.' And David removed his jacket, rolled up his sleeves and knelt down by Mum.

'A useful man; fancy that,' said the lady paramedic. 'I've just administered Syntometrine, and here comes the placenta by the looks of it.'

Everyone worked together and Ryan stood in the doorway, watching. David was calm and caring and helped the paramedics pull out the placenta and cut the umbilical cord. They spent a long time examining the placenta. It was "complete", David said. Then they decided a cup of tea might be good for everyone. Ryan went downstairs, where Billy was waiting, pacing the kitchen.

'Is everything OK up there?' said Billy.

'Yes. Mum's had the baby. The ambulance people are taking care of her. David's helping too. They've got the placenta out and cut the cord. Mum needs a cup of tea.'

'And the baby? It's all right too?'

'He's fine.'

'Were you there when he was born?'

'Yes. Only me. I caught him.'

'Bloody hell, Ryan. You're a hero, mate! I'm surrounded by midwives. Let's get this kettle on.'

They all had tea, and Mum seemed not to notice that it wasn't coffee, and even Ryan, who never had hot drinks, enjoyed a cup. The paramedics also had a cup each, because between them and David they had decided that both mother and baby were fine and there was no rush to get them into hospital.

The baby was "premature", David said, but not "dangerously" premature, and fortunately with no apparent problems. The baby was breathing, suckling, and was sturdy. Everybody, apart from Mum, who remained on the bathroom floor cuddling her baby, stood around on the landing as they drank their tea and ate digestive biscuits. Billy had found them in the cupboard. He always thought of biscuits.

And Ryan was filled, for a moment, with an uncontrollable thrill of happiness, excitement, something formidable and good flowing around his veins. Ryan thought it was all so strange and unreal and he didn't feel at all tired even though it was gone three in the morning and the world outside was black and cold and still. Somebody must have thought to turn on the heating because the radiators were gurgling and popping. So, Ryan thought, other things did happen at this time of night. Good things. Not just bad things. He remembered Lex's face in the fridge light. He remembered the black helmet sitting on the table, ready to go. He remembered that his new brother would never meet his dad. Ryan slipped off to the other bathroom, locked the door behind him, and cried long silent sobs.

'How's he doing?' Billy asked, peering his head round the bathroom door. He grinned broadly at Joanna.

'Less of the he,' whispered Joanna, and she half cried, half laughed. 'I knew it would be a girl.'

'Ah, bless her. Have you told Ryan yet?'

'No. Send him in, could you?'

Joanna carefully pulled back the towels that were keeping the sleeping baby warm. She waited, and after a minute or two, Ryan peeped his head round the bathroom door.

'Come in here and say hello properly to your little sister,' said Joanna.

Ryan looked at the sleeping baby. Joanna wrapped her up again and held her to her breast and the baby stirred and suckled.

'He's actually a little girl?' said Ryan, eventually.

'He is indeed.'

'But she's beautiful,' said Ryan.

'Of course she is. Thanks for all that you did tonight, Ryan. Lex would have been so proud of you.'

Ryan shrugged. The baby suckled for a while, then stopped, and Joanna passed her to Ryan, who took her in trembling arms. He looked down into her tender, placid face. 'Hello, my little sister,' he said.

'Somebody needs to take some photos. Lex's camera is in the bedroom.'

'You won't call her Sian, will you?' said Ryan. 'Or Liberty?'

'No. They're no good. I've had a better idea.'

Her name was Alexandra Nicholson. Ryan agreed with Mum that it was right to name her after her father. She would be called Xandra for short. Ryan liked the name and he thought Dad would have liked it too. Xandra was a healthy baby and after just a few hours in hospital, she and Mum were sent home. Billy and Ryan picked them up.

'Thank God we're out of there!' said Mum, as Billy pulled out of the car park.

Billy took them home, and after settling Mum on the sofa, making her a drink, and chatting to Ryan about nothing in particular, he left them. They needed bonding time, he told them. Or some such. Billy was not airy-fairy, Ryan knew. And it felt strange after Billy had left; the three of them in Lex's "cottage", without Lex. He would have been making the drinks, ensuring Mum was comfortable and was getting some sleep, he would have kept Ryan company, he would have laundered the baby clothes and nappies, cuddled his baby daughter.

Last night's euphoria had evaporated. Ryan felt hurt all

over, like he'd been beaten up. Mum was hurting even more, he guessed. There was so much to do and so much to share, and no Dad to share it with.

Three days after Xandra's birth, Mum was clearly exhausted. The midwife who visited advised her to ditch the reusable nappies. Nobody, *nobody* would blame her for turning to disposables. Mum needed to be "realistic". The midwife herself went to the shops and bought nappies and wipes. Mum had seemed grateful; she used the disposables and said how amazing they were. She had used towelling squares and plastic pants with Ryan when he was a baby, to everybody's amazement. But she liked to be responsible. Ryan? Didn't she? Yes. Yes, she did. *But disposables are fine, Mum.*

Ryan worked hard to help. He loaded the washing machine daily, he hung the clothes out to dry, Xandra's tiny white baby things fluttering on the line like butterflies breaking out of a chrysalis. He washed up, he made coffee, plates of sandwiches. He tried to keep up with his studies, and he made sure Mum saw him doing that. Ryan hoped that would be enough. He felt he was making a difference, and standing in Dad's shoes, a little bit.

And then the crying started. Only it wasn't Xandra who was crying, it was Mum. Xandra barely made a noise. She was calm and contented, most of the time. She slept a lot. Ryan heard Mum snivelling at night to begin with. Then he would find her crying in the kitchen while trying to prepare breakfast, or crying quietly when she was breastfeeding Xandra, or changing her nappy. Ryan tried to cheer her up, but he didn't know any jokes because jokes never sunk in with him, so he tried to think up funny stories and really there wasn't much to laugh about, no stories to tell, so he stopped that. And Mum wasn't listening anyway.

But at least now there was something to be glad about, which was as good as laughing, Ryan thought, in the circumstances. His baby sister was adorable. Surely Mum knew that? Why did she have to cry so much? He supposed their life was still tragic. There was a hole, wide and yawning. Xandra helped fill it, but only a little. He thought Mum felt Xandra's comfort too. Maybe she didn't. Ryan found that thought unsettling; it was frightening. How would she ever cope without Lex if even having his baby to look after didn't comfort her?

'Are you all right, Mum?' Ryan asked one morning over breakfast. Xandra was ten days old, and already becoming rounded, and her skin was peach-like, and Ryan swore she was smiling at him when he looked down at her and smiled at her and spoke to her and twirled some of Mum's ribbons around so she could enjoy the movement and the colours. Xandra was easy to talk to. Not so Mum. Her eyes had a red rim and they were puffy. Her hair, once so glowing and curling and healthy-looking, dangled limp and sour over her shoulders. She was oddly silent. When she did the online grocery shop and he asked for cola, he got it. Frozen pizzas and pies too. This was not good. This was not Mum. Was it because he'd called her a bitch? He hadn't meant it, not really. Didn't she know that? Should he bring it up?

'I'm fine, love,' Mum said, appearing to make a huge effort to crack her face with a smile. Ryan wasn't convinced.

Another week went by. Xandra grew bigger and stronger,

and Mum's crying became more frequent. If only Lex were here, Ryan thought, he would know what to do or say. Mum was a mess these days, she had always been so pretty and she had always worn nice clothes, even when she was pregnant. Since Lex had gone, Mum had given up looking nice and enjoying life. And she was dirty, she actually smelled. There were stains on her clothes and she seemed to wear the same stuff day in, day out. A bit like him with his socks, until Dad had bought him those comfy new ones. Ryan guessed she had given up showering. Was she even brushing her teeth? She was smoking again. But she made no effort to hide it, as she had always done up until now. Her cigarettes and her lighter were strewn on the kitchen counter for all to see. She still smoked outside, but no longer at night, in secret. He watched her smoking. Surely it was no good for Xandra? Surely it would get into the milk? His mother was disgusting. It was undeniable. Something would have to be done, but he had no idea what.

'Billy?' said Ryan. It was a rainy Saturday afternoon, and Billy had brought fish and chips over for their tea. Mum wasn't up to cooking much, if at all. Ryan couldn't remember the last time she *had* cooked. It was all sandwiches and crisps and "freezer crap".

'Yes, mate?' said Billy, shaking salt onto his chips. Mum was upstairs changing Xandra, so her chips were still wrapped up, keeping warm for her. She probably wouldn't even eat them. She was getting thin, for a woman who had not long ago had a baby. Ryan wished she was fat again, shoving doughnuts in her mouth and arguing with Dad about flying, or conglomerates.

'Mum's not happy,' said Ryan. 'I know Dad died but I

thought she'd be a lot happier than this now that Xandra is born.'

'Oh, she'll be all right, Ryan!' said Billy. 'It's all got to settle down, that's all. I expect your mum's hormones are all over the shop.'

'She keeps crying.'

'All the time?'

Ryan considered.

'Too much of the time,' he said.

'Why don't I have a chat with David about it? It could be postnatal depression.'

'What's that?' said Ryan.

'Some women get… down, after they've had a baby. It's not their fault. And your mum has more than most mums to be down about, doesn't she? She can't share Xandra with Lex. It must be upsetting for her, eh?'

'I suppose so. But she's got me.'

'I know and you're doing a sterling job, but… a woman in your mum's position… she must be feeling it right now. Why don't we give her time, and I'll mention it to David. I promise.'

'She stinks,' ventured Ryan. Billy had to know. He had to understand. Ryan had to get things through to him. Even if it meant saying unkind things about Mum. He'd already said unkind things about her, and to her. *Bitch*. 'She smokes too.'

'I knew she stinks, Ryan,' said Billy. 'And I know she smokes. I've always known she smokes. It kind of gives itself away, doesn't it?' He gave Ryan a sympathetic nudge. 'Tell you what, after she's eaten her chips, I'll see if I can't persuade her to have a nice long soak in the bath, eh?'

MAY 2007

The smoking was silly. It was more than that. It was bad for Xandra and it was bad for her, and it was irresponsible and it was selfish. But she couldn't stop. She was smoking four, five, six cigarettes a day, shamelessly, in broad daylight. The cigarettes didn't even help, so why on earth did she do it? She knew Ryan watched her, disapprovingly, from the kitchen as she sat on the patio puffing smoke into the warm spring air. She knew it saddened and disgusted him.

And how disconnected she felt, from all that had happened. She couldn't even think about Lex anymore. She could not conjure him in her mind. She felt nothing. She was too tired to care. He was dead, that was the stark fact, he had been killed, but something else had got a hold on her now and she felt powerless. She felt like she could die too, perhaps she should, to make life easier for Ryan and Xandra. Sometimes she felt she could just laugh about all of this, laugh about her life and laugh that Lex had died, he was dead, dead, dead, it didn't seem real, yet it was real, hence her state of mind and body. She couldn't see Ryan these days either, she just didn't know him. Who was he anyway? Was he her son? Or was he Lex's son? And Xandra, this baby, who she knew she must take care of, or something dreadful would happen to them, something they might not recover from, and she realised that had already happened, and the baby made no difference, none of it mattered. And Ryan was trying to talk to her.

'Please try to stop smoking, Mum. I don't like it. It's bad for you.'

Bad for you, bad for you, she was sick of bad for you—

'Life is bad for you, Ryan. Haven't you worked that out yet?'

He shook his head, and retreated back into the kitchen, closing the door on her, and then she realised she hadn't spoken to him, she'd said nothing at all, her words had been silent in the May morning.

It was postnatal depression. David said so. Mum went to the doctor and he gave her some tablets to make her feel better. But they didn't work. They made her worse. She stopped talking, she stopped trying to make meals, even sandwiches, for Ryan and for herself. She no longer even looked at the laundry pile, and it was becoming a mountain that Ryan struggled to keep on top of. She did manage to care for Xandra, but only just. The health visitor came round every day; she was "concerned". And then social workers paid a visit, and they chatted to Ryan in the kitchen. It was bad, Ryan knew, if social workers were involved. Mum sat at the table, pale, deep-eyed, saying nothing, while a social worker spoke to them.

'You may need to spend some time apart from your mum,' said the social worker, named Becci. She had short black hair and long dangly earrings. She was actually nice, and Ryan realised she was there to help, but he wondered if she would just make things worse. She wouldn't understand. 'Just for a while, until your mum gets better.'

Ryan didn't like the sound of that. He looked at Mum, for support, for a defiant flash in her eyes, for a "No way!" rapped out in her clear, crystal voice. But she said nothing. She didn't even appear to be listening.

'Perhaps in a foster home?' said Becci. 'You could go back to school.'

'School?' said Ryan.

'Yes. You need an education, Ryan. It's the law. And your mum needs space to recover and get herself together. Your mum tells me you don't go to school, but she's worried that she's not doing enough for you right now. How does the idea sound, eh? Even if it's for a while, until your mum's back on track? We're here to help, Ryan.'

Ryan sat up in bed that night hugging his knees and crying almost as much as Mum. Billy was staying over for the night, on the advice of the social workers. Mum should not be left alone. Xandra should not be left alone with her mother. Ryan was glad he was still in his own home, in Lex's cottage, where he'd felt so safe those months when Dad had been with them. There was talk of Mum going into hospital for "proper" treatment. But how would that help him? He could end up living with strangers, eating strange food on strange plates, sleeping in strange beds. What if they had a cat? It wouldn't be Seamus! What if they had yellow things? What if their house smelled of bananas? He huddled in his bed, closed his eyes, and hoped for sleep. It didn't come. Comfort did not come. Dad did not come.

The morning after Becci's visit and her terrifying suggestions, Ryan walked to Sharon's house, which was on the other side of town. He didn't want to leave Mum, but Billy was there, so he slipped out, unnoticed. He rang Sharon's doorbell.

'Ryan?' said Sharon. 'What are you doing here, love? I mean, it's great to see you, of course. Come in, you look cold. Zephyr! Ryan's here.'

Sharon rang Mum. She gave Ryan lunch. She said they were planning to go swimming that afternoon with a few of the other home ed families. Did Ryan want to come with them? He could borrow Zephyr's spare trunks. Then Sharon could drive him home. How would that be?

The pool was loud and splashy and cold, but Ryan enjoyed the feel of the water, and he powered up and down the pool for several lengths. It was almost like being on the back of Dad's motorcycle. Had Dad been a swimmer? He didn't know. It was something else they had not discovered about each other.

In the camper van, on the way home, Sharon insisted Ryan sit up front with her. It was supposed to be Clover's turn, and she sulked.

'Ignore her,' said Sharon.

'Mum's ill,' said Ryan. He wanted to talk. He thought Sharon wanted him to talk, which was why she had said he should sit in the front. He wasn't stupid. Neither was Sharon.

'I know she's ill,' said Sharon. 'She'll get better, though, I can promise you that much.'

'She doesn't wash.'

'Oh, blimey.'

'She smells bad. Billy got her to have a bath at the weekend but she hasn't washed since then.'

'That's not nice, is it?'

'And she smokes.'

'Ouch.'

'They want her to go to hospital for a bit. They want me to go to a foster carer.'

'You are joking?' Sharon turned to look at him, and she looked horrified. She bit her lip, and looked again to the road.

'No. I'm not joking. They keep popping round. They want me to go to school too.'

'School?!'

'Yes. I'm not going, though. I'll run away first. I'll go anywhere. As long as it's nowhere near social workers.'

'Well, don't do that, Ryan, please. The last thing your mum needs right now is to worry about you if you run away. Oh, what a mess. I wonder… look, I'll try to speak to Joanna when we get you home. Don't worry, Ryan. I'll try to sort something out.'

Ryan could stay at Sharon's house for a while. Becci the social worker spoke to Sharon, and Mum agreed it would be fine; a private arrangement between the two friends. It would be a good thing and it would give Mum time and space to "regain her strength". Billy would help too, if Sharon needed a break. Ryan could stay with him, "no sweat", for a night or two, if he wanted. Nobody, absolutely nobody, not even Becci it seemed, wanted Ryan to go into care. Ryan was glad of Mum's friends, who, he was beginning to feel, were also his friends.

He was calling, calling for Dad. He was running, running along a beach with soft sand, a hot sun burning in a huge blue sky. He called and shouted until his voice was hoarse, until he couldn't shout anymore. And then Dad was there. Dad ran towards him, his arms outstretched, his face smiling all over. He called out to Ryan, 'Come here, come here!' and he stopped a few metres away, and he beckoned. Ryan walked towards him, and he reached out to touch him, but Dad had gone, he had faded away into the sea, and nothing was left on the sand except his black motorcycle helmet. Ryan picked it up and something fell out. A ticket.

Ryan woke up with a jump, and sat up, galvanised. He was sleeping on Zephyr's bedroom floor on a blow-up mattress. He'd been here for two days. Mum was in hospital, with Xandra. Mum was getting "proper" treatment. He was missing her terribly. He was missing Dad even more… but now… this latest dream… now he had a plan. He knew what he needed to do. He would do it. But how? Not on his own, no. He wouldn't be able to *think* of things. Who could he call on?

Ryan's lips curled into a slow smile as he thought of the one person who could help. The person who could do anything, it seemed, with impunity. The person who had the charm, the nerve and the head to help him. He woke Zephyr and told him he was going to the library; he had things to look up for his history project. Before that he needed to go into town. To get some money. He wanted to buy Mum some flowers or chocolates or something, to take to her in hospital when he visited. Zephyr grunted, rolled over and snored loudly. Ryan dressed, and quietly left the house.

'You want to go where?' said Beau in disbelief. Ryan poured out the story of Social Workers and Hospital and Foster Homes and School and his mum wearing dirty clothes and smoking like a chimney and not washing, because she was loopy, and him sleeping on Zephyr's bedroom floor which was OK because Sharon had saved his arse.

'It's seven o'clock in the morning,' said Beau. 'I've got school later.'

'Never mind that. Can you help me?' said Ryan.

'I don't know. Have you got any money?' said Beau.

'I can get some.'

'Are you sure about this?'

'Lex wants me to go.'

'Lex?' Beau scratched his head.

Ryan told Beau about his dream.

'That's freaky,' said Beau.

'Will you help me? Please?'

Beau looked at Ryan. Beau sighed.

'Yes. But we'll end up in the shit. There'll be trouble. It's a long way.'

'But I have to go. Lex promised to take me. We were going to go up there together on the Harley. We were going to camp. I was gonna love it. He wants me to go. He's gonna be there. He said I should go. I have to do this.'

'Ryan, you do know... you do get that Lex won't actually be there, don't you?'

'He'll be there. I have to go.' Ryan sobbed.

'All right, Ryan. We'll sort it. Don't—cry. Come in. I'll get you a drink. And a crumpet. We'll go up to my room. Come on.'

Ryan entered. Beau closed the door behind him.

216

The plan was watertight. It was all so easy.

Later that day, after Beau's mum had left for work, Ryan left for Dad's cottage. He let himself into the house with his own key and listened for noises. There were none. The house was horribly silent, like a... like a mortuary, Ryan thought, and he pushed the thought away, hard, like he would a bullying boy: Beau, once. Morgue, mortuary. He wondered what these places were like. They were like a quiet house, he supposed, emptied of people. Even Seamus wasn't there, but Ryan didn't stop to wonder what had become of him. Mum kept her credit card in her desk drawer and only used it for online shopping. Ryan knew that she didn't need to be so cautious with money these days but Mum hadn't got that far yet, she wasn't used to having enough money. He was one step ahead of her yet again.

Ryan and Beau walked to the train station and bought tickets. Ryan knew Mum's PIN because she had gone through a stage of not recalling it, and had asked Ryan to memorise it for her. Which was ridiculous because her PIN was his day and month of birth and what kind of mother doesn't recall the birthdate of her child? It was just another example of how crap she was. How crap she had always been? Ryan didn't want to feel that Mum was crap, because he felt sorry for her, but he feared she was crap and he feared it was partly his fault. He was difficult. He'd called her a bitch at a time in her life when she'd really needed not to be called a bitch. That was unforgivable of him, and he knew it. He would have to say sorry, even though he hated to do that. Mum was not a bitch. She was just bloody useless and sad. And dirty. Almost he wished... almost he wished Dad hadn't come back. None of this would have happened. It would just be him and Mum and Road to California and craft fairs.

The tickets were expensive. The boys could not decide who should look after them. In the end Beau decided he would do it, and he carried them home carefully and put them under his laptop on his desk in the corner of his bedroom. Ryan would look after the credit card.

'Don't lose it, Ryan, for fuck's sake,' said Beau.

Later, the two boys went to the cashpoint at Tesco on the outskirts of town with Ryan's cash card and took out £200. He had his own account with savings of £600. Dad had set it up for him before he'd married Mum. He really had thought of everything. The boys bought simple provisions; a bottle of cola each, some crisps, and chocolate bars. They were supposed to be for tomorrow's train journey, but were all gone by lunchtime.

In the afternoon, the boys walked into town to The Old and New Bookshop and bought the *Rough Guide to Scottish Highlands and Islands.* It was good to be clever, Ryan thought, feeling proud of himself, and proud of Beau, and he glanced as his friend, grateful for his presence. Where Ryan would panic, Beau was sensible and prone to calmness. It had been one of Dad's qualities too.

'What are you doing for the rest of the day?' said Beau, as they left the bookshop.

'I don't know. I should go back to Zephyr's house. But I'm worried the social workers might come for me.'

'I thought you said that was all sorted.'

'It depends, though.'

'On what?'

'If my mum stays ill for a long time, and she can't leave hospital. She's on the loony ward, you know. Did you know?'

'Yeah.'

'She's got her own room so she can be private with my sister. But Sharon won't be able to put me up forever. I can't stay at Billy's all the time. I'm not their kid, am I? So what will happen?'

'You're worrying too much. They won't just turn up out of the blue, Ryan, will they? Don't these things have to be arranged? Court orders or something? Nobody's going to kidnap you. You could stay at mine tonight? We could ask Sharon if we can have a sleepover. Tell her you'll go back tomorrow or whatever. My mum will be fine with it. She lets me do what I want, more or less.'

'That could work. I really need to make this journey tomorrow.'

'Stop your worrying, will you?'

'And your mum's all right with Ryan staying is she, Beau?' said Sharon. Her hair, green today, was piled up on her head. Ryan thought it looked like a bird's nest. He realised he hadn't thought about birds and their nests and their eggs for weeks. Was the passion waning? He hoped not. He just had other things on his mind. Sharon and Clover were making clay pots in the messy conservatory. Zephyr had gone to a friend's house. Ryan eyed the clay warily; he didn't like the wet-dry feel of it on his hands. It made him feel dirty.

'Yes, she's fine with it,' said Beau. 'We're going to watch Rocky III and eat popcorn.'

'That sounds good,' said Sharon, wiping her hands on an already grimy apron. She was so nice, with her hands covered in clay and the small ring through her nose that Ryan didn't entirely approve of… but, oh, she was just *nice* and Ryan felt more than a pang of guilt that he was deceiving her. 'If you like that sort of thing,' she added. 'Can't say Rocky films do much for me.'

'So I need to get my clothes and toothbrush and stuff,' said Ryan, and he beckoned Beau to follow him upstairs.

'All right, love. Oh, did you get your shopping?'

Ryan and Beau froze. 'Shopping?' said Ryan.

'You went out this morning for chocolates, Zephyr thought you said.'

'Oh. I got them, thanks.'

'So are you visiting her later?'

'Umm. No. I think I'll save it for another time. She seems to cry every time she sees me. It might be best to have a… a break.'

'It's not you that makes her cry, Ryan, love. But all right, I can see where you're coming from. I'm popping in later and I'll tell her what you're up to. I expect she'll be glad you're having some fun, eh?'

Ryan and Beau went upstairs to pack up Ryan's things.

'You can't take those,' said Beau, as Ryan attempted to squeeze his favourite copy of *A Kestrel for a Knave* into his rucksack, along with the copy of *The Great Gatsby* Dad had bought for him.

'Why not?'

'You won't have time to read. You've already got the guidebook. That's a… tome.'

'You think it's too cumbersome?' asked Ryan.

'Dunno. It's too heavy and too bulky,' said Beau.

'We'll be on a train for a long time,' said Ryan.

'Shh!' said Beau, closing Zephyr's bedroom door.

'Sorry.'

'Leave those books here. You need your toothbrush and toothpaste and a towel and shit. Not heavy books. Besides, won't you want to look out of the window? That's the best part of a train journey.' And Beau gently eased the books from Ryan's pale hands and put them back on Zephyr's bedside table.

Eventually, Ryan was done with his packing. He had fitted the stuff Beau deemed he needed into his blue rucksack. He checked his pocket to make sure he still had Mum's credit card. He did. He was ready to leave.

Ryan stood awkwardly in the kitchen and said goodbye to Sharon. He felt another pang of guilt – hell, it wasn't a pang, it was a gong, a thud, a heavy heartbeat. What if social workers came for him, even if it was just to see him for a "chat", as Becci liked to do sometimes, and he wasn't there? Sharon would end up in trouble. She was entrusted. He was betraying her.

And what about Xandra? Would they take *her* away? Would she have to go into a foster home? Mum was breastfeeding her, so surely they couldn't? It wouldn't make any sense.

He would have to stop worrying. If he was going to make this journey, keep this promise, he would have to stop thinking, and just do it. He was too young to worry, wasn't he? He didn't feel young. He didn't feel old.

'Have fun, then, Ryan!' said Sharon. 'Enjoy your Rocky

movie. I'll let your mum know what you're up to later. You'll be back tomorrow?'

'Yes, tomorrow… afternoon,' said Ryan. 'We're going to watch all the Rocky films. So we'll be tired in the morning.' Ryan worried that Sharon might point out that Beau would have to go to get up for school, so they surely couldn't stay up too late, but of course, she didn't think of it. Daft hippy, as Billy would say. But Sharon wasn't daft. She was bloody great.

'OK. Wow. Whatever lights your fire, I suppose. No problem, as long as Beau's mum doesn't mind. I'd better take your phone number, Beau. Just in case.' She passed an old envelope and a pen to him. He scribbled down a number. Sharon watched him.

'In case of what?' said Ryan.

'Oh, I don't know. The hospital may ring? I might need to contact you. Ah, thanks, Beau, love. I'll pop it on my pinboard. Oh! Ryan! I forgot. It's the science museum trip tomorrow! The coach leaves at eight thirty sharp. You mustn't stay up too late. I won't accept an OD of Rocky films as an excuse, you know!'

'I'd forgotten,' said Ryan, looking sheepishly at the floor. Sharon had bought and paid for his coach ticket, which was kind of her. It was one of the group's big outings for the year and Ryan had been looking forward to it. After… afterwards, he'd pay Sharon back out of what was left of his money in his savings account. He'd have to. It would only be fair.

'You will absolutely need to be back for that,' said Sharon. 'Guess it's just Rocky III after all? Most of us in the group are going, it'll be a fab day. Zephyr's hoping to sit at the back of the coach with you.'

They did watch Rocky III, and they did eat popcorn, so it wasn't all lies.

Then Clarissa called round. Beau's mum sent her upstairs and the unsuspecting girl poked her head round Beau's bedroom door. She jumped when she saw Ryan.

'What the fuck is *he* doing here?' she said. Clarissa ventured further into the room, staring at Ryan like he was a bird-eating spider.

'Ryan? He's – er – he's…' Beau had no explanations.

'I'm watching Rocky III,' said Ryan. He felt he ought to say something.

'Boring,' said Clarissa, and her super-straight hair and plentiful black eye make-up withdrew onto the landing.

'Clarissa?' called Beau.

'What?'

'Come in. Make up with Ryan, will you? We've been hanging out for a while now. I was going to tell you. He promises not to hit you ever again.'

'Really?' And Clarissa entered Beau's bedroom and sat on the bed next to Ryan.

'I promise,' said Ryan.

'I can't believe you two hang out,' she said, looking hard at Beau. 'I'm sorry about your dad. Beau told me what happened. He said he'd heard. He didn't say how he'd heard, though.'

Ryan shrank from her. 'Thanks,' he said. Clarissa had about her, always, an overpowering smell. Ryan guessed it was nothing more than cheap body spray, or perfume; which was better, he had to concede, than the smell of unwashed body and cigarette smoke.

'I'm sorry I hit you,' said Ryan.

Clarissa shrugged. 'So what are you two really up to?' she asked, chewing on her ever-present gum.

'Watching Rocky III,' repeated Ryan.

'What's with the tickets?' said Clarissa.

Beau had been looking at them, making sure they had definitely got the right destination, which they had. And the tickets were on the bed, alongside the *Rough Guide to Scottish Highlands and Islands.* And Clarissa was leaning across the bed, reaching for the tickets. It was all in slow motion, like it wasn't really happening, but it was, and slow, slow, but quick, and Ryan wanted to do something to stop her but it was too late, her long fingernails were on the tickets. Thank God the cash was in Ryan's bag, thought Ryan, as he watched Clarissa's… *talons* reach out. Her hand closed in and she took up the tickets.

'Nothing!' said Beau, and he snatched them from her.

'Nothing? Let me have them!'

Clarissa grappled with Beau, she tickled him and he giggled, like a little girl, and she giggled too, and they were a tangled giggling mess, and Beau dropped the tickets. Ryan stared at Beau and Clarissa in disbelief. Clarissa grabbed at the tickets and her eyes widened as she read the destination on them. Ryan stared at her in horror. *No, no, no.*

'Where the fuck is that?!' said Clarissa, peering at the tickets. She picked up the guidebook.

'Don't say anything, Clarissa, please!' said Beau, red-faced.

'What's it worth?' said Clarissa.

'It's worth everything,' said Ryan quietly. He took a step towards her, even though he felt repelled by the smell of her, the over-made-up face, the huge hoop earrings. 'I'm going to Loch Coruisk, which is on the Isle of Skye in Scotland, because that's where my dad told me I should go and he was going to take me there. So I'm going anyway and Beau here, who's my friend whether you like it or not, is coming with me. He knows how shy I am and he will make up stories so people don't get suspicious. And I really need to do this and please don't mess it up for me. And I am sorry I hit you. I meant to hit *him*.' And Ryan indicated Beau, who was slumped, shame-faced on the bed, looking from Ryan to Clarissa.

Clarissa handed the tickets and the guidebook to Ryan. He took them in trembling hands and Clarissa must have noticed because her face changed.

'OK,' she said. 'Apology accepted. You really hurt me that day but I suppose I wasn't very nice to you. Let's just forget about it. And I won't say anything to anyone. But on one condition. I'm coming with you. D'you get me?'

Beau was right. Ryan didn't need to bring his favourite books. The day had been clear and bright since sunrise, and Ryan had spent most of it looking from windows, enjoying the changing scenery, which was becoming more dramatic with every turn of the train's wheels. Beau and Clarissa sat opposite him, and were both asleep, Clarissa leaning on Beau's shoulder. They had bought Clarissa a ticket before they boarded the train early that morning, using Mum's credit card again. Clarissa had also insisted on a can of cherryade, a packet of Monster Munch, and a copy of *Glamour* because journeys were boring. Did they get her?

They had been travelling for eight hours now, and had changed trains three times. Clarissa had wanted to stay in

Edinburgh. But Ryan had shaken his head. No. She knew where they were going. He still half-wished she hadn't come with them; but she was good at acting older than her fifteen years, and she was good at ordering food and drinks, and she had a certain brand of confidence that Ryan, and even Beau, lacked. She was proving to be useful, despite her gum chewing, her whining and her stupid magazines. (She had exhausted *Glamour*'s possibilities and had moved on to *Cosmopolitan*.)

Ryan wanted to wake them up to see the scenery. They were missing so much. But he didn't want to disturb them, so he enjoyed it, alone, his thoughts his own, and his thoughts were mostly of Dad. The mountains, lochs, the ever-changing skies, seemed to be flying past while he sat, still and quiet, on the train. He realised that he was searching for Dad, waiting to spot him, hurtling loch-side on the Harley, or pitching a tent.

He wouldn't allow himself to wonder if he had been missed back at home already. Where exactly was home nowadays? Mum hadn't yet sold their old house. The cottage was still very much Dad's. Ryan was currently living in neither. Of course, by now, he understood, he would have been missed. Sooner or later, but he hoped later, Sharon, or Beau's mum, would work out that they were "missing". Probably Sharon would "raise the alarm" when he didn't turn up for the science museum trip. He hoped she would just get on the coach with her kids and forget about him for the day. But he knew she probably wouldn't. Mum would be worried to death, if she could be bothered to worry, of course; pulling at her hair, clutching Xandra to her chest. Ryan could imagine

Mum's wild face, her tortured questions, her stupid constant tears. How she had changed, and for the worse, and he hated to see her in such a state and he was furious with her for descending into it. Pull yourself together, he'd told her. But she hadn't.

Forget it, kid. Your mom can take care of herself. But go easy on her, will ya? And just get here.

Joanna, curled up in her hospital bed, stirred. She turned from Xandra, who was sleeping, quiet and unaware in her Perspex cot.

Lex?! It was him! He was here, in her room!

No. No. It was Sharon. Sharon was in her room.

Joanna sat up, feeling groggy, and peered at her friend.

'Oh. I thought it was… I dreamed about him. Jesus. That was… sorry. I'm sorry.' She rubbed her eyes. She sat up, she ran her hands through her matted hair. How frail she felt; diminished. 'Sharon. How lovely. What time is it?'

'It's about midday.'

'Really? I've lost track. All I seem to do is sleep these days. How are you, anyway? Come and sit down. There's a chair under all that junk.' Sharon cleared the chair of its baby paraphernalia. She sat down.

'Listen, Joanna, there's a bit of an issue with Ryan—'

'What's the matter? Is he OK? He hasn't visited me for two days. I can't tell you how I miss that boy.'

'He's… umm… he's gone.'

'Gone?' Joanna sat up straight, pushing hair off her face. Suddenly, she didn't feel so frail.

'We think with Beau. We think they've… run away. Don't panic, Joanna. It's all… in hand. Sort of.'

Joanna sprang out of bed. Xandra stirred; she started to whimper.

'I'll have to feed her!' said Joanna. She picked Xandra up. 'Shit! I can't do anything until she's fed… Ryan's run away? Are you sure?'

'We think so.'

Joanna shook her head and cried.

'Why? Sharon, why?'

'We don't know. Billy thinks it might be the social workers with the fostering talk. Ryan's scared, we think.'

'Oh God! This is all my fault. Where's Billy?'

'At your house. Lex's house, that is. We've had a good look around and we think he's taken your credit card.'

'How long have they been gone?'

'I don't know. I'm so sorry… I got hold of Billy this morning when Ryan didn't turn up for the trip—'

'The science museum trip?' Joanna had stopped crying. You can't think clearly and cry at the same time; something she had learned from bitter experience. But she had remembered the trip, she was "with it" enough to have remembered. Ryan had told her about it, and she had listened.

'Yes. So I rang Billy and we've been over to the… cottage and nobody was there so we got hold of Diana, Beau's mum, and there's stuff missing from her house, Beau's stuff has gone. And Ryan's stuff. Ryan stayed over at Beau's house, you see, last night. Toothbrushes have gone, that kind of thing. They told me they were going to watch Rocky III… never mind. At least we know they've planned something.'

'Oh, God. Beau's mum will be furious with me… Will they be safe, Sharon? Will they?'

'I think so, yes.' Sharon hesitated. Joanna stared hard at her. 'Beau's sensible, isn't he?' Sharon tried.

'So's Ryan,' said Joanna.

'Yes, I know. I meant… I meant together they'll be fine. We think Clarissa might be with them too.'

'Really? But that's good. That's good. There's safety in numbers. And she's a girl, isn't she? She'll have some sense.'

Xandra suckled greedily while Joanna gazed blankly into a distance she could not see. Sharon moved from the chair to sit alongside her on the bed. She rubbed Joanna's back and said small consoling things. Once Xandra had finished feeding and was asleep, Joanna handed her to Sharon.

'What are you doing?' said Sharon, holding the baby uneasily, as Joanna began to throw things into her bag.

'What do you mean?' said Joanna, checking the contents of her wash bag, and zipping it up. She didn't know precisely what was in it, but it looked full of "things", so that would do.

'Don't you need to stay—?'

'I'm getting out of here. I'm going to get my son back. Wherever he's gone, or whatever he's doing, I'm bringing him home.'

The Kyle of Lochalsh; three lonely figures standing in silence on the platform. They were a long way from home. They were tired and hungry, and cold, and breathing the strangely whispered air of the highlands, cool and clear, a little shocking to the lungs. It was sweet, Ryan thought. He felt clean. He felt… *replenished*. He hoped they would spot an eagle at some point. A sea eagle, a golden eagle. Any eagle would be amazing. The air was cold, mountainous, and sounds were different here... more echoey; sharper. The town was tiny, more like a village. A village with a train station. The end of the line: one way in, the same way out.

Clarissa looked tired, worn, her make-up bleary. She chewed her gum, slowly. Beau looked... pensive, unsure, doubtfully flicking through the *Rough Guide to the Highlands and Islands*. Nobody noticed them; their fellow passengers had scattered to their various destinations already, and the train had already left to go back again.

'What now, then, drongos?' said Clarissa. She grinned stupidly, Ryan thought, but at least she was still grinning. It meant they were all right, things were OK. He didn't want his friends to worry. He didn't want his friends to lose heart.

'I don't know,' said Beau. He slammed shut the guidebook.

'I thought you dickheads had a plan?' Clarissa said.

'Ryan?' said Beau.

Ryan looked at them both.

'We need to get to Loch Coruisk,' he said. It was all he could say.

'It's night-time,' said Clarissa, shivering. 'It'll be dark soon. We need to find somewhere to sleep and we can go to this loch thing tomorrow. In the guidebook it said it's tricky to get to. You need to get a boat or traipse over some mountains. I know which I'm doing. And we can't do either tonight. D'you get me?'

'We'll have to blag our way into a hotel or something,' said Beau. He opened Ryan's rucksack and pushed the guidebook into it. 'And then we'll need to work out how we're going to get to the loch tomorrow. It's quite a long way from here. We'll have to look into getting buses and all that shit. Ryan, you've got your mum's credit card safe?'

'Of course I have. I've still got cash too.'

'Do not lose either of those things. We're fucked if you do.'

'We need to find a hotel or something, then,' said Ryan. 'But just for tonight.'

'So who's going to do the talking?' said Beau.

The boys looked at Clarissa. She rolled her eyes skywards.

The guest house was quaintly shabby and old-fashioned, like anyone's grandparents' house. Their "family room" was drab, but neat; it was dust-disturbed and smelled of bleach and potpourri. The woman had looked at them doubtfully, as Clarissa asked for a room and explained: Beau and she were brother and sister, Ryan was their cousin, and they had travelled up by train, and the rest of the family, their parents, aunts and uncles, their… grandmother, and their younger siblings and cousins… they were a large family, did she get her… they were following on in cars, but they had got held up… in traffic and were staying in a motel near… Edinburgh, and would be travelling on from there tomorrow. The family were gathering for a holiday.

So, they needed a room, just for tonight. She was eighteen but she had no identity on her: apart from her own credit card. Would that be all right?

There was a room with a double bed and a single, the lady said doubtfully.

'The boys can have the double and I'll have the single.

231

It sounds perfect,' said Clarissa. 'To be honest, we're all really tired.'

The woman took the credit card and Clarissa filled in a form, Beau watching carefully to make sure she did it right. 'Joanna,' he whispered. Clarissa got it. She was hot on pretending to be an adult, but not too good with spelling. And her hand writing was undeniably that of a teenager, so Beau had instructed her on the train, if she had to sign Joanna's name at some point, not to put circles above the "i"s, just dots, and definitely not hearts.

The old lady examined the credit card carefully. Clarissa entered the PIN with no hesitation. She had remembered the number by heart, of course. Thank you, said the woman as she handed back the card and the receipt. Clarissa smiled sweetly at her.

Was there a chip shop nearby? asked Beau. There was. The weary travellers, after leaving their bags in their room (Ryan laid claim to the single bed immediately, by unpacking his bag and spreading its contents across the pink eiderdown), found the fish and chip shop and greedily they ate their meals, and washed them down with cherryade, Clarissa's favourite. "Try it, Ry. You'll like it."

The evening was even colder now, and quiet. They were such a long way from all that was familiar to them, and that was becoming ever more obvious. But Ryan was glad they had come this far. Beau, and even Clarissa, seemed to understand how important this trip was to him. They didn't want to let him down, he could tell; they didn't want to complain too loudly or voice any doubts, so they tried to act cheerfully, they tried not to moan about being cold and tired and a long way from home.

Dad had been here, thought Ryan, he must have travelled through here to go on to Skye. Ryan wondered if he'd stayed in the same guest house? Probably not; it wasn't Dad's style. Ryan thought he would have camped, everything he needed packed up in the Harley, which was now as dead and gone as Dad; but Ryan hated that thought, and maybe the motorbike was dead and gone, but not Dad. Not really. It wasn't possible. And tomorrow Ryan would be on Skye. He could see the lights on the island as he ate his chips; Skye was close to the mainland, almost not an island at all, which disappointed him, a bit. The bridge ruined it. But he felt, he thought, further on, across the island, its "beauty" and its "splendour" (Dad's words) would reveal itself. And Dad would reveal himself, somehow, he would be there, he was waiting for him. *Come on, kid, hurry up now, would ya? I'm getting cold here.* And there was no doubt in Ryan's mind whatsoever about this. He knew. Dad was waiting for him.

Joanna discharged herself from the hospital and ignored the worried nurses, the staid advice of a junior doctor. A quiet fuss was made, persuasive words were uttered and ignored, a gentle hand on her back was shrugged off and was not proffered again. They understood her anxieties. And she had not been "detained", of course, so she was free to go … but it was unwise… her medication … Joanna ignored them all, and she insisted that Sharon drive her and Xandra home. The plan was to head for Lex's cottage, meet Billy, and Beau's mum, and decide what on earth they were going to do.

Sharon's camper van was bumpy, noisy, smelly; but it

was taking her home, her and Xandra, and Joanna was thankful for it.

Joanna knew, as soon as she entered the living room and saw Lex's framed print of Loch Coruisk hanging over the mantelpiece, where Ryan had gone. She had possibly guessed already; she wasn't sure. But it became obvious when the large photograph loomed before her, the craggy grey mountains hanging over the loch, reflected in the glass-like water.

'Put a stop on your credit card,' suggested Billy.

'No. No, he'll be needing it,' said Joanna. She stared hard at the picture. Billy followed her gaze. 'He's gone to Skye, Billy, I'm sure of it. Lex told him about Loch Coruisk and Ryan wanted to go. They planned to go together, you see? It's Ryan's way of… I'm not sure. Of coping? He's going to feel closer to his father, I think, if he travels there. I know my son. He's spiritual, in his own way. That's behind all this, I'm sure of it. It's the place in the picture. Look.'

Seamus, who seemed remarkably well-fed and groomed for a neglected cat, coiled about her legs. Ryan was not running away, she felt sure; he was running towards something. She knew it. She would not panic. Nobody must panic. They heard the crunch of gravel on the driveway, a car door slam, and seconds later David joined them. He and Billy hugged. Billy brought him up to date.

'… so, Miss Marple here thinks they've dashed up to Scotland. I still think we should go to the police,' said Billy.

'No!' cried Joanna. 'We must not do that. Whatever we do, we can't do that. Ryan needs to make this journey. I'd…

I'd like to go and meet him. Billy, leave a message on Beau's mobile, could you, please? Mine's not charged. Tell him we know where they are. I'll go and meet them, and bring them home.'

'How the hell are you going to do that?' asked Billy, as Sharon and Diana glanced uneasily at each other.

Joanna ignored the glances, the doubts looming all around her, like the mountains over Loch Coruisk. 'I'm going to hire a car and drive up there,' said Joanna. 'If I leave now, I'll be there by morning.'

'Drive up to Skye?' said Sharon.

Joanna waved at the photograph. Everybody stared at it. Silence. Nobody knew what to say. They all looked uncomfortably at each other, there was some shuffling, and avoiding of Joanna's gaze. She stood by the picture. She reached out, ran her hands over it. Silent contemplation filled the room.

'Right. I'm driving you up there,' said Billy. 'David, you stay put in case they come home. We need somebody to stay here. Is that all right?

'Of course,' said David.

'Widow Twonky here could be way off.' And Billy pointed at Joanna, who glared back at him, and then tried not to laugh at her friend's outrageous sense of humour. Thank God for it, she thought. Thank God for him. She had the best friends in the world. 'But she knows her own son better than the rest of us so... let's work on this premise that they're heading for the back of fucking beyond. Diana. You coming?"

'Yes, of course I am,' said Diana. Joanna flashed a grateful smile at her. 'It's my son too.'

'Great,' said Billy.

'Well, if you're going, we are,' said Sharon. 'What an opportunity for the kids. How often in life do you take an impromptu trip to the Isle of Skye? They'll talk about this for years. It beats the science museum hands down! And it will be good to know Ryan and his friends are all safe. I reckon they are. They know what they're doing.'

'You definitely don't want to involve the police?' said Billy to the room at large. 'Diana, how do you feel about that?' Diana was fumbling with her mobile.

'It's fine by me. I know Beau will be all right, he's got his head screwed on. I'm going to nip out for a cig and then I'll ring Clarissa's mum. She won't be too bothered, I expect. Clarissa does as she chooses.'

'They're safe, Diana,' said Joanna. 'I know they are.' She reached out and took Diana's hand. 'Thank you for trusting me. I just want to go and meet him myself. And bring them all back safely. I'm going to have a quick shower, I'll bath Xandra, pack a bag and we'll go. If that's all right with everyone?'

They were ready. Lifts home given, bags packed, and the party assembled back at Lex's cottage, ready to leave. Diana climbed into the camper with Sharon and Zephyr and Clover. Billy kissed David goodbye, and Joanna kissed him too.

'Thanks so much. I'm sorry for stealing your man,' she said.

'Get along with you. Just bring them all back. I'll ring you if there's anything to report.'

'Help yourself to the crap in the freezer. There's wine

to be found too, somewhere. Let us know if you hear anything, anything at all.'

David promised he would be in touch if there was anything to report. He helped her strap Xandra's car seat into the back of Billy's car. And just after four o'clock Billy's car and Sharon's camper van crept along Lex's crunchy gravel driveway, and turned left, heading for the main road, and whatever waited beyond.

The lady at the guest house told them which bus to catch, and where and when.

'But shouldn't you wait for the rest of your family?' she asked, as she served their breakfast. The eggs were greasy, the sausages overcooked and shrivelled, the tomatoes and mushrooms cold. But the landlady, Mrs Roberts, was kind, so all three made an effort to eat at least some of their breakfast.

'Won't your family want to meet up with you here?' She was getting persistent.

'No, no, we want to get there first,' said Clarissa. 'It's turned into a race, and we're going to win.'

Mrs Roberts looked at the girl doubtfully, although it was not her business, she realised. But she wondered if she was being told the truth, and she suspected that she wasn't; but paying guests were paying guests, and Lord knew she needed those. She hoped they weren't in trouble.

'I've had a text from Billy,' said Beau. 'He sent it last night. I didn't have a signal.'

'What does it say?' asked Ryan.

They were on a bus, taking up the bumpy back seat,

rattling across Skye towards Loch Coruisk. Clarissa was looking at a leaflet.

'It looks like you can just turn up,' she said, 'and get on one of these boats. We might see dolphins. Oh! I really hope we do. We might even see a whale.'

'It says, "We are coming up, J guessed ur heading 4 Loch C on Skye. R U? Don't do anything daft, we'll b there tomoz."'

'I knew she'd guess,' said Ryan.

'You know what, if you'd asked her, she probably would have brought you up here herself,' said Beau.

'No. I had to do this alone.'

Beau and Clarissa exchanged looks.

'Anyway,' continued Ryan, 'she's a loony, and I don't know when she's going to get better and my dad wanted me to come now. Before I have to go to a foster home and go back to school.'

'I don't reckon either of those things will happen,' said Beau. 'You worry too much.'

'Are you going to reply to Billy?' said Ryan.

'Yep, texting now. Then all the parents can quit worrying.'

'You don't think they've told the police, do you?' said Ryan, panicked.

'No. We're not babies. This is what I've texted back. "OK, we are on bus heading for Loch C should be there by lunchtime. We all fine. Clarissa with us 2". Is that all right?'

'Yes.'

'Oh, I really want to see a dolphin!' said Clarissa, chewing her gum.

Shortly before midnight the convoy of worried (but no longer desperately worried) mothers and mildly-worried-but-really-quite-thrilled-by-the-adventure hangers-on crossed the border and entered Scotland. They had made OK time, considering the M6 traffic, and with a tiny baby and a couple of kids in the party. They had stopped just north of Birmingham, and again at Tebay services. They'd eaten supper there, and Sharon had insisted Zephyr and Clover have a wash and brush their teeth before they set off again.

'You're joking?' said Zephyr.

'No, I'm not. And for heaven's sake, make sure you go to the loo,' said Sharon. 'We want to press on.'

Back at the van, the kids changed into fresh joggers and T-shirts and snuggled under blankets. They were to try to sleep. Diana would stay awake, she said. She'd even try to drive the camper if Sharon needed a break. Sharon laughed. Her camper was a law unto itself, she said. It had taken her months to become its mistress. She wouldn't inflict that on anybody. She just hoped nothing would fall off on this journey.

Joanna tried to insist on having a turn at driving. Billy insisted she could not. What about her medications? Should she drive? Besides, she looked all in, and should try to sleep.

'Joanna, be sensible, for Christ's sake.'

'I haven't been taking any medications,' said Joanna. 'I took a couple to begin with but they made me feel horrible. So I hid them under my tongue and spat them out later.'

'What the bloody hell for?' said Billy. 'You need them, Joanna.'

'I'm breastfeeding Xandra! They said the meds were OK with breastfeeding but I don't want to take anything. Not even paracetamol. Don't you understand?'

'Bloody hell! But, yes, I understand. You're probably right. We don't want you turning into a zombie.'

'Right. And I'm… I'm zombie enough as it is, wouldn't you say?' Joanna looked at Billy, who glanced at her; he smiled reassuringly, then looked back to the road. He was a safe driver.

'You're no zombie, woman.'

'Says you.'

'Well, either way, you're not driving. Sleep, darling. Just sleep.'

Billy won the argument, for once, and on they drove, and he didn't bother waking Joanna when they crossed the border.

'Elgol?' said Beau. 'It sounds like something from The Lord of the Rings.'

'Wait until we get to the loch,' said Ryan. 'You'll think you're in The Lord of the Rings.'

'I hate those films,' said Clarissa. 'Boring.'

The bus journey was over. To Ryan, it had been fascinating. Over and again on this trip he'd imagined Dad in the landscape, taking in a view; strolling along a beach. It seemed as though this place belonged to Dad, and that Dad was here, where he should be, somewhere beautiful, somewhere secret and silent, waiting for his son. The feeling, Ryan knew, would never leave him. This was the place. Perhaps California too? If they ever got there… if his stupid mother would grow a pair of… wings. Another

240

time, perhaps. First things first. He was on Skye. The most beautiful place in the country. His dad had said so, and his dad was right.

There wasn't much in Elgol. A small harbour, a tiny school right on the edge of the sea; a hut selling boat tickets. They were tired and hungry (again), not having managed a great deal of Mrs Roberts's well-meant breakfast. Clarissa made noises, dangerously close to whining, about finding something to eat and drink: chocolate, crisps, cherryade, anything. But Ryan could almost smell the loch now; and he could smell fish, and he screwed up his nose.

'I hate that smell,' he said.

'Unlucky,' said Beau. 'It's a harbour, what do you expect?'

'I don't like it, either,' said Clarissa. 'Let's go and get these tickets and get out of here. This loch had better be worth it,' she added, looking hard at Ryan. He handed her Mum's credit card.

'Knock yourself out, sis,' said Beau. With a toss of her hair, Clarissa stalked over to the little hut where the boat trip tickets were sold.

The sun rose early. The mountains and the lochs glowed golden-bright. All was cold and light. The landscape was endless and grand and frightening. But Joanna liked it. And Ryan was here, and soon she would be with him.

They spotted a Little Chef in the distance. 'We'd better stop,' Billy said. They were in remote country now, and there probably weren't that many more Little Chefs to be found. This was bloody Scotland, after all. Beautiful, of course, but...

'There's not much here,' said Billy. 'Do you know, this is my first visit to Scotland?'

'Mine too,' said Joanna, looking round to check on Xandra. She was stirring, her little head quietly writhing from side to side, a grimace gathering itself into a cry. Yes, they should stop, eat, she should feed and change Xandra. Joanna took up Billy's phone to text Diana. The phone beeped.

'A message!' cried Joanna. She opened it and read it eagerly. 'Thank God,' she said. 'It's from Beau. All three are heading for Loch Coruisk. I told you, Billy. I knew.'

'That's great, darling, really great. Aren't you the clever one?!'

'I just know my son.'

They pulled into the Little Chef car park.

'No wonder... he... loved it so much,' said Joanna. They were on Skye. Joanna texted Beau: "We're not far from you now. Keep safe and stay together."

'Billy?'

'Yep?'

'Do you think Lex knew?'

'Knew what, babe?'

'That he didn't have long... left.'

'How on earth could he have known? He wasn't ill. He had an accident.'

'Incident,' corrected Joanna. She pictured Ryan's bitter face, she heard the bitter tone of voice. It was an *incident* that killed Lex.

'I know it sounds stupid but... he wanted us to get married so soon and he bought the house as quickly as he could and...'

'No, Joanna. No. He was just dead keen to get on with his new life with you and Ryan and Xandra. That was all. He couldn't possibly have known what was going to happen.'

'You're right. I loved him so much. Ryan adored him too. I don't know how we're going to get through this.'

'You will. You have no choice. You've got two great kids who need their mum and you'll pull through. You're the toughest person I know, woman.'

'Thanks for being such a good friend, Billy. I mean it. Ryan and me, we'd be lost without you.'

'Shut up. Get some rest. This is going to be a long day.'

'Look at the seals!' squealed Clarissa, running from one side of the small boat to the other. 'Oh, look at the little ones!'

The seals were frolicking in the water, indifferent to the boatload of visitors so enchanted by them. A group of Japanese tourists wrestled with cameras, indulgently smiling at Clarissa's enthusiasm. The boat rounded a small island where more seals basked on the rocks, enjoying the spring sunshine. The boat sailed slowly past, its engine chug-chugging, to allow time for the photographs. Soon the boat slowed even more, and pulled up alongside a simple wooden jetty, and the passengers disembarked, and were asked to report back to the boat in two hours. And not to be late because there might not be places on a later boat for them to sail back on. There was a timetable and it was important to stick to it. It wasn't high season just yet… but it was good weather, and there were quite a few passengers around today.

People moved off in their little groups, the three youngsters dragging behind. Ryan wanted to stay away from other people, he said. He hated crowds. They followed a path as it rounded rocks and tussocks of grass, and soon Ryan found himself in a place he could not have imagined, a place he could not have described. The silence overtook him, and he moved as in a dream, and he wandered down towards the shore of the loch, Beau and Clarissa following him. And they stood, together and silent, and looked around at the mountains, the sky, the water, and a magic took hold and grew in Ryan; yet he had known this was how he would feel, this was how it would be. Dad had known, he'd felt this, he'd known how Ryan would feel here; it was Dad's gift. Ryan drifted from the others to be alone. He sat on the grass, he lay back on the earth and filled his eyes with sky. He rested, but did not sleep. He did not want to dream. He wanted to be alive, awake, in touch with himself, his senses; in touch with his father.

After a while, the three convened and sat on a rock and gazed at the water, so blue, the sky reflected like a sheet of silk, pure and smooth. There was a gentle breeze. Beau and Clarissa said nothing. They held hands, and Clarissa, tired, leaned again on Beau's shoulder. Ryan, later, got up and walked, and his friends watched him go. He wandered along the edge of the loch; then he followed a path as it rose a little, and he wandered off across rocks, and he stopped once to look back. Beau waved.

Dad was here. Ryan felt his presence in every twirl of the breeze, every swish of the grass, every call of a seagull; the only noises in this silent place. Then Ryan saw it, a soaring eagle, circling towards him, over the loch, and Ryan thought the eagle was a sign from Dad, in fact it could even *be* Dad, reincarnated into a creature wild and free and ferocious, and Ryan was embarrassed by even thinking such a thought. It was silly, but the thought lingered, and he watched the eagle as it circled, until gradually it glided away, becoming smaller. Ryan fancied nobody else had spotted it, and he was glad. But of course, this eagle had been alive for some time, years probably, and Dad had only been dead for two and a half months. It could not possibly be him, even if there was such a thing as reincarnation; Ryan suspected there wasn't. Even so, it was a sign, and he took it as such.

He sat on a rock beside the loch for a long time, and was only pulled from his silent reveries by a gradual awareness of movement, animation, in Beau and Clarissa's direction. Their numbers had swelled, and Ryan could see it was over, their runaway trip; they had been found. Mum was there, with others; he couldn't take it all in at once, but he saw Sharon standing next to Clarissa, her arm round her shoulder, and Billy was there, shielding his eyes and looking in Ryan's direction, and so Ryan stood up on the rock, and he waved. Mum, her tousled blond hair always recognisable, carrying a bundle; Xandra of course. And Zephyr and Clover. And was that Beau's mum? Ryan watched as Mum handed Xandra to Billy, and left the group, and made her way towards him. Ryan stood up.

She didn't know what she would say. He seemed to have grown. He was lankier, manlier, more Lex-like. Why hadn't she noticed before? Damn her and her stupid self-obsessed grief, this stupid depression that had suffocated her. Already she was feeling free of it; she was pushing it further from her with every step she took towards her son, as he stood, alone and motionless, waiting to greet her, she hoped.

Here was a place where it was easy to breathe. She could feel perfectly why Lex had loved it so much. It was one of those rare places that insinuates itself into you, where you mesh into it, become part of it, and if you love it, you carry it with you forever, and never forget it. Lex had felt this, she knew. She thought she might, too. And looking at Ryan now, she knew that he was under its spell, and she knew she had done the right thing not to get this trip of his curtailed, not to panic and call the police and ruin everything. It was a pilgrimage, and Ryan's alone, and it was Ryan's business. She was tired. She knew she was going to cry as soon as one of them spoke, if not before. She knew she cried too much, and it was time to stop, and be strong again, like she once had been. She was tough, Billy had told her so. She thought he might be right. Close now, and closer, and she swallowed, once, twice. She stood still, two paces away. Ryan avoided her gaze, as he usually did. Joanna had hoped for more, something rare and trusting.

'I saw a sea eagle,' he said. Joanna tried not to cry but a single sob escaped. She wiped away determined tears. 'But it's gone now,' he continued.

'That's a sh-sh-shame,' said Joanna, her voice shaking, her throat burning with the effort to hold back the sobs. 'I would have liked to have seen it.'

They sat together then, lowering themselves in tandem onto the rock, and they looked over the water, blue and still, and listened to the sounds of nothing but life, and they knew that Lex would have loved this more than anything, he would have been there with them in equal silence, absorbing it all into his being, thankful that his family, his wife and son, were at one with him, appreciating the beauty and peace of it, allowing it in, letting it settle over them like balm.

Of course, they missed the allotted boat back. Zephyr and Clover wanted to explore, and ramble and scramble around, and they clambered over the rocks, and Clarissa gamely played hide-and-seek with Clover. Sharon said the loch was "mystical". Billy strolled round with Sharon and Joanna, baby Xandra peaceful in her sling; and even Diana, not an outdoor woman, sat on a rock enjoying a cigarette with a view. The adults were all so subdued and becalmed, and the youngsters knew it. Ryan watched them, and thought how cool it would be if adults could be this laid-back all the time, instead of freaking out over impossibly small things.

Zephyr announced he was hungry, and then of course everybody was hungry. Reluctantly they made their way back to the small jetty, a straggling bunch of adventurers who were all far more tired than they wanted to admit. Mum walked with Ryan at the rear of the group, and she stopped and gently took his hand in hers. He didn't pull away.

'I'm not going back into hospital,' she said. 'That's over, Ryan, all right? We're going home, you and me and Xandra, and we're going to be fine. I promise you. I'm going to be…' She swallowed. 'I'm going to be tough. For you and for Xandra. I'm going to get a grip.'

Ryan nodded. He looked at Mum, and for once, perhaps for the first time, he held her gaze fully in his own, and they smiled at each other, and something was lifted from them, by the hands of giants.

Mrs Roberts looked from face to face, and was certain she had not seen a grandmother among them. What had happened to her? Had they left her in Edinburgh? Unless one of the ladies was… but no, they were all far too young, none of them over forty, or not much over, she was certain of that. And one of them with a wee baby… she at least was no grandmother. They made a merry party, if rather bedraggled, and they filled her tired old guest house with laughter and chatter. The children (she was habitually nervous of young people), were well-behaved, even if one of them did appear to be named "Zephyr". Each to their own, of course. Oh well, grandmother or no, she was glad the young people had been reunited with their family, and she was glad they had all chosen to spend tonight in her establishment. Things had been quiet all winter and a full house was just what she needed. The sleeping arrangements seemed a bit topsy-turvy but, of course, as she told her neighbour the following day, paying guests were paying guests.

JUNE 2007

'February 16th 2007

Dear Mr and Mrs Jones,

You don't know me but my name is Alexander Nicholson and I recently married your daughter Joanna. I hope that's not too much of a disappointment for you, that you didn't attend the wedding. I would have loved for you to be there. It was a real nice wedding, with Joanna's close friends and our son Ryan present. He's fourteen years old.

I was in love with your daughter years ago when she got pregnant with Ryan. I played dad for a while, but I wasn't up to the job, and I chickened out. I didn't want to be a father. So I left Joanna to it. I was mean and selfish and it's something I'll regret until my dying day. But I have been given a second chance. I have been allowed back into Joanna's life. Ryan had some problems and his mom figured he needed a man around, a father, to sort things out. I'm not sure that's true, as Joanna is more than capable. I guess she was just tired of it all. I tried to help and I think Ryan is doing OK now. I'm proud to say that Joanna is expecting another baby, so there will soon be another grandchild.

My own mother passed away a couple of years ago, and she never met Ryan, which is something else I'll always regret. I'd love my kids to have grandparents.

I know Joanna is proud and she told me once that you guys were proud too, and that's where she got it from. Could you let your pride slip a little, please, for Ryan's sake? He is a great kid, and you couldn't fail to grow to love him, like I have done. I know that if you bite the bullet, Joanna will also, and Ryan won't be the only one who benefits.

Joanna doesn't know I have written you, that girl would half kill me if she did! But I guess you know your daughter pretty well by now, even if you haven't seen her in a long time.

Please consider getting in touch. I'm including all our contact details in this letter. I'll square it with Joanna in the end. There's no point in lying about it and she'll work it out for herself. She's one smart woman, and Ryan is a smart kid. You will be so proud of him.

Yours in hope,

Alexander Nicholson'

'We didn't know how to react at first,' said Eric – "Grandad" – 'and tragically… well, we thought about it for too long. In the end we decided to write back. And we heard nothing. Then yesterday, Joanna rang us and told us Lex had died and that you'd run away and she told us about the journey to bring you home… well, can you imagine…?'

'I'm sorry,' said Ryan.

'But you're back now, and you're safe and sound. That's all that matters,' said Eleanor – "Grandma" – and she put a chubby arm round Ryan's shoulders. 'We are the sorry ones. To think we missed out on fourteen years of your life… we've been so stupid!' And she wiped away her tears. Ryan thought she wasn't at all proud. She was just a granny.

'I was pretty damn stupid, too,' said Mum, 'but we're together now and starting today, we'll rebuild this family. Lex has gone… but … well, we are here. And Lex would have been thrilled. I know he would.'

They sat together in the kitchen, each in their own silence, thinking about the past, and excited about the future. Even Xandra was quiet. But of course, she was blessed with thinking only of the present. Ryan clutched the letter Dad had written to his grandparents. He could keep it, they said.

It was a week after the impromptu trip to Loch Coruisk. Upon their arrival back at Lex's cottage – "*our* cottage," said Mum, firmly – there was a letter propped against the coffee pot in the kitchen. David had left it there. It was addressed to Lex. Mum had opened it and had sat at the kitchen table and sobbed.

'Oh, dear Lex!' she'd cried, and showed the letter to Ryan, who'd read it in silence. He had never regarded himself as having grandparents, but here they were, writing a letter to his dad, asking to meet up.

'Lex wrote his letter to them a week before he died,' Mum said, pointing at the date.

'Wow,' said Ryan, reading through Dad's letter again.

'And we finally wrote back to him,' said Granny. 'But he had already gone. He'd gone.'

251

Of course, Ryan had insisted Mum ring her parents straight away, and let them know what had happened. It was only fair. Ryan had listened to her on the phone, and she had sounded so quiet at first, stumbling over her words, stammering of course, unsure of herself. Then, as the conversation went on, she became brighter, more relaxed. Arrangements were made, and Ryan was going to meet his grandparents. He couldn't believe it. He'd grown up without them; he wished he hadn't, but there was no point in being angry with Mum about that. She had to do what she had to do, as Dad might have said, and besides, in the end, before it was too late, at least for Ryan and Xandra, she had got in touch and arranged the reunion. She was learning, maybe? And she seemed happy, as happy as anyone could be in her situation, and she seemed glad to be with her parents again. Dad had done it. He'd sorted everything out before he'd died.

Ryan was in bed. Eric and Eleanor were going to stay in the spare room, for a night or two. They had nothing to rush home for, they said. The garden could keep and they would much rather stay and become reacquainted with their only daughter, and get to know Ryan and cuddle little Xandra. She was "the spit of Joanna at the same age", according to Eleanor. Grandma.

And had he really gone to Loch Coruisk, with Beau and Clarissa? Was it all a dream? No. They had gone. Dad had told him how beautiful Loch Coruisk was, and now Ryan, and the others, people he thought of now as his friends, knew it was beautiful too. He would never forget the silence that had taken them over, as they sat and looked over the still blue loch to the grey mountains beyond, an unearthly quiet surrounding them. It was something they had all shared and felt. There was a bond between him and Beau and Clarissa that he thought would not be broken.

They still had Dad's ashes, hidden away in a cupboard in the living room. Mum said it was "morbid" to keep them, it made her feel uneasy and should they take them up to Loch Coruisk? Ryan thought it was a good idea… until Mum reminded him that Lex had loved California too, he'd loved lots of places, and would it be right to carry the ashes to California and scatter them there, to take the ashes to Lex's childhood home?

'But you don't fly,' said Ryan, and Joanna shrugged.

'So what? Besides, I do fly, as from now, and we'll go, you and me and Xandra, when she's a bit older. We'll visit.'

In the end they decided they would bury the ashes in the back garden. It was the right thing, Ryan felt, it was simple, and Dad would have approved. As Mum said, he'd been falling in love with this place, his "cottage"; it was his first proper grown-up home, and now it was theirs.

He closed his eyes. He heard voices wafting up from the kitchen, those of Mum and his new-found grandparents. The voices were comforting and Ryan smiled to himself. He had grandparents after all. He had proper grandparents with grey hair and square glasses and sensible shoes. And perhaps it would take Mum a while to get used to them again; perhaps she was still a little cross with them; but as she said, she was to blame too. They would work it out. He slept.

Ryan walked down towards the loch. He walked on soft sand that gave easily under his feet, and it was cold. He was alone. But in the distance a figure appeared and as the figure approached him, seemingly flying across the water, Ryan saw it was not an eagle, but it was Dad, and as he reached the near shore of the loch, Ryan saw that he carried a picnic hamper and Ryan stood and watched as Dad took out all the lovely food and spread it out on a huge red and white and blue patchwork quilt.

'Your mom made a quilt for me!' said Dad. 'Isn't it great? I knew she'd make me one!'

'I knew she would too,' said Ryan as he sat on the quilt. They smiled at each other, languorous smiles that hid nothing.

'Eat,' said Dad, and Ryan picked up a slice of pizza, with tomato sauce that tasted of tin, but that didn't seem to matter anymore, and a bottle of cola. They ate and drank in silence, staring out across the loch, and occasionally smiling at each other. After they had eaten all they wanted, Dad looked hard at Ryan.

'You made it. I hoped you'd make it.'

'How could I not?' said Ryan. Dad smiled. He ruffled Ryan's hair. He paused.

Then: 'She came for you, didn't she?'

'Yes.'

'I knew she would. She'll be OK now, kid. So will you. You just got to believe in one another.'

Ryan looked across the blue water. So did Dad, and for a few peaceful moments, all was silent.

Too soon, Dad spoke again. 'I have to go now. You understand?'

Ryan nodded. He understood. He would not cry.

Dad stood up and held out his hand to Ryan. Ryan

reached out and felt Dad's large, warm, strong hand envelop his own.

'Keep looking after your mom,' said Dad. They stood facing each other, Ryan wanting to drink in every last ounce of this time with Dad, this time that he knew was not real, in this dream that he knew was a dream; but he could convince himself it wasn't, if he kept on believing, concentrating. The lochside had become a wide beach with warm, white sand, and blue skies above, and a hot sun. Probably, they were in California, because in dreams you can drift and shift from one place to another. The places come to you.

'I promise,' said Ryan. 'I'll look after Mum.'

'And your sister.'

'I will.'

'And look after yourself. Don't take crap from anyone, ever. Don't dole crap out either, OK? Be a good friend. And remember what we had. It could have been nothing at all.'

'It was everything,' said Ryan. They held each other then, until finally Dad drew back.

'I'm done. I'll see you, kid.'

And he was gone, in a swift, smooth dilution. No fuss. And just the half-empty pizza box and potato chip bags and cola bottles remained, strewn all over the quilt that lifted gently along its edges in the lilting breeze. Ryan gathered up all the rubbish in the centre of the quilt and tied up the four corners. Then he turned to go back the way he had come, pulling the quilt behind him, carving a soft channel in the sand.

3

THE ROAD TO CALIFORNIA

PART II

JUNE 2017

I never dreamed about my dad again. But I did look after Mum. I promised, so I had to. And she looked after me. I was the man of the house, she said, and I had to behave like one. So I did. I tried. But she was the boss, always. And she had travelled to Loch Coruisk for me, of course. It was her I went there to meet, I realise now. I had to bring her back to me, and thereby take myself to her, because my dad had gone and we needed each other more than ever.

I didn't return to school, not quite. I studied for my GCSEs at home and went into my old school to sit my exams, a year later than my year group, but that didn't matter. I had some catching up to do. There was a new head teacher at the school by then, and she was fine with me sitting the exams there. I was kind of a cult figure among the kids at school. Nobody really knew who I was, I didn't wear uniform and I just flitted in to sit exams, and out again. *Is that Ryan Jones*? I heard it a few times, but I just smiled and said nothing. Because I was not Ryan Jones. I was Ryan Jones Nicholson.

I did go back to school for A levels, and I studied English Language and English Literature and History; I took a course in American Studies at University. I didn't take a gap year. In life, there are no gaps. Uni wasn't always easy for me; I almost gave up a couple of times. I got a diagnosis of "high-functioning autism" while I was a student. I find life tricky and I don't always understand this world. But I'm working on it.

After Uni, I came home and started writing. I can't stop writing. Of course, I'll never be a vet; that really was just a pipe dream. But, I did get Mum on a plane, eventually, last year; she, Xandra and I went to California. We had a ball. We went to the places Dad had told us about. We met my dad's cousins in Salinas, who put us up for a few nights, and told us some stories about my dad that I'll not forget. There's talk of them coming over here for a "vacation", in a year or two.

My mum made a quilt for my dad, of course she did, with red, blue and white patches. The pattern is Road to California, of course. We use it as a throw over the sofa in the lounge and we still call it Lex's quilt. I know he would have loved it.

My mum's business eventually picked up where it left off after my dad's death, and is now doing brilliantly, and Mum and her team of talented seamstresses run a successful business, with their website and their high-street shop. Road to California is thriving and it brings to my dear mum a joy the rest of us can only guess at. I know she would be lost without it.

I have some people I need to thank. This project has been a labour of love and at times it wasn't easy. It's also been a joint effort. Thanks to my mother, Joanna Jones Nicholson, for helping me to recall some of our more heated discussions. And thank you to her for filling me in on some of the conversations I wasn't privy to. She has a good memory and, I think, a fair one.

Thanks to my friend Beau Stirling, now a maths teacher of all things. Clever guy! Also Clarissa Cooper, who is a nurse, and a fine one too. Beau and Clarissa were married last year. Their wedding was beautiful.

Thank you to Sharon and Zephyr and Clover, those crazy, *crazy* people, our loyal friends. Clover is an actress (and waitress), and Zephyr is somewhere in India as I write. We'll all go back to that loch one day. Promise?

Billy Plumb and David Johnson continue to be wonderful, generous friends to my mum and to me, and the best kind of godparents to my little sister, Xandra, who is funny and cheeky and blessed with our dad's looks; and our mum's determination! But she can't sew, not yet, in fact she hates sewing and knitting and crocheting. Poor Mum can't fathom that. But she thinks Xandra will come round in the end…

Thanks to my grandparents, Eric and Eleanor Jones, who are both alive and well, despite the advancing years. They're always on my side. Nobody could ask for more.

Finally, many thanks to my writing mentor and my friend, Mrs Elizabeth Marchant, who said I should write it all down.

ACKNOWLEDGEMENTS

Big thanks to Susan Davis, Jennie Rawlings, Eliza Dee and Hannah Vaughan: "Team California", and what a team!

For reading the novel so early, and for their enjoyment of it, I'm grateful to generous book bloggers Anne Williams (Being Anne), Nicola Smith (Short Book and Scribes) and Katherine Sunderland (Bibliomaniac).

Thanks to my Aunty Mandy, for partly inspiring Joanna and for being perennially young, creative and such a fun person. Love you!

Big thanks and love as always to my children Oliver, Emily, Jude, Finn and Stan.

And thanks to Ian, who is still making everything possible…

And finally many thanks to all the fabulous home educating families I've had the pleasure of meeting and befriending over the years. You are all inspiring!

★

Louise tweets @LouiseWalters12
and her website is at louisewaltersbooks.co.uk